OLD SINS,
LONG MEMORIES

OLD **SINS,**
LONG **MEMORIES**

ANGELA ARNEY

ROBERT HALE · LONDON

© Angela Arney 2014
First published in Great Britain 2014

ISBN 978-0-7198-1368-9

Robert Hale Limited
Clerkenwell House
Clerkenwell Green
London EC1R 0HT

www.halebooks.com

2 4 6 8 10 9 7 5 3 1

Typeset in Minion Pro
Printed in Great Britain by Berforts Information Press Ltd

CHAPTER ONE

IT WAS RAINING on the day Darren Evans was to die. Brutal, violent rain and Darren was to die the same way. Brutally. Violently. Not that he knew that when he got up later than usual that Thursday morning. The hour of the day didn't worry him. Neither time nor weather bothered Darren. He did what he wanted, when he wanted. Only his fix was important. Not the past, not the future, only the next fix.

But that morning he felt unusually unsettled, and it was Dr Browne's fault. The day before he'd collected his prescription for methadone, his heroin substitute, although, as usual, it was never enough. Dr James, his own doctor, had been off and he'd seen the new doctor, Dr Browne. She'd not quibbled about his need for the methadone, although he was sure she guessed he was mainlining heroin as well. She'd hardly questioned him at all, and yet he'd had the strangest feeling; for the first time in years he'd felt that here was someone he could talk to. That maybe there was a chance of help to get away from the vicious circle of drug dependency. But the surgery was full, and she was rushed, although she had told him to come back, and he sensed she meant it. Of course, he said he would but didn't intend to. He always said that. But this morning he changed his mind. Yes, he would see Dr Browne again. Next week. Perhaps he'd even tell her the whole story from start to finish. Years of guilt weighed him down. It was time he talked to someone.

That morning he followed his usual routine, took his methadone, then topped it up with heroin – although it was getting more and more difficult to find a vein – before eating half a tin of baked beans with a dirty spoon, cold, straight from tin. Now, at just after midday, he decided he had enough energy to face the task of changing the rusted-through exhaust on his old van.

Looking out at the sodden scene outside through the grimy net curtains draped across the window, he shivered. Rain was lashing the bedraggled December garden, flattening the early snowdrops, which, against all odds, had succeeded in growing, only to be beaten down, so that now they lay like little dead things amongst the lank grass. Darren didn't notice them; he only saw the rain and felt the cold. Changing the exhaust was not a job he relished. But it had to be done. Noise from the broken pipe attracted attention. The last thing he wanted. He'd grown used to being invisible. It was how he liked it. Therefore, much as he disliked physical effort of any kind, the exhaust had to be changed.

Entering the lean-to garage, which was tacked on to the side of the shabby bungalow he inhabited, Darren carefully shut the doors. The rain was blowing that way, and would soon penetrate his cotton T-shirt if the doors were left open. Even with the doors shut he started shivering violently; there was not a spare ounce of flesh on his thin body to keep him warm. Rubbing his hands together and blowing on his fingertips, he got to work. First he raised up the van on an old jack. It didn't look man enough to do the job, but a desultory push with one hand satisfied him as to its safety before he slid beneath the vehicle and began unscrewing the bolts holding up the rotten exhaust system.

The garage, built in the 1930s, was a single-walled brick affair with an asbestos corrugated roof, and the heavy rain thudding down drowned all noise inside and out. It drowned the noise of the person walking purposefully up the side path of the bungalow towards the garage. It drowned the noise of the door opening. Only when the rain blew in on his face was Darren aware that someone else was there, and turned. He saw the barrel of a gun. That was all he saw in his last fleeting seconds of life. Noise and pain followed. A deafening explosion, momentary agony, hot and burning; a blinding red mist. Then there was nothing. For Darren Evans even his daily fix ceased to matter.

The jack was wrenched roughly away. The van crashed down on Darren's inert form. Then the driver's door was opened, and someone climbed in and started the engine. Broken exhaust roaring loudly, the van shot backwards and forwards. Not out through the open doors, but just far enough to crush the body. It came to a stop so that one of the wheels lay near what had once been Darren's head.

The engine coughed into an abrupt silence.

The sound of rain drummed out the pattern of death with a rhythmic tom-tom beat on the asbestos roof.

Darren Evans would not be visiting Dr Browne again.

CHAPTER TWO

THERE WAS NO mistaking the Moppits' van; it had two lurid orange mops splayed cross-sword fashion as a heraldic design across the side of the sliding doors. The van drew up in the leafy suburb of Blackheath, London, outside number 27 Heathview Road, at exactly the same moment as Lizzie, travelling by cab from Waterloo, arrived.

Lizzie paid the driver and watched the orange mops switch places as the sliding doors of the van skimmed open. It had been sensible of Louise to recommend she hire cleaning contractors to do the final spit and polish of the house before she handed over the keys.

'Much more sensible than you working yourself up into lather over it,' Louise had said. 'I know of a terrific firm. They're friends of mine. I'll hire them.'

Momentarily, Lizzie had wondered at the wisdom of letting Louise doing the hiring; her friends were not, as a rule, conventional. But Moppits was a comforting-sounding name, and Lizzie had envisaged a pair of homely, middle-aged ladies armed with mops and buckets. However, as the van disgorged its occupants no such reassuring figures emerged. Two young men, sporting various forms of body piercing on ears, noses, and lips, and dressed in frayed jeans, and leather bomber jackets, leapt out then proceeded to unload large pieces of cleaning machinery as well as the conventional mops and buckets. One was tall and thin, the other short and stocky with the beginnings of a beer gut.

'Are you Dr Browne?' the taller of the two inquired.

'Yes,' said Lizzie, advancing cautiously. 'I assume you are Moppits personnel.'

'Nope,' came the reply. 'We *are* the Moppits. What you see is all there is.'

'Oh,' said Lizzie. Mentally crossing her fingers, and hoping Louise had known what she was up to when she'd hired them, she opened the door, and began directing them towards the various rooms.

'No need,' said the tall one. 'We got a plan of the house from the agents. We've worked it all out on a computer, that's how we do our quotes. Everything's computerized. Saves time. By the way, my name is Ned and this is Darren.'

Darren gave a wide grin, showing that he had a silver tongue stud as well as earrings and a nose ring.

Darren. The name reminded Lizzie of the pathetic drug addict she'd seen the day before at her surgery at Stibbington. The Darren standing before her now looked well fed and healthy, whereas the Darren in Stibbington looked as if he hadn't eaten a proper meal in years and was anything but healthy. Not usually overly sympathetic to drug addicts, she'd seen too many, there was something different about the boy that made her want to help. He exuded an overwhelming sense of sadness and worry.

'We'll start upstairs,' said Ned. 'It shouldn't take long. I see all the furniture has gone, thank God.'

Lizzie concentrated on the present. 'Yes, all the furniture has gone.' She felt annoyed that he was pleased about it, because she was vacillating about the sensation she'd felt when she'd walked into the empty house. Belongings made a house personal. Now it was just an empty shell, waiting to be cleaned ready for its new occupants. Lizzie clamped down firmly on the suspicion of a trickle of self-pity. This was not the end. This was the beginning of a new life, and she had to remember that.

'I've already done the master bedroom,' she said, 'although there are still some books up there that I need to sort through and pack up. No need to do that.'

'Okay,' said Ned, adding quickly, 'but the price quoted stays the same. We can't afford to do it for less.' He set off up the stairs, vacuum cleaner in one hand, and electric polisher in the other.

'We're artists,' Darren told Lizzie conversationally, unzipping a bag from which he took an assortment of dusters. 'We need the money to fund the studio rent as well as painting. There's no money in art unless your name's Damien Hirst.'

'I see,' said Lizzie. Everything fell into place. That must be how

Louise knew these two, from her work in the art gallery. Her daughter's world was much more exotic than her own. It consisted of artists, dealers, and assorted media people, all, to Lizzie's eyes, slightly bizarre.

'Louise has organized a show for us in three months' time,' said Darren, tongue stud gleaming. 'We've got a lot of painting to do before then if we're to fill the space.' Then, dusters stuffed in pockets, and mop and bucket in hand, he too climbed the stairs.

Lizzie put off following them; she'd sort the bedroom books later. Instead, she wandered into the kitchen and made a cup of tea. This roomy house in Blackheath, a gracious part of London, the place she'd called home for a large part of her life, was empty now. But it still smelled of the vanished occupants. At least, it seemed so to Lizzie. Although empty, the house echoed with a resonance, the detritus of more than twenty years of marriage. Another woman would perhaps have been in tears, or agitated during the last moments in the ex-conjugal home, but not Lizzie. She was determinedly in control. It was something she prided herself on. Whatever happened she remained calm.

Even so it was impossible to put the brain into a completely neutral gear. To Lizzie the essence of life was analytical thought, which led to rational outcome. Mike had always said she was more scientist than woman. At one time she'd taken that as a compliment, but now it rankled. Nevertheless, while sipping the comforting cup of tea, she studied her past life with a cold, clinical eye, the same way she would have studied a specimen beneath the microscope: scientifically, without prejudice, and with a ruthless clarity, bearing in mind all the relevant facts. That she was a successful career woman was not in doubt. That was a fact and one which she skipped over effortlessly. It was her role as a woman with a capital W that was the point in question. Was she different from other women? On reflection she thought not. She'd been married, was now divorced, had a daughter and was in her early forties. Even allowing for a touch of vanity Lizzie knew she wasn't bad looking. Hair blonde, with artificial assistance – everyone was allowed to manipulate nature a little – she still had a good figure, although was a bit on the thin side. All in all quite attractive, although not exactly the last word in nubile sexuality.

Mike, it seemed, preferred the latter. Lizzie had known about the affair for months, had given it some thought in her usual measured manner, but hadn't panicked because she thought she knew what it was. It was lust, not love. She and Mike had their own kind of love, comfortable as an old shoe, and about as exciting. This suited Lizzie. She'd always got her excitement and challenge in life from her work as an inner-city GP. Mike was having a mid-life crisis. He'd get over it.

There was good reason to think this. Mike was a ditherer. Always had been. Could never make up his mind about anything. So why, she'd reasoned, should he be any different this time? Once his ego had been satisfied he'd come back to the fold. Besides, he'd always relied on her for money. As a freelance journalist and novelist his earnings had been precariously intermittent. So she was totally unprepared, and it had come as a nasty jolt of surprise, when Mike had suddenly asked for a divorce.

As with everything else Lizzie considered it carefully. Mike was aggressively determined on the divorce, and never one to waste time on lost causes, Lizzie had agreed. Pride, as much as anything caused her to acquiesce without too much argument. Pride, and the need to keep control, and remain dignified. Now the divorce was final, and she'd been left to sort out the final bits and pieces before the new owners moved in. This was Lizzie's final day in the ex-marital home. Trust Mike, she thought, finishing the tea and feeling more irritated than angry, he always left everything to me.

Ned and Darren, in a flurry of intense activity, like two genies let out of a bottle, whisked through the house, vacuuming, polishing, scrubbing, mopping, and using copious amounts of scouring and bleaching agent.

'You wouldn't win prizes for being environmentally friendly,' grumbled Lizzie, hating the smell, which was eradicating all trace of human occupation.

'Can't afford to worry about that,' said Ned briskly, obviously the mover and groover of the pair. 'We get paid to clean, and we do it the quickest way.' He gave the upstairs lavatory a flush then poured bleach in the bowl and down the sink waste. 'Kills all known germs,' he said, waving the plastic bottle with a flourish.

They finally departed, floating out of the house on a billowing wave of potent disinfectant, Lizzie's cheque in Ned's pocket. Left alone, she finished sorting through the books, the only thing left now in what had been the master bedroom. Most of them were Mike's and those she put in a box in the porch for him to collect later that day; the rest were out of date medical text books, which she dumped in the wheelie bin feeling guilty because she hadn't taken them down to the recycling yard. But there was no time. She had to get the train back to Stibbington.

Turning the key in the lock for the final time she had a strange frozen feeling, and found herself wishing that she would wake up and find it had all been a bad dream. That Mike had decided to stay, that their comfortable, if passionless, marriage would continue. But reality prevailed, and she turned the key firmly. She was leaving to catch the train and embarking upon a different, if uncertain, phase of her life. The trouble was, if there was one thing Lizzie hated it was uncertainty.

The train pulled out of Waterloo Station on its journey westwards, and Lizzie, breathless from running across the entire width of the concourse to catch it, stumbled towards an empty seat in the carriage and trod heavily on the foot of the woman sitting opposite.

'I'm so sorry.' She looked down. The woman's shoes, pale beige suede, had a big black mark where Lizzie's wet foot had been. 'I'm sorry,' she repeated.

The woman lowered the newspaper she was reading, acknowledged the apology briefly with a slight nod of the head, then returned to reading. Lizzie settled down in her seat. There'd been no time to grab an evening paper and as she had nothing to read she allowed herself the luxury of immersing herself wholly in her own little puddle of gloom.

It matched the weather outside. A grey December rain swept across everything in the City, casting a pall of dark mist over late afternoon London. In Regent Street, Lizzie knew, the Christmas lights would be giving a cheerful sense of purpose to the scrabbling crowds of Thursday late-night shoppers with their bulging Christmas carrier bags. Something she always enjoyed. But, away from the crowds and lights, total gloom pervaded. The perfect day for me, thought Lizzie moodily.

'Remember, one door closes and another opens,' her daughter, Louise, had told her breezily over the phone that morning before she'd set off from her cottage in Stibbington back to London for the last time. 'People get divorced every day.'

'I don't,' Lizzie had snapped irritably. 'Besides, what do you know about it? You've never even been married.'

'Well . . . ' began Louise.

Lizzie interrupted even more crossly. 'And for heaven's sake don't give me advice. You're my daughter not my mother.'

But Louise, not Lizzie's daughter for nothing, was not put off by a bad-tempered mother. 'You know perfectly well what I mean, Mum. Come on; don't make a mountain out of a molehill. Be honest. It isn't as if you and Dad were ecstatically happy. He's not a bad man, and I do love him, but he's rather weak, and personally, I think you should have given him the order of the boot years ago.'

Probably true, but Lizzie was not in the mood to admit it. Besides, she felt guilty that Louise was taking sides. It was unfair to Mike. Damn him! She felt she had to try to explain. 'It's the humiliation, Louise,' she'd said slowly, 'to suddenly realize that you no longer have any leverage, that you no longer matter to someone. Besides, you can't wipe out years of marriage at the drop of a hat. It leaves an indelible print on your life.'

'Your pride has had a dent. That's what it is.' Louise was emphatic with all the certainty of youth. 'You never used your leverage with Dad. You just kept it handy as a comfortable backstop. But you never needed it.'

'Have you been leafing through my psychology books?' said Lizzie suspiciously, beginning to feel as if she were in an analytical session.

True to form Louise ignored her. 'Look at life positively. You've walked straight into another well paid job, although why you had to take a partnership in general practice down there in Hampshire I'll never know. Another city, *any* city, would have been better than being right out in the sticks. Nothing will ever happen down in Stibbington; it's as quiet as the grave, to coin a phrase.' There was a pause and then Louise delivered the *coup de grace*. 'And you'll never meet another man there.'

'I don't want another man,' said Lizzie, and meant it. Mike was a habit that wouldn't be easy to shake off, but Louise wouldn't understand that. She wondered briefly if all mothers and daughters misunderstood each other. Much as they loved each other they never seemed to be on the same wavelength. 'One man has been quite enough for me,' she said decisively. 'I'm happy to go solo. And as for Stibbington, well, I know I shall enjoy living there. Already I love my cottage. It may be old, but it has all the mod cons I need.'

'Ha!' muttered Louise, sounding unconvinced.

'Wait until you've visited before you jump to conclusions.'

The house in question, Silver Cottage, was situated in a remote winding lane called Deer Leap Lane. It was a small house with a thatched roof, surrounded by a thick privet hedge; a country cottage looking as if it belonged on the pages of a fairy tale book. That, and the fact that it was on the edge of Stibbington, away from everything else, had attracted Lizzie. And despite Louise's reservations, Lizzie thought Stibbington a dream of a place. Small and ancient, on the coast and yet in the New Forest, it clung to the banks of the meandering river Stib as it made its way out into the Solent opposite the Isle of Wight. It was the perfect mix of country and seaside, giving the impression of a place permanently on holiday. Quiet, it was true, but relaxing.

'Mother,' said Louise. Lizzie knew she was serious. Louise always called her *Mother* when she was being serious. 'I rang because I wanted to wish you luck when moving out of the big house today. I don't want to argue with you. And you know I wish I could be there in person, but the gallery has a private view tonight and I've got to get everything ready today.' Louise's job in the Fine Art gallery in Cork Street was a cross between receptionist, curator, and general dog's body. Lizzie had always wished she'd opted for a better paid, more academic career, but Louise loved it.

'Thanks,' said Lizzie, immediately feeling guilty. 'I know you'd help if you could, and I'm sorry I snapped. But I must dash now or I'll miss the train to London. I'll speak to you this evening when I get back to Stibbington.'

'I shall be out. Private view, remember?' said Louise. 'And then tomorrow I'm off to Valencia at the crack of dawn to organize an exhibition there. I'll ring you when I get back to London.'

They'd left it there, and Lizzie had come up to London feeling even more guilty. Louise's intentions were well meant; she'd been trying to cheer her up. But on that particular day nothing could cheer her. She felt a failure. She, Lizzie the achiever, prizes at school, at university, a medical practitioner, an important member of society, had failed to hold her marriage together. That was the thing that really stuck in her gullet: failure. She couldn't bear failure. It meant one had lost control.

The train rolled onwards through the open countryside of Surrey into Hampshire. It was pitch black now save for the occasional light from an isolated farmhouse. After Winchester where half the passengers disembarked, the remaining passengers sped on to Southampton.

After that would soon be Piddlehurst, the nearest main line station to Stibbington. Lizzie waited until the serried arms of the cranes and floodlights of Southampton's container port disappeared into the rain-lashed darkness, then struggled into her still wet raincoat. Collecting her bags and umbrella she waited in the corridor beside the door ready to leap out the moment the train drew to a halt. Silver Cottage and a glass of wine were high on her agenda.

It was only as she was collecting her car from the railway car park that she noticed the woman she'd trodden on had also alighted. Lizzie could see her, beneath the station lights, surrounded by several suitcases, talking to Piddlehurst's one and only taxi driver. Unlocking the car door she wondered where the woman was going, then forgot all about her as she struggled to drive through torrential rain with a misted-up windscreen.

On the other side of Stibbington a car skidded to an abrupt halt. 'Damn! That's all I need. The water-splash is flooded again. Why the hell hasn't a flood warning sign been put out? We could have taken the other road if we'd known.' Black water lapped at the side of the car. and Detective Chief Inspector Adam Maguire swore again and said, 'Grayson, you may have to push if this thing stops.'

'Perhaps we should go back.'

'Don't be a fool, man. Are you suggesting we do a three point turn in this depth of water?'

'No, sir.'

'Then we go on.'

'Yes, sir.'

Sergeant Steve Grayson slumped down in his seat wishing that he hadn't begged a lift back home with his superior. Adam Maguire was dour at the best of times, had been ever since the death of his wife. But for the last few weeks he'd been positively vitriolic. Grayson thought he knew why. Boredom had a lot to do with it. All they seemed to do these days was toil with mountains of petty paperwork generated by the higher echelons of bureaucracy. Not a single interesting case had come their way in weeks. What was the point in being a detective, he thought moodily, if there was nothing to detect? Petty thieving at Stibbington's weekly market didn't rate as high as a gold bullion robbery, although the thieves were just as hard to catch. There was Mrs Armitage and her shoplifting, he supposed, not that anyone took much notice of that. She did it on a regular basis and her husband always paid up so the shop keepers never prosecuted; in fact Grayson thought they positively encouraged it. Sometimes he found himself praying that she would steal something really big, something that would enable them to charge her and get her to court. But Mrs Armitage perversely specialized in large pink knickers with elasticated legs and waists, bras big enough to put a baby in, and tights, with the occasional foray into men's underpants, usually with sexy messages printed on them. Never anything expensive, and always very large; Grayson thought this even more bizarre as both Mr and Mrs Armitage were tiny, wizened creatures.

All this was a certain recipe for bad humour and on top of everything else there was the ever-present threat of closure hanging over Stibbington police station. Plans were afoot to move them all to Southampton where they'd be swallowed up into the huge new glass and concrete police headquarters. 'We'll be like ants in an anthill,' Maguire had said. It was enough to depress anyone. Although I have a wife to go home to, reflected Grayson, not an empty house. However, that didn't help now, not when he was stuck in a flood with a bad-tempered Maguire. Once again he cursed his old banger for letting him down thus forcing him to ask for a lift.

Maguire slipped the car into gear, edging slowly forward, and obviously thinking much the same, said, 'About time you got yourself a decent car, Steve.'

'We've got one good one, and I can't afford another. Not on a sergeant's pay.' Grayson looked anxiously out of the window. 'I hope Ann got through before the water-splash flooded. I don't want her breaking down out here in the dark, not now that she's pregnant.'

'Not at any time,' Maguire said gloomily. 'Even country lanes are not safe places these days. Rape and pillage everywhere according to the popular press. Don't know what the world is coming to.'

Grayson grinned. 'Wishful thinking, sir?' he asked wryly. 'If you ask me, we could do with a bit of rape and pillage to liven things up; something to make a change from pen pushing.'

Maguire gave a ghost of a smile. 'Too damned right.' Then he changed the subject. 'How is Ann, by the way?'

Just thinking of Ann had a cheering effect on Grayson. 'She's fine. She had the car to go into Southampton for a scan today. With any luck

I'll know the sex of the baby when I get home.'

'What's lucky about that? Better to have a surprise. More natural,' said Maguire, sounding bad tempered again.

Grayson didn't answer but wondered if Maguire regretted not having a family. Too late now. His wife was dead, poor thing, stricken with cancer in her early forties, and Maguire, although only forty-seven, seemed an old man to Grayson. He couldn't imagine him with another woman.

The car started to move and they both breathed audible sighs of relief as it crept slowly out of the flood water. The engine coughed and the car juddered to a halt as Maguire jammed on the brakes to dry them. Soon they were on the tree-lined approach to Grayson's road on the edge of Stibbington.

Maguire dropped him outside his house. It was an old police house. Grayson had bought it when Hampshire Constabulary were rational-izing their assets and restructuring the force, which, as Adam Maguire had cynically observed, was a fancy way of selling off police property and making policemen redundant. But it's an ill wind, thought Grayson now gazing with pride at the square, red-brick house, with its pocket handkerchief-sized gardens front and back. Ugly but practical. Not everyone's cup of tea but it suits me and Ann.

Lizzie following Adam Maguire and Sergeant Grayson on her way from the railway station was not quite so lucky when she came to the flooded water-splash. Water seeped under the door of her low-slung Alfa Romeo, soaking the floor. It was a totally impractical car, but she loved its design and the roar of the engine. In the Alfa she felt adventurous, although tonight her spirit of adventure had been somewhat dented by the weather, and the fact that now the exhaust was coughing and spluttering worryingly. In her rear mirror she could see steam rising from the hot exhaust. She was uneasy. She remembered someone telling her that the water-splash, although normally only a trickle of water across the dip in the road, could flood badly, and was prone to flash flooding. Once, apparently, someone had even been swept away and drowned. Crossing her fingers, she prayed she wouldn't be adding to the list of fatalities. The car coughed again, and Lizzie held her breath. If it broke down in London, which was not unknown as the carburettor was inclined to be temperamental, all she had to do was leave it, hop out and hail a passing cab. Here there was nothing and no one to hail, although her mobile phone was a comfort. Automatically, she tapped her raincoat pocket, feeling the reassuring bulge which was her contact with the outside world. However, the Alfa did get through the flooding, albeit reluctantly, with the engine sounding like a forty-a-day smoker, and Lizzie eventually saw the welcoming lights of Silver Cottage blinking through the rain.

She'd remembered to set all the timers – heating, lights, cooker – and the cottage was warm and bright, with an appetizing smell coming from the kitchen where she'd left a chicken casserole in the slow cooker. Dumping her bag and wet raincoat in the hall she poured herself a large glass of wine. She would have liked to have chatted to Louise, but as that was impossible she switched on the television and watched an American medical soap where all the doctors and nurses were impossibly glamorous and led incredibly active and complicated sex lives. It was so ridiculous that it cheered her up. Lizzie chuckled into her wine and chicken casserole. There was something very relaxing about being single, celibate, and able to watch rubbish without anyone disapproving.

For Adam Maguire walking into the house he'd once shared with his wife Rosemary, but now lived in alone, the reverse was the case. Nothing was switched on. The house was dark, smelled damp, and to make matters worse the dog had been sick on the kitchen mat.

'Damn, Elsie Clackett,' he muttered crossly. 'Why will she always feed the dog when I ask her not to?'

The dog, an old golden Labrador, sidled up to him, apologetic, sorrowful-looking, and rubbed her sleek sides against his leg in apology. 'It's all right, Tess.' Reaching down he fondled her silky ears. 'I know it's not your fault.' He opened the kitchen door and shooed her out into the garden. The dog hung back, reluctant to go out. He gave her a shove. 'I know it's raining, but you go out and do what you've got to do. Then you can come back in.' Smiling, he watched her broad golden back hurtle across the sodden lawn into the darkness as she made for the shelter of the bushes at the bottom of the garden. Then turning back into the kitchen he cleaned up the mat.

Later that evening sitting in front of the television, with Tess by his side, a pre-cooked dinner for one on a tray and a glass of whisky in his hand, he looked about him. The house was small, a typical two up two down forest cottage which had once accommodated a farm worker and his family. Now, such cottages were highly sought after by wealthy weekenders. Rosemary had wanted the house. Adam would have preferred something more modern, but she enjoyed being trendy, and Adam had always been happy to go along with whatever she wanted. Everything in the house was neat and tidy, thanks to Elsie Clackett, who came in twice a week to clean. Everything that should be polished was polished. Everything in its right place. In fact, everything was just the same as it had been the day Rosemary died. So why was it so depressing? What was different about the room, or indeed the whole house? He knew the answer: it was *too* tidy, and it was empty. There were no little touches of someone else's hand; a vase of flowers, scattered magazines, a half-finished book lying upside down. He was living in a vacuum and had been ever since Rosemary had gone from his life. *Passed over* as Elsie Clackett said. 'Passed over what?' he always wanted to shout. 'She hasn't passed over anything. She's dead!' But the words remained in his head, known only to himself.

Everyone, relations, friends, colleagues, all said, 'time heals'. But Adam doubted it.

Not feeling hungry he gave Tess most of the microwaved meal. She ate it all as usual. Casserole, cottage pie, sausages, whatever he gave her, she ate it. Tonight it was cottage pie and sprouts and she polished the plate, chasing the last sprout around and finally chomping on it with a smile of satisfaction on her whiskery face.

'Dustbin,' Adam said affectionately, and poured himself another generous measure of whisky. On the TV he switched over from the medical soap. He hated anything to do with hospitals since Rosemary's illness. Idly, he watched a thriller flickering across the screen, then became irritated. Why was it on television all the detectives, usually middle-aged, ended up in bed with glamorous young women? Exasperated, he switched it off and put on a CD – Vivaldi's *Four Seasons*, that should chase away the black bear sitting on his shoulder. 'Music has charms to sooth a savage beast,' he told Tess, who followed her master across the room.

She followed a tall, grey-eyed man, black hair streaked with silver at the sides, and a face which, although handsome, was much too thin, with deep lines either side of the mouth. Whenever he looked in the mirror to shave, about the only time he bothered to look at himself,

Adam saw the lines and thought of Rosemary. 'Laughter lines,' she'd always said. But lately there'd not been much to laugh about, and sometimes in his blackest moments he wondered if he would ever *really* laugh again. Music washed into the room, the notes of the solo violin throbbing joyfully. Adam felt a little more cheerful, and poured himself another whisky. Definitely the last, he decided, and raised his glass. 'Bring me an interesting case,' he said to no one in particular. 'Something to occupy my mind.'

Tess wagged her tail, anxious to please, and watched him intently.

While Lizzie, Adam Maguire, and Grayson were making their various ways home, the woman from the London train had asked Andy Watson, the only taxi driver to do regular duty at Piddlehurst Station, to take her to the House by the Hard at Stibbington.

'I believe it's a good guest house,' she said.

'Been recommended, has it?' said Andy. He didn't like Mrs Matthews, the owner of said guest house. She was very friendly with his wife. He didn't like his wife much either but was stuck with her. One of the reasons he was always out and about with his taxi was because he'd do anything to get out of the house and away from Marge Watson's nagging. 'Don't step there!' 'Mind that settee with those trousers!' 'You know that's the cat's chair!' Anything, in fact, to stop him from settling down comfortably in his own home. This was the reason he was the only taxi outside the station on the black, wet December night.

'No. I read about it in the *Stibbington Guide Book* and came down yesterday to get the feel of the place. I decided then to stay, so now I'm returning with my luggage. It's an ideal spot for me.'

'Ideal if you want to be stuck out on the end of the hard,' said Andy putting the woman's suitcases in the boot. 'All right in the summer, I suppose, if you like that sort of thing. But quiet. Very lonely this time of year.'

'That's what I want,' said the woman. 'Peace and quiet. I have a book to write.'

'Well then,' Andy opened the door for her. 'Peace and quiet. That's what you'll get. As the saying goes it's as quiet as the grave down there.'

CHAPTER THREE

THE FOLLOWING MORNING was Friday, and the first thing Lizzie thought about when looking out of the window at the cottage garden was that getting a gardener was a high priority. The privet hedge surrounding the garden gave privacy, but, and this was not something that had occurred to her before, it also grew. Now she looked at it more closely she realized that since she'd bought the cottage it appeared to have grown at least two inches. She felt vaguely surprised; weren't things supposed to stop growing in the winter? And the garden itself, which was full of bushes and plants, all of which appeared to be of the dark green, crawling variety, seemed to be encroaching upon the house itself. There was no doubt about it. She needed a gardener, and soon. If she delayed much longer there was the distinct possibility that she'd have to carry a machete to hack her way through the undergrowth to get in and out of the house. Gardening was unknown territory to Lizzie, but she'd envisaged, when she'd bought the house, that she would eventually have a typical cottage garden full of old-fashioned flowers. It would be crammed with pansies, lupins, hollyhocks, and roses, a cheerful, brightly coloured place of relaxation. She looked out of the window. Anything less cheerful was difficult to imagine. The whole scene was dank, dark, and very, very wet.

Last night she'd felt surprisingly content, but now in the cold light of dawn she suddenly felt very alone: on her own in a town she didn't yet know, with a house and garden she hadn't fully sussed out. Plus a job in a country practice where most of her patients, as far as she'd been able to make out, were in their eighties living in isolated cottages. A far cry from the drug addicts and unemployed people she'd been used to dealing with. Perhaps Louise was right, she thought uneasily, and she was going to find Stibbington too quiet and dull.

On the other side of Stibbington down by the estuary, unfazed by the bad weather, Emmy Matthews busied herself in the kitchen of the House on the Hard. It was early morning, and there was no sign yet of her one and only guest, a female, but she bustled about nonetheless preparing a full English breakfast. Strange woman, she thought, popping up out of the blue like that, staying one Wednesday night, then leaving early Thursday morning before breakfast saying she'd be back that evening. At the time Emmy hadn't believed her. In fact thought it merely a ruse to get away politely; people were like that, saying one thing and meaning another. Besides, she'd paid her for the single night. People who paid like that didn't usually come back. But, true to her word, Mrs Jean Smithson, that was her name, had returned with her luggage and announced that she had made up her mind and would be staying for at least a week. Maybe more.

'Probably wasting my time with the breakfast, though,' Emmy muttered as she prepared the food. A widow, living alone, she was used to talking to herself and no one answering her. In fact, she much preferred it that way. Her late husband had the irritating habit of interrupting the flow of her monologues. Not that Emmy thought it a monologue. She called it conversation. Looking on the black side of life was second nature to her. Not content with having an unexpected guest out of season she was now wishing that Mrs Smithson were a man; they ate more, but Emmy didn't mind that. She always puffed out her rather meagre bosom with pride at the sight of someone tucking into whatever she'd cooked. A man always did justice to the food and appreciated her cooked breakfasts, whereas women were usually too worried about their weight. She took a sugared grapefruit half, a selection of mini packets of cereal, and some milk through to the dining room, setting them out on the table before straightening the damask napkin in its wooden ring. No one could ever say she was mean with food. The visitors' book in the House on the Hard contained many flattering comments about the food written by previous guests. She was justly proud of that.

Mrs Smithson came into the dining room just as Emmy was leaving through the door into the kitchen. The dining room had a polished wooden floor and the sound of her shoes clacking on the surface alerted Emmy. She turned, glad to see her. 'Ah, Mrs Smithson, I was wondering whether or not you wanted a full English breakfast.'

'Yes, please.' Mrs Smithson took her seat. A tall, thin, lonely figure in the empty dining room. She looked around. 'Do you have any other guests at the moment?'

Emmy shook her head. 'No one at the moment.'

'Ah,' said Mrs Smithson.

Emmy thought she sounded almost pleased. 'But as I told you yesterday I have the Walsh family booked in next week until after Christmas, although they'll only be taking breakfast here. The rest of the time they'll be with Mr Walsh's parents, who have a small flat down by the quay. Until then I'm empty. Not many people come to Stibbington in the winter. Will you be wanting to stay over Christmas?'

'Probably not. I hope to finish what I came to do by then.' The woman bent her head and concentrated on the grapefruit in front of her. A clear dismissal.

But Emmy, never one to take a hint, was not to be so easily dismissed. She liked to know about people. Gossiping with her fellow landladies about her guests was the only thing worth talking about in Stibbington. 'The taxi driver told me you're a writer.'

'Yes.' Mrs Smithson's tone was not friendly, but Emmy didn't notice. 'And for that reason I like to be left alone. I need to concentrate.'

'Of course,' said Emmy, brightly impervious. 'You just let me know if there's anything you want, and I'll make sure you get it.'

'There is something.'

'Yes?' Emmy took a step back into the centre of the dining room, eager to please.

'I shall be keeping the key to my room with me, and I should be glad if you would not go in and disturb anything.'

Emmy tossed her head back with a little smile. The woman couldn't be serious, surely. 'Now don't you worry about me disturbing anything. I shall be very careful when I make the bed and dust, and I shall—'

But Mrs Smithson was serious. Very serious. 'I would prefer it if you did *not* make the bed.' Her voice was quite harsh. 'Please stay away from my room.'

To say Emmy was astonished was putting it mildly. She was an old-fashioned seaside landlady, and, although anxious to make her guests comfortable, ran her guesthouse with an iron rod. She was used to her guests acquiescing to her suggestions, not giving her instructions. No one had ever done that before.

'But I can't leave you in a dirty room,' she spluttered. 'What about changing the sheets?'

A spoon clattered loudly into the grapefruit bowl. That Mrs Smithson was exasperated, in fact, very annoyed, finally penetrated Emmy's consciousness. 'You may change the sheets when I tell you, Mrs Matthews. Not on any other day. And you may do a little light cleaning at the same time. But until I give you permission please leave my room and everything in it alone. I shall have piles of paper everywhere, and I really cannot tolerate any interference with my things. If this is not convenient, then I'm afraid I shall have to find other lodgings for my stay in Stibbington.'

After opening and closing her mouth for a moment, but saying nothing, Emmy began to retreat. The last thing she wanted was to lose a paying guest, even if she was rather strange, and logic told her she shouldn't complain; no housework meant an easier life. But she couldn't leave without saying something. 'I shall change the sheets as you wish,' she said in a businesslike fashion. This statement was met with stony silence and Emmy began backing into the kitchen. 'I'll start cooking the breakfast. Do you want fried mushrooms or tomatoes?'

'Both,' came the reply in an uncompromising tone of voice.

In the kitchen, Emmy put on the bacon, sausage, tomatoes, and mushrooms to fry, and poured herself a cup of tea. The little contretemps with her guest had left her feeling bothered and bewildered, not least because of the uneasy feeling she had about Mrs Smithson. Someone more sensitive than Emmy Matthews would perhaps have tried to pin the feeling down to something positive, but Emmy fell back on her 'catch-all' solution. It was her stomach. Something had made her feel bad. Upset her stomach, in fact. She was very prone to stomach upsets. And if she felt that way, or *bad*, as she always described it, there was only one thing to do, and that was to go to the doctor. Emmy had implicit faith in the doctor. Especially Dr Jamieson. He was a wonderful man. He always knew which pills to prescribe, and she always felt better after a visit because he set her mind at rest. Yes, an appointment with Dr Jamieson was just what was needed and she'd organize that the minute she'd delivered Mrs Smithson's breakfast.

Carefully scooping out the now cooked bacon, sausage, tomatoes, and mushrooms, she eased a slice of bread and some slices of black pudding into the sizzling fat. She'd show Mrs Smithson what a *real* cooked breakfast was like. No one would ever be able to point a finger at her and say she didn't look after her guests. Even if some of them were a bit strange.

'Honeywell Health Centre.' Tara Murphy balanced the phone between one ear and her shoulder while her hands shuffled and sorted a pile of repeat prescriptions.

'Mrs Matthews here. I want to see Dr Jamieson. And I want to see him this morning,' said Emmy fiercely, anticipating opposition. That uppity Tara Murphy, who seemed to think she was there to keep patients away from doctors, might push other people around but she was not one of them. What right had that girl to be so snooty anyway? Her father had arrived in Stibbington only twenty-five years ago, an Irish labourer with not a penny to his name. Just because he could charm the birds from the trees, and had married the local garage owner's daughter, eventually inheriting the business, didn't make the Murphy family special. Tara Murphy had nothing to shout about.

'I'm afraid Dr Jamieson is fully booked,' said Tara firmly. 'All day.' There was a moment's silence while Emmy digested this, then Tara said, 'I can book you in for next week if you like.'

Emmy thought Tara sounded very uncaring. Doctors' receptionists, in her view, ought to *worry* about patients. What use was next week? She felt bad now. 'I could die in the meantime,' she sniffed.

'If it's urgent you can see Dr Browne. She's new to the practice. She's taken the place of Dr Burton, who is now retired.'

'I know.' At first, Emmy was not happy, but then she cheered up; it would be an opportunity to see what the new lady doctor was like. Not that she had much faith in women doing what she considered to be men's work. That was another thing she didn't approve of. These days young women seemed to be doing everything and anything. Doctors, priests, lorry drivers. Emmy disapproved of them all. 'All right. I'll see this Dr Browne. About eleven will be convenient for me.'

'Half past eleven is convenient for Dr Browne. I'll put you in the computer.' The phone clicked dead leaving Mrs Matthews glaring and impotent. That Tara Murphy was much too big for her boots.

Morning surgery had finally finished and Lizzie was running late. Emmy Matthews had taken much more of her time than the ten minute slot she'd been allocated. Hastily grabbing a cup of coffee she popped her head into the senior partner's office.

'Sorry, Dick.' She gulped back the hot coffee. 'But I'll have to tell Mabel, I'll catch up with my letters this evening. I'll do them myself. I don't want them to be late.' It hadn't taken Lizzie long to find out that Mabel was always late with the typing no matter what time of day it was given to her. If she wanted something done the same day it was quicker to do it herself on the computer.

Dick Jamieson regarded Lizzie with fatherly exasperation. 'Drink your coffee, girl, and have a sandwich before you go off on your visits.' Glad of the excuse Lizzie obediently sat down and took the sandwich Dick proffered. 'I should have warned you about Mrs Matthews,' he said mildly. 'I assume she is the cause of you running late.'

Dick exuded an air of tranquility about him; nothing appeared to faze him, and Lizzie began to relax. She pulled a face and agreed. 'Yes, Mrs Matthews is the reason. What a woman. As soon as I thought I'd got her sorted out she presented me with another symptom. Headache, earache, stomach upset, and—'

'Bowels,' interrupted Dick, and roared with laughter. 'That woman is healthier than either you or me,' he said. 'Give her a prescription for a laxative of some kind and she'll go away happy.'

'I'm afraid I suggested something different,' said Lizzie, who didn't agree with prescribing things just to keep patients happy. 'It seems that the last prescription you gave her isn't working. To use Mrs Matthews' exact words, "A sachet after breakfast fails to produce anything".'

Dick raised his bushy eyebrows. 'So what did you give her?'

'Nothing,' said Lizzie, biting decisively into the sandwich. A mistake. The sandwich, made by Tara's mother at the garage shop, filled with tuna and sweetcorn, splattered its contents in all directions. After mopping up the errant sweetcorn she continued. 'I told her to get plenty of exercise, drink more water and eat apples and broccoli.'

'And no prescription?'

Lizzie shook her head. 'No prescription,' she said firmly. 'I told her that I believed in nature being given a chance.'

Dick's eyebrows went even higher. 'Watch it. She'll be telling all and sundry that you are into complementary medicine or some such nonsense.'

'Dick,' said Lizzie severely. 'Good diet and exercise is usually the best medicine. You know that.'

'Ah yes, of course I do. But you know as well as I do that some patients prefer a prescription, and Emmy Matthews is one of them. It's something tangible she can hold in her hand. That piece of paper on its own can make them feel better.' Dick leaned forward and regarded Lizzie with a quizzical expression. 'You've got a piece of sweetcorn on your cheek.' Lizzie hastily wiped it away with a paper serviette. Dick grinned, 'Did you recommend diet and exercise to your London patients?'

Lizzie, regaining her sense of humour, grinned back, and throwing the serviette in the wastepaper basket shook her head. 'Point taken. No I didn't because most were too poor to buy fresh fruit and vegetables even if they had access to them. And when they did have money, burger and fries were the cheapest option, and the one they all preferred. And as for exercise! Well, pounding the streets of Whitechapel is not only dangerous, it's enough to send anyone into deepest depression. I never recommended it. But it's different here. People are not so poverty-stricken.'

'We have our poor too,' said Dick. 'You'll meet them soon enough.'

Lizzie finished her coffee just as Tara Murphy came in with a pile of patients' notes in their brown cardboard envelopes, which she put down in front of her. 'I've taken another two calls for you, Dr Browne,' she said. 'That makes ten visits in all.'

'Thanks, Tara.' Lizzie took the notes and stuffed them into her leather bag. 'With luck I'll finish these calls in time for evening surgery. I'm sure one day I'm going to get lost around here. I'll have to programme the satnav with all these addresses.'

Dick tutted, but Tara beamed. 'I'm trying to persuade everyone to go electronic,' she said. She looked at Dick Jamieson, 'You will have to soon, as soon as we have the new system installed. You'll have all your visits programmed on to your laptops – no more old brown folders.'

Dick groaned and Lizzie disappeared clutching her brimming black bag. She couldn't wait for the new laptops.

The satnav proved invaluable. The New Forest around Stibbington was riddled with minor roads. Lizzie found that often patients listed for a visit lived at the end of tracks which were marked on the map by a series of dots, and she suddenly realized, with gratitude, that Dick and the other partners had been giving her an easy ride up until now.

Previously, they must have sorted out her visits, giving her all the ones within a confined area of Stibbington so that she didn't get lost. Today her patients were scattered much further afield.

It started raining again, and the car, its carpets still wet from her encounter with the flood of the night before, now smelled stale. The windscreen steamed up in the dampness and cold rain, and she had difficulty in keeping it clear, finally resorting to periodically wiping the screen with the back of her coat sleeve, the duster in the glove compartment proving useless. It was at times like this that she did wonder at the wisdom of buying an old but snazzy-looking car as opposed to a dull but modern one with air conditioning and other mod cons. But too late. She had the Alfa.

The bare branches overhanging the lanes seemed menacing, dripping great plops of water on to the roof of the car, and Lizzie began to feel uneasy. Would she settle down in the country? It all looked depressingly dark in the rain. And there was so much mud. Mud had never been a problem in Whitechapel. After just five visits her rather elegant black leather shoes looked as if they would never recover and her feet felt cold, damp, and uncomfortable. She made a mental note: waterproof footwear of some kind was an essential item for her shopping list. Was there such a thing as a fashionable Wellington boot?

It had all been so different on the days she'd made the initial reconnaissance trips visiting the practice. Three whole days in Stibbington and every one of them a glorious day. A sharp autumn frost had brushed the bracken and trees with silver, the sky had been a brilliant, sunny blue, and the River Stib and the estuary had glittered cerulean in the clear air. Of course, common sense told her it was bound to rain in Stibbington the same as it did everywhere else. But this seemed more than just ordinary rain; it had the ferocity of a tropical downpour without the heat. Everything was so cold. The rain was freezing, the mud was freezing, she was freezing, and Lizzie, irrational though she knew it to be, felt cheated.

The route to her last patient took her along the hard, past Mrs Matthews – the hypochondriac patient's – guesthouse, The House on the Hard. It looked almost aggressively well kept, thought Lizzie, and quite different from the run-down bungalow next door. On fine days she could see that the guesthouse must have had a beautiful view, but today the river looked anything but inviting; a great slab of muddy-coloured water surging in the wind against the gravel of the hard. Would it ever stop raining? A motorcyclist passed her. He was too close, and much too fast for comfort, spraying mud all over her windscreen. Using an unladylike epithet, Lizzie stopped, cleared the screen, then started off again, peering out through the gloom, looking for the turning for Candover House, the address of her last patient, Wayne Girling.

She found Candover House at the end of a long track stretching away from the sea, in a small clearing beside a pine plantation. It was such a grand sounding name that Lizzie had expected it to be a Georgian mansion. Instead she found a small farm cottage, overshadowed by dark pines, with a chicken run and coop on one side of the path in the front garden. Some miserable, unhealthy-looking chickens, half their feathers missing, were scratching about in the mud. So much for free range, thought Lizzie. The opposite side of the path was planted with rows of Brussels sprouts and leeks. A long-haired lurcher type dog rushed up the path towards her barking loudly, but following an ear-piercing shriek of 'Rover!' rushed back the way he'd come and vanished behind the house. A woman emerged at the side of the house, and then disappeared like the dog, only to reappear at the front door, which opened just as Lizzie put her foot on the doorstep.

'Mrs Girling?'

The woman nodded. She was tired-looking, and could have been any age between thirty and fifty. But she had a fine-boned face, and Lizzie could see that she must have been beautiful once, although years of neglect had taken their toll. She was wearing a wrap-round pinny over a dress and her feet, complete with slippers, were in a pair of rubber galoshes. She waved Lizzie in and through the hall without a word.

Lizzie found her patient, Wayne Girling, a very small, undernourished-looking little boy of ten, sitting wheezing on the front room settee. It was obviously the best room and rarely used, having the musty chill of a permanently closed place.

She smiled encouragingly at her small patient, and said, 'Have you a warmer spot, Mrs Girling? The kitchen perhaps?' Wayne sat staring, swinging his puny little legs and wheezing, seeming entirely disinterested in everything. The smile from Lizzie failed to get a reaction.

Mrs Girling twisted her hands, plucking at the edge of her overall, and looked uncomfortable. 'The kitchen is in a terrible muddle,' she said in a low voice.

Lizzie guessed that the whole house was probably in a terrible muddle. The poor woman looked washed out; having a child so late in life had obviously knocked the stuffing out of her. 'Don't worry about that,' she said, trying to put Mrs Girling at her ease. 'I'm used to that. My own kitchen is always in a terrible muddle. But a warm kitchen would be much better for Wayne. Muddle doesn't matter; it's part of everyday life.'

A ghost of a smile flickered briefly across Mrs Girling's face, and Lizzie felt she'd made some headway. Together the three of them went back through the freezing cold hall – no central heating, noted Lizzie – into the warmth of the kitchen.

'It's his chest,' Mrs Girling said somewhat superfluously; the short trip had left Wayne sounding like a pair of worn out bellows. She placed him on a chair near the source of heat, an old-fashioned kitchen range. 'He's always been chesty, although my other son was always as fit as a fiddle.'

Lizzie had to worm her way through Wayne's uncooperative jumper, shirt, and vest in order to place her stethoscope on his chest. 'How many other children have you, Mrs Girling?'

'Only one. Tarquin. But he's older. Twenty-seven now.'

'Grown up, then,' said Lizzie conversationally, still trying to put the woman at her ease.

'I suppose you could say that.' Mrs Girling sounded doubtful, as if she were not certain on that fact.

After taking Wayne's temperature, Lizzie thumped his chest. Unsurprised she found he was choked with mucus. 'Did he have a cold before this wheezing set in?' she asked.

'Yes. But he's always getting colds, and he's always wheezing, although not as bad as this. That's why I called you. I'd have brought him to the surgery, but he said he felt too wheezy to walk.'

'You did the right thing in calling,' Lizzie assured her. She flicked through Wayne's sparse notes, noting that he'd rarely seen a doctor, which presumably meant that Mrs Girling had coped alone during Wayne's previous wheezing attacks. 'Has any other doctor ever suggested that Wayne might be asthmatic?'

'Certainly not.' The mother was immediately hostile and defensive. 'No one in our family has anything like that. Everyone is very healthy, and Wayne has never been neglected.'

Lizzie ignored the hostility and began to write out a prescription. 'I'm not suggesting that he's been neglected, Mrs Girling,' she said quietly. 'But he needs some treatment now. I'm going to give him some antibiotics for the chest infection, and an inhaler to help with his breathing. It's very important that it's used correctly so read the instructions carefully.' She searched through her bag and found a sample pack of antibiotics. 'I'll give him two of these now, and leave you with enough for tonight. But he must continue with them tomorrow and start the inhaler as soon as possible, so the prescription needs to be taken into a pharmacy now. Is there someone who can do that for you?'

Mrs Girling jerked her head towards the back of the house. 'Tarquin can do it,' she said. 'He's only out the back there, fiddling with his plants as usual. Never does anything useful like earning money, or taking me out in the car when I need it. But he'll have to help out now. Now that his little brother is ill.'

Lizzie thought Tarquin could have helped out earlier and brought his mother and brother to the surgery, but said nothing. She snapped her bag shut and passed the prescription over. 'Get Tarquin to go and fetch it straight away. There's no time to lose.' She ruffled Wayne's tousled head and held out the tablets. 'You stay here in the warm, young man. I'll soon have you feeling better.'

Wayne said nothing. He swallowed the tablets Lizzie gave him, then took a sip of water before wiping his nose on the back of the frayed knitted cuff of his jumper.

Mrs Girling escorted Lizzie back to the front door, the hostility dissipating a little. 'Thank you for coming, Doctor.' She paused, and then said, 'You've moved into old Mrs Burnett's house, haven't you? Silver Cottage in Deer Leap Lane.'

'Yes.' Lizzie wondered where the conversation was leading.

'Tarquin used to do the garden for Mrs Burnett. She found it too much. He tidied it for her once in a while.'

Lizzie thought of the wildly overgrown garden, which needed much more than a tidy. A radical overhaul by a landscape gardener was more the requirement, but Tarquin Girling would be better than nothing to start with. At least he could clear up a bit. 'Tell him to come and see me,' she said. 'I could certainly do with some help.'

Again a fleeting smile lit Mrs Girling's tired face. 'It would have to be for cash in hand,' she said quickly. 'That's how Mrs Burnett always paid.'

Lizzie understood the unspoken message: Tarquin was fiddling the benefit system. But so what, she thought, feeling sorry for Mrs Girling. Judging by the state of the house there appeared to be precious little money to go round, and she was not going to give away such a small deceit.

'Of course,' she agreed. 'Cash in hand. The same as before. Ask him to come and see me tomorrow afternoon, Saturday. I'll be in then.'

'He'll come,' said Mrs Girling firmly. 'I'll see to it.' It seemed the prospect of a little money gave her the impetus to be positive.

CHAPTER FOUR

THE RAIN HAD stopped, but clouds hung overhead, dark and heavy with moisture, necessitating use of the car headlights even though it was only early afternoon. Tyres squelching, Lizzie made her way back down the track and supposed that the unseen Tarquin must possess four wheels of some sort if he were to go to the pharmacist, and visit her tomorrow, or go anywhere else for that matter. Candover House was so isolated; no wonder Mrs Girling looked frazzled and depressed. She wondered if there was a Mr Girling, and made a mental note to look up that fact.

At the end of the track, surrounded by mud banks and wispy sea grass stood an old wooden clapperboard warehouse building. Lizzie hadn't noticed it on her way to the Girlings', but now it loomed into focus in her headlights demanding attention. Faded lettering on the side of the timbers indicated that it had once been a ships' chandler where boats had put in for supplies, but the river had silted up and now it was a good hundred yards from the waters' edge. Paint peeling, isolated and forlorn-looking, it stood empty. Some of the boards were loose and flapped spasmodically in the wind. All in all it was a depressing hulk. Just as well it's out of sight of the town, thought Lizzie; its air of decay doesn't sit well with the affluent atmosphere of Stibbington itself. Past the chandlery she turned on to the made up surface of Shore Lane, which wound its way alongside the River Stib towards the hard. She'd nearly got as far as the first bungalow when her attention was caught by the sight of Mrs Matthews. She was running down between the brambles and the remains of the previous summer's nettles in the overgrown driveway from the bungalow towards the lane, and waving frantically. Lizzie gave a silent groan. She had no desire to see Mrs Matthews again for at least a week. Twice in one day was above and beyond the call of duty. But she had to stop. The woman was obviously distressed. So distressed, in fact, that she could hardly speak.

Lizzie stopped the car and turned off the ignition and waited for her to catch her breath.

Emmy Matthews leaned against the side of the Alfa, wheezing, and alternately clutching her ample bosom and pointing in rapid succession. It reminded Lizzie of a clip from a silent movie and would have been funny had not she been so agitated.

'It's . . .' Emmy drew in a deep breath, coughed, clutched her chest and pointed again. 'Darren,' she gasped. 'Van. Accident.' She took another deep, shuddering breath. 'You *must* come.'

Without a word Lizzie got out of the car and followed her up the drive towards the bungalow. Slipping and sliding in the mud, she wondered what kind of accident she was about to find, and was worried. It had been a long time since she'd dealt with any on-the-spot trauma. Most accidents in London were dealt with by the emergency services that possessed all the latest hi-tech equipment. What did she have in her bag? Would it be sufficient to deal with the situation? She made to go towards the house, but Mrs Matthews, still breathless and unable to speak properly, shook her head and, grabbing her arm, dragged her towards the garage.

'Oh my God.' One look and Lizzie knew that nothing she had in her bag would be of the slightest use. Nothing could resuscitate the mangled body lying beneath the van. Force of habit made her kneel down and feel for a pulse. Of course there was none. How could there be? The man's brains were splattered all over the garage floor, and had been there for some time judging by the dried-up appearance of the mess and the overpowering rank smell of stale blood. She scrambled up off her knees, and noticed in a detached fashion that there was blood on the bottom of her winter coat. 'I think we'd better ring for the police,' she said.

'Is he dead?' Emmy seemed unable to take her eyes off the awful sight.

It was a needless question, but Lizzie could see that Mrs Matthews was not in a fit state to think properly. She stepped between the crushed body and Emmy, blocking her view, then gently taking her arm, she led her away. 'Yes, he is dead,' she said quietly. 'Is there anyone in the house I should speak to?'

Mrs Matthews shook her head silently then took a deep breath and started gabbling very quickly. 'Darren Evans lived alone. If you can call it living. He never looked after himself properly. I brought him up a meat pie. It was spare because Mrs Smithson didn't stay in for lunch. I was thinking she would, so I made the pie. But she disappeared without so much as a word, and I had the pie left over. So I thought Darren would like it, and I brought it up for his supper tonight, but. . . .' Her voice petered out tearfully, and she was silent again for a moment. 'I used to be friendly with his mother when she was alive. But that was before. . . .' She stopped, dabbed at her eyes, and then said. 'Oh well, none of that matters now.'

But Lizzie had stopped listening. Retrieving her mobile from her bag she punched out 999. 'Yes, police. There is a dead man here at—' She stopped a moment and got the exact address from Emmy and imparted the information. 'No, the man is definitely dead. I am a doctor, believe me, there is no chance of resuscitation. Yes. Yes. I can wait until they get here.' She closed the phone and put it back in her bag. It began raining again. A hard, straight, drenching downpour, unremitting in its ferocity. Emmy stood and looked expectantly at her, seemingly impervious to the pouring rain. 'Do you want to wait in my car with me, Mrs Matthews?' Lizzie asked. 'I think you should stay here until the police arrive, as you were first on the scene.'

They settled in the car, both dripping wetly on to the floor and seats. Lizzie wound the window down a fraction to try and help ease the fug that was already building up. They sat in uncomfortable silence. Darren Evans; the memory of the young man who'd been to see her earlier in the week was etched on her mind. Perhaps if I'd given him more time. Perhaps if. . . . If what? Too late now. Lizzie, unable to get the picture of the pulped head out of her mind wondered if it was bothering Mrs Matthews too, and thought it probably was. She looked pale, and wasn't talking.

They were not there long before a police car arrived. A horn blared and a man stuck his head out of the window. He looked impatient and slightly bad tempered. Lizzie wound down her window and got drenched by a particularly ferocious blast of wind and rain through the opening. 'Move it!' he shouted, 'and be quick about it.'

'He might have said please,' grumbled Lizzie, but at the same time she was glad of the interruption. It brought back a sense of normality to an abnormal situation. Shoving the Alfa into gear and rolling over to the right as far as she could, she let the police car pass, then followed it up the drive and parked behind. She and Mrs Matthews waited while the two men went into the garage. 'Do you know them?' she asked.

Emmy Matthews nodded. 'The older one, the one who shouted, is a newcomer to Stibbington, Adam Maguire. He's a widower, lost his wife to cancer not long after they moved here about three years ago. And the young one lives over on the other side of Stibbington, in one of those old police houses. He married Ann Palfrey. She comes from an old Stibbington family, although his family, the Graysons are new, have only been here since the war.'

Lizzie gave a wry smile. She'd already found out that country people had long memories, and had resigned herself to being a newcomer in Stibbington until her dying day. If I stay that long, she now thought, because if it keeps on raining the way it has been for the past couple of days I won't be able to bear it. She always found rain depressing at the best of times, but the countryside in the rain was even more depressing, and that was the last thing she needed at the moment. Illogical though she knew it was, rain made her think of Mike. It had been raining the day he'd told her that he was moving on to another relationship with someone else. Someone younger, more attractive. Stop it, she told herself. Don't start mulling over the past. Stop it. But she couldn't. Not entirely. She would never have moved down here if it hadn't been for Mike leaving her. It was his damned fault she was stuck out in the country in a sea of mud and in the pouring rain, waiting to be interviewed by the police because one of her patients, head smashed to smithereens, lay on the concrete floor of a freezing garage. To make matters worse she was stuck in a car with Mrs Matthews. Every doctor's nightmare patient. A hypochondriac. Suddenly the pavements of London held an allure they'd never possessed when she'd lived there.

Adam Maguire came out of the garage first. He strode through the mud in an enormous pair of green wellington boots, and wrenched open the door of the Alfa. 'I'm Detective Chief Inspector Maguire. Which one of you is the doctor?' he asked, but already he knew. The older woman had an unfashionable Stibbington air about her and looked pale and shaken; the younger of the two looked sophisticated and in command. Her dark hair was well groomed, and she had an air of brisk professionalism about her. Not pale at all. It seemed that it would take more than one mangled body to shake her. Adam didn't bother to analyze his feelings, other than to briefly acknowledge that she looked the capable kind of woman who always made him feel uncomfortable. He preferred dealing with men. He knew where he was with men. Never had to guess.

'Me,' said Lizzie. 'I'm the doctor. I rang in and reported it.' She nodded towards the garage, 'but Mrs Matthews found him first.'

'I'll take a brief statement. We can do it in more detail later as I understand that you both live locally.' He looked towards the bungalow. 'I expect it's a mess in there, but it's better than me standing out here in the rain and getting soaked. Let's go in.'

The bungalow was, as he rightly surmised, a mess. Sparsely furnished, with dirty curtains so grey it was impossible to hazard a guess as to their original colour. The whole place looked as if it hadn't been cleaned for months. Certainly, the washing up hadn't been done for a week or more.

'Never seen so many dirty coffee cups,' said Mrs Matthews with a sniff of disapproval.

'And most of them with inches of mould growing in them,' said Lizzie, picking one up.

'Please don't touch anything. Forensics will need to go over this place with a fine-tooth comb.' Maguire was annoyed. Surely the woman knew better than to disturb evidence; heaven knows there were enough crime programmes on TV these days. No excuse for anyone not knowing the rudiments of police procedure.

'Sorry,' said Lizzie, hastily putting the cup back.

'I thought forensics were only called in if it's a murder,' said Mrs Matthews, showing that she for one *did* watch TV and knew the way the police worked. 'But this is an accident. Poor Darren couldn't have jacked the van up properly.'

Adam Maguire didn't confirm or contradict her statement. He remained silent and got out a notebook. He hated taking notes, something Steve Grayson should have been doing, but he had to wait outside to organize the backup team and direct the forensic pathologist to the body. Body, not scene of the crime; he was too well disciplined to allow himself to jump to conclusions. Probably Mrs Matthews was right. The van had not been jacked up securely. 'Tell me how you came to be here, Mrs Matthews?' he said.

She went through her story of the meat pie, and how Darren Evans had always neglected himself, and finished up by saying, 'It's terrible for such a dreadful accident to happen, but of course it was inevitable, I suppose. Retribution, you might say.'

'Retribution?' He quizzed Mrs Matthews' by now slightly tearful face. 'That's a strange word to use.'

'Oh!'

The woman was flustered. Worried. Almost guilty-looking. Adam wondered why. He saw Lizzie watching Mrs Matthews, a quizzical expression on her face, and guessed she was picking up the same vibes. That was the trouble with a place like Stibbington: everyone knew so much about each other, and he, as a newcomer knew nothing. He'd ask Steve later on. He must know something about Darren Evans. 'Yes. Tell me why you think that, Mrs Matthews,' he said.

To his disappointment the woman seemed to recover her composure, and a blank looked settled across her face. 'Well, because Darren was always so careless,' she said. 'He never seemed to care what happened to him. His whole life was a tragedy. From start to finish. A tragedy,' she finished firmly.

'Thank you, Mrs Matthews.' Maguire knew that was as much as he was going to get from her today. Might as well let her go. 'Go and ask Sergeant Grayson to get a constable to run you back down the lane to your house in a car, there should be another squad car out there by now.'

He turned towards Lizzie. She was watching him intently. He noticed her eyes, a mixture of green and brown, and found himself thinking she would have been attractive if she were not so thin or impatient-looking. It was obvious that she couldn't wait to get away.

As if to confirm his analysis she looked at her watch, and said briskly, 'I hope you won't be too long with me, Chief Inspector. I have an evening surgery to do before I can go home.'

'I'll be as brief as possible. Just tell me how you became involved in this,' he hesitated, then said 'accident.' It was better to leave it at that for the time being. Gossip would spread like wildfire through Stibbington soon enough, no need to fan the flames until he was sure.

Lizzie told him her name and how she'd seen Darren Evans as a patient the previously Wednesday, but didn't know he lived at the bungalow until she'd been waylaid by Mrs Matthews. Adam Maguire listened and made a few notes. She had a nice voice, he thought. Calm and quiet. Obviously not local, no trace of a Hampshire dialect. Come to think of it, he hadn't seen her around before and he knew most of the doctors in Stibbington personally. Then he remembered. Dr Burton had recently retired and a woman had taken his place. His mind drifted for a moment. Dr Burton. Nice man. He'd looked after Rosemary during her final days. Rosemary. Would he ever get over the feeling of emptiness that swept through him whenever he thought of her? Trouble was that although he felt her loss as keenly as ever, he was beginning to forget what she had looked like. In the beginning she'd been so real that he'd felt he could almost see and touch her. Almost. But now, three years on, her image had faded, leaving him with only brief insubstantial glimpses. But those glimpses made him feel lonelier than ever. He couldn't bear to let her go, yet the mere act of continuing to live without her was forcing her further and further away.

'Of course, it doesn't look like an accident to me.'

Lizzie Browne's statement jerked his mind back to the present. He looked at her. She was standing near the door, ready for flight, bulky doctor's bag in one hand, car keys in the other. She looked impatient. Adam suspected that she knew his mind had been wandering, and it put him on the defensive. 'Really, Dr Browne. Speaking as an expert, are you?' he asked.

'I've seen my fair share of death. Natural, unnatural, and violent. This obviously was not natural, and in my opinion looked far too violent to be a plain accident. The weight of a car falling on someone's head would do serious damage, but I doubt that it would smash it like an eggshell. In my opinion that van was driven over him.'

'Thank you for your opinion, Dr Browne. But I'll be glad if you would keep your thoughts to yourself until we've had a proper report.' Adam knew he sounded stuffy, a regular Mr Plod, in fact, but something about the woman raised his hackles. Annoying thing was, he couldn't explain why. He noted the impatient swing of her medical bag with irritation. 'I know you've got to get to your surgery so I won't detain you any longer, although as we shall need to speak to you later I shall need your address.'

Lizzie gave the address briskly. 'Silver Cottage, Deer Leap Lane, Upper Stibbington.'

Feeling guilty Maguire tried to make amends and inject a note of friendliness into the proceedings. 'Silver Cottage. I know it. A very pretty little thatched cottage, with a vast garden. Your husband will have his work cut out to tame that wilderness.'

'I don't have a husband. I shall be employing a gardener.'

She turned and in a moment was gone. A faint whiff of perfume lingered, and Maguire was left with a vague feeling of uneasiness knowing that he could have handled things better. But there was no time to worry about antagonizing a local doctor; there was work to be done. He left the bungalow and returned to the garage.

Steve Grayson had been busy. The area around the cottage was now sealed off with blue and white plastic tape secured to stakes in the sodden earth. The tape flapped dismally in the wind and rain, making a sharp clicking sound, a contrast to the hiss of the steady downpour. A screen was in the process of being erected to protect the garage and its contents from prying eyes. Even in a small town like Stibbington local people and the press could be intrusive, as both Adam and Steve knew to their cost. At the end of the drive one very unhappy, wet policeman stood on guard for the same reason. Adam Maguire was inclined to share Lizzie Browne's view that Darren Evans's death was no accident, although he was saying nothing for the moment.

He walked down to where Grayson was talking to the officer on guard. 'Okay?' he asked the duty policeman.

'Yes, sir,' came the mumbled reply. It was the newest recruit to Stibbington police station, Kevin Harrison. Adam felt sorry for him. A rotten job. He could well remember what it was like to stand on duty in the rain, a steady stream of water plopping with monotonous regularity from the brim of his helmet on to his nose.

Steve Grayson was buoyant. 'At last, a case to get our teeth into,' he said.

'Don't sound so bloody cheerful; that poor sod back there is dead.' Adam stood back as a photographer came past, lugging his gear into the garage. 'Get a move on,' he told him, 'the pathologist will be here any minute, and he won't want to hang around waiting for you to finish, not in this weather.' He turned to Steve. 'Where is Merryweather? He has been informed, hasn't he?'

'Of course. And I told him it was the kind of gory case he likes.'

Yes that was true. Phineas Merryweather, local forensic pathologist, was doctor, poet, musician, bon viveur, and connoisseur of fine wines who also loved a 'bit of gore' as he was fond of saying. Adam Maguire, on the other hand did not. Sometimes he wondered whether it was his subconscious desire for a quiet life that had made him choose the job at Stibbington. He had escaped from Liverpool and the never-ending string of inner-city crimes to the relative peace and security of rural Hampshire. Rosemary had wanted to leave the city, and he had wanted whatever she wanted. Now, though, he could move, in fact had been offered promotion to do so, but he lacked the motivation. Besides, if he were honest, he rather liked the slower pace of life in Stibbington. The people were friendly in small, unobtrusive ways. And there were not many cases like the one he was faced with now. Murder, and against his better judgement he knew he'd made up his mind, was a rare event in Stibbington.

He went back to the garage, and stood watching the photographer. Lights flashing, the photographer dodged about taking pictures from every conceivable angle. Adam felt sorry for the boy on the floor. Death had already robbed him of personality. It always did. Darren Evans was now a statistic. All that remained of a life. The photographs would show a bloody corpse with a splattered head, a thin body with legs like sticks protruding from beneath the van. The pictures would be looked at, commented on, then put in a file, and that would be that.

'What have you found out about him?' he said to Steve Grayson who joined him in the garage.

'Not much,' replied his sergeant. 'Twenty-seven years old. A registered addict. Heroin.'

'I know,' said Maguire. 'Dr Browne prescribed his methadone only this week.'

'Well,' continued Grayson, 'he'd been on the stuff for years. Got his regular prescription for methadone from Dr Jamieson, Honeywell Health Centre, but mainlined as well judging by the state of his arms. Born here. He left Stibbington after school, had a short spell in prison for aggravated burglary, came back here when he got out and has kept his head low ever since.'

'Did you know him? You've lived here all your life.'

Grayson screwed up his face. 'I've been trying to think. Name seems vaguely familiar. I'll run it through the computer again when we get back. But I've never met him.'

'What about when you were at school?'

Grayson rolled his eyes heavenwards. 'I'm six years older than he was, sir. I'd left secondary school just as he was starting. Then I moved away for five years.'

Maguire sighed, he should have realized. Trouble was twenty-seven or thirty-three, it all seemed the same to him. Incredibly young. 'Have we been keeping an eye on him?'

'Not us at Stibbington. No reason to. Hampshire Drug Squad has been vaguely interested. They'd like to know how he could afford drugs and to buy this place, which apparently belongs to him. Although God knows why anyone should want to buy it.' Grayson looked around at the tangled garden and run down bungalow, dismissing it with a glance. 'It's a dump. But apparently he managed to pay all his bills on time, and his state benefit wouldn't have covered it. So they guessed he was doing a bit of dealing.'

'Have they got anything on him for dealing?' asked Maguire.

'No. And according to them they haven't got the time or resources to follow up little people like Darren. They go after the big boys, and just wait for something to happen to the small fry.'

'And it has,' said Maguire thoughtfully, his professional mind slipping into gear, and with it the familiar stirring of interest. It was good to have a challenge. He had a gut instinct that this case would prove to be interesting. 'Well, tell them to back off,' he said. 'This is our case. And who knows, if there are any big boys involved, maybe we'll be able to give them some answers to their problems in the not too distant future.'

'You're thinking it is murder then,' said Grayson, sounding excited. 'How can you be sure?'

'I can't. But I'm as sure as I can be at this stage. So go and find out if he had any friends. And don't be afraid to milk the drug squad for information, although don't give anything away. Not until we're good and ready.'

Grayson grinned. 'As I said right at the beginning, it's good to have something to get our teeth into.'

Maguire grinned back. 'Push off,' he said, not unkindly.

'That's no way to speak to your subordinates!' A portly figure appeared at the side of the tarpaulin tent, and Phineas Merryweather, small, rotund, and rather pink in the face, puffed in. His breath rasped before him like little spurts of steam in the cold wet air.

'God, Phineas, you sound like a bloody train,' said Maguire. But he was glad to see him. 'Take a look at what we've got here.'

Phineas bent down with some difficulty, wheezed more than ever, and peered beneath the van. 'V is for very dead,' he said.

'I don't need a forensic pathologist here to tell me that.'

There was no reply. Phineas needed all his breath to struggle into his protective clothing. With much grunting and puffing he succeeded and then lowered himself to the ground and crawled under the van. He made his initial examination then shouted for the van to be hauled away, before scrambling upright. 'I'll give him a good going over once I get him on the slab. But I doubt there'll be a lot more I can tell you.'

'So far, Phineas,' said Adam, 'you've told me absolutely nothing. All I've heard is a series of grunts.'

'You'd grunt, my boy, if you were my age and size trying to examine a corpse under a van.' He clasped the bulge that ballooned forth over his belted waist and sighed. 'Wife's put me on a diet, but I must say it doesn't seem to be working.'

'It never will, Phineas. You like your food and wine too much. Now, come on, tell me what you've surmised about Darren Evans here.'

'That his name?' said Phineas without interest, while struggling out of the protective suit. 'Well, he is, or rather was, a drug addict, but you probably know that. And he's dead.'

'I know that as well, for God's sake.'

'Don't be impatient, my dear boy. I was going to say he's been dead for at least twenty-four hours, and it wasn't an accident. Head's too bashed about. So much so, in fact, that I doubt I'll be able to draw definite conclusions as to the cause. But never mind, we'll scrape him up and have a good go. It's always amazing what you sometimes find when you're picking about amidst the pieces. Turn over one little piece of flesh, and hey presto! A revelation.'

Adam closed his mind to the unsavoury image. 'When can I have the report?'

'On your desk first thing tomorrow morning.'

43

CHAPTER FIVE

Lizzie slept badly that Friday night. Darren Evans had been murdered. She was certain of that, no matter what that supercilious Inspector Maguire might say. Keeping an open mind was one thing, but ignoring the blatantly obvious was ridiculous in the extreme. Yes, it was definitely murder, and that meant the murderer was somewhere out there in the darkness of Stibbington. Suddenly, the isolation of Silver Cottage, which had made it so attractive when she'd bought it in the autumn, became intimidating.

She felt alone and vulnerable, and found herself thinking of Carly, a student friend who now practised in the States. When she'd visited Carly, who also lived alone in a small village near Cape Cod, in an equally isolated house, she'd laughed at Carly's insistence on keeping a gun in her bedside locker. Now she wished she had access to one. But even if she had possessed such a thing, leaving it in the bedside locker would be illegal; firearm laws in Britain were much tougher than those in America. Besides, there was another major disadvantage: she wouldn't know how to fire the damned thing. So a gun was out of the question. Perhaps she ought to get a dog. A dog would be company. A dog would bark. But acquiring a dog in the middle of the night was also not the most practical of ideas. There was nothing for it but to keep the demon thoughts at bay.

But after tossing and turning for another hour, she finally went downstairs and got the heavy brass candlestick which stood in the hearth for ornament. Lying in bed with it beside her also proved impracticable; it was cold, hard, and dug into her ribs. But once carefully positioned by the side of the bed she felt more relaxed and safer. Her last thought before drifting off to sleep was that if anyone came in the night she would hit them first and ask questions afterwards.

When Saturday morning dawned she looked at the candlestick and felt slightly silly at being so panicky the night before, but she didn't move it. It could stay there. Her insurance policy against any unwelcome visitors.

Wrapping a thick towelling robe around her she slipped her feet into a pair of huge hedgehog slippers. A silly present from Louise when she knew her mother was moving to the country. 'Just to remind you that you'll be living side by side with nature', she'd said. Lizzie looked at them now and smiled. Then smiled again as she remembered that it was her Saturday off. In fact she was off duty for the whole weekend. It was her first chance to explore Stibbington since she'd taken up residence.

Outside, a wet and windy night had turned into a grey and dismal morning, although it had at least stopped raining. But the silence got on her nerves, which was absurd because she'd longed for peace and quiet, but now she wished there was someone around to talk to or even argue with, and that there was the roar of traffic in the background. She switched on the radio; the chatter of the newscaster's voice was comforting.

After a breakfast of toast and coffee Lizzie decided to try out Stibbington Market. Everyone at the practice had assured her it was excellent and now, she reasoned, was as good a time as any to go.

The market at Stibbington ran the length of the High Street. The stalls stretched either side of the road, all the way from the top of the hill down to the quay by the marina at the bottom. Although it was a cold and windy winter's morning it was crowded, and the first person Lizzie bumped into was Emmy Matthews.

'How are you, dear?' she said, lowering her voice confidentially. 'Got over that nasty little experience we had last night? I thought about you. It's very lonely out there in Deer Leap Lane. I do hope you weren't too worried and were able to sleep.'

'Yes. I slept perfectly, thank you,' Lizzie lied.

'Of course,' Mrs Matthews continued. 'As you know it's very lonely where I live, *and* it's next door to where Darren . . . well, enough said about that! I don't want to say the word.' Lizzie wondered which word she had in mind but didn't inquire, but Mrs Matthews was unstoppable. 'Anyway, thank goodness, I wasn't on my own last night, nor will I be for the foreseeable future. I've got a lady guest until Christmas. And at Christmas I've got a family staying. So I'm all right.'

'I'm so glad,' said Lizzie edging away.

'There she is over there. Mrs Smithson, my paying guest, I mean.' Mrs Matthews peered nosily. 'Whatever can she be shopping for? She doesn't need to shop for anything. Not while she's staying with me. I provide everything. Hello, Mrs Smithson.' She waved energetically and called but the woman didn't acknowledge her.

Lizzie realized that it was the woman on the train she'd accidentally trodden on. And she was still wearing the same suede shoes by the look of it. She walked awkwardly, which was hardly surprising. High heels and cobbles were not a happy combination. What women do in the name of vanity, thought Lizzie. She glanced down at her own feet, sensibly clad in sturdy walking shoes. No point in being vain, there was nobody she wanted to impress; besides, she didn't fancy crippling herself on the cobbles. Mrs Matthews shouted again, but still the woman didn't turn around. 'She didn't hear you,' said Lizzie.

'No, I suppose not.' Emmy Matthews' eyes darted around. 'Oh, I must dash. There's Marge Watson from Picklehurst over there. I must pop over and tell her about Darren Evans. She'll want to know.'

She darted off leaving Lizzie to wander down between the market stalls in the wake of Mrs Smithson, who seemed to be looking at everything and chatting to stallholders. Looking but not actually buying. Lizzie bought half a dozen fresh free-range eggs – laid the day before or so the girl assured her – farmhouse butter, cream, some broccoli, apples and potatoes then discovered that her arms were nearly being wrenched out of their sockets by the weight of her shopping. She looked at the other women in the market, all scurrying about with their laden shopping trolleys. Maybe I should get one, she thought, and then immediately dismissed the idea. No, she had definitely not yet reached the stage of using a trolley, and she would rather dislocate both shoulders than be seen wheeling one.

Halfway down the High Street was a small delicatessen. Antonio's Delicatessen, a permanent shop, not a market stall. It was packed with Italian goodies, and Lizzie succumbed and went in to buy a packet of pancetta and a lump of fresh parmesan. Now she had all the ingredients for a carbonara. It was only when she was inside the shop that she saw that Adam Maguire was being served.

'Your usual, Chief Inspector? Two granary loaves and a jar of bolognaise sauce?'

'Yes, thanks, Antonio,' said Maguire.

Antonio was small and dark, and looked to be of authentic Italian extraction. He was also bright and breezy and Lizzie guessed he was a gossip. 'I've heard you're involved in a bit of excitement,' he said, putting the loaves into brown paper bags.

'If you can call death exciting.' Maguire sounded morose.

Antonio rattled on happily, oblivious to the other man's mood. 'Danny Bayley was in here this morning. He always comes in on a Saturday to pick up his three P's for the week: pizza, pesto and pasta, that's his regular order, every week. That will be three pounds and ten pence, please.' Antonio tapped out the amount on the till and held out his hand. 'He told me that Darren Evans had been murdered. Fancy that, a murder, here in Stibbington. You'd never think it, would you? It's such a quiet place. Everyone so respectable. I can hardly believe it.'

'It's not the first murder here, nor will it be the last.' Lizzie listened more carefully. So he *had* decided it was murder. Or rather it had been *proved* to him that it was murder. The police were like the medical profession in that respect. They always wanted proof before committing themselves. A fact which Lizzie often found exasperating; she believed in intuition as well as hard evidence. Maguire handed over his switch card. 'Could you give me twenty pounds cash back, please, the cash point isn't working.' Antonio obliged and Maguire pocketed the money. 'And for your information,' he continued, 'respectability and murder often go hand in hand. Although no doubt Danny Bayley will totally misreport it and the *Stibbington Times* will have some stupid lurid headline.'

Antonio took a practical viewpoint. 'Of course it will. He's in the business of selling newspapers, and he's got to say something different from the TV people. It was on the TV early morning news this morning, but only a brief mention. Did you see it?'

'No,' said Maguire.

'Have you arrested anyone yet?'

Maguire made no reply and turned to leave. Lizzie was unsurprised at his silence. No policeman worth his salt was going to bandy news about in the local delicatessen. She stood back out of the way to let him pass, and in doing so noticed Mrs Smithson. Partially hidden by a wicker stand, which held an assortment of freshly baked bread and biscuits, she was rummaging amongst the packets of biscuits and had a packet of cantucci in her hand. Idly, Lizzie wondered if Mrs Matthews's cooking was not as good as she said it was, and maybe the poor woman was hungry and was looking for something to nibble on in the privacy of her room.

On his way out Maguire saw Lizzie and paused beside her. 'I need a fuller statement,' he said quietly. 'Will it be convenient if I call round this afternoon? At about three?'

'Yes, I suppose so,' said Lizzie reluctantly. Waste of her time and his, really, as there was nothing more she could tell him. If he'd written everything down yesterday afternoon this further visit wouldn't be necessary.

She paid for her purchases and left, noting that Mrs Smithson darted across to the counter, cantucci in hand, the moment she'd gone. Lizzie got the impression that the woman was morbidly inquisitive and had been listening to Maguire's conversation but had not wanted to be observed.

Adam had a luncheon appointment with Phineas Merryweather. It was not his idea. Phineas had insisted.

'Look, man,' he said over the phone. 'Anyone can see that you're not eating enough, and I bet you were up half the night on the Darren Evans case. Lose any more weight and you'll have a breakdown or be a walking cadaver. Meet me at the Royal Oak in Sewley Village. They do a wonderful venison steak there, and their fries melt in your mouth.'

Adam weakened at the thought of a good meal and human company rather than a microwaved meal in the company of an aging Labrador. 'What about your diet? And what about your wife?'

'The diet can wait, and Lucy is visiting her sister in Bournemouth today. She's left me a cottage cheese salad, which I really don't fancy. Come on, you can tell me more about what your boys found in that garage, and I can regale you with a few theories of my own. It'll be a working lunch. But one which will do you good. Meet you at the Oak at about one o'clock – I'll book a table.'

Five minutes before the appointed time Adam parked his car in the small gravel car park in front of the Royal Oak, heaved Tess out from the back seat, stood shivering while she found the right bush beneath which to have a pee, and wondered what on earth had possessed him to tell Lizzie Browne he'd visit her when he could just as easily, in fact, far more easily, have asked her to come down to the station. A mixture of emotions buzzed about vaguely at the back of his mind, a desire to banish the antagonism between them, and what else, he thought hard, what else? He didn't know. Perhaps Phineas was right, he would have a breakdown if he didn't look after himself.

The threatened rain still had not come, although the sky was as black as early evening and the outside lights were on. To make it feel even more miserable a cold wind had sprung up. It whistled through the lattice of bare branches, bringing down the last few remaining leaves from the surrounding oak trees. Adam shivered. Two horses, with blankets thrown over their backs, were tied to the wooden fence which ran along one side of the pub. They stared balefully at Adam as he passed them. Something about their unfriendly stare reminded him uncomfortably of Lizzie Browne. She didn't want to talk to him, and he couldn't blame her. He could have asked Steve Grayson to go and interview her, but he wanted to do it himself. Next to Mrs Matthews she was first on the scene, and there might be something she saw, something which she subconsciously registered. He needed something, anything, to give him a lead on what appeared, at the moment, to be a senseless killing by a person or persons unknown.

The Royal Oak was decked inside with holly and dried hops sprayed with golden paint, and interspersed with fairy lights. It reminded Adam that Christmas was only two weeks away.

Phineas was already there, sitting at a scrubbed wooden table by the open fire perusing the menu. 'Jolly, isn't it,' he said, waving vaguely in the direction of the decorations. 'I love Christmas. It's the one time in the year Lucy doesn't try to stop me eating.'

'Good God, Phineas, can't you ever think of anything but your stomach?' Adam sat himself on an upturned beer barrel, which served as a seat, and stretched out his chilled hands towards the fire. He kicked the log over with his foot, shooting a spray of sparks flying up the wide chimney. The log began to flame.

Phineas passed over the menu and looked quizzically at Adam. 'What are you doing for Christmas?'

'With any luck I'll be working. Another interesting case, I hope.'

'You can come to us if you like. Lucy always cooks enough to feed a regiment. My two daughters and their husbands and children are coming so it will be pretty noisy, but you are very welcome.'

'Thanks, Phineas, I'd like to, but it all depends on work.'

It was a lie. He had no intention of going. Never had a family Christmas in his life. At least not the sort of Christmas Phineas was talking about. As an only child his Christmases had been quiet. Years later, with Rosemary they'd been quiet too, no children to rush around making a noise. Now he hated the false jollity and commercialization of the season. Now Christmas started in October and worked its way up to saturation point in the last couple of weeks before the actual day; senses assaulted on every side, radio, TV, High Street shops, blaring out carols and jingles, crammed with games, food, and presents. It all served to remind Adam that he was quite alone in the world. No brothers or sisters, no cousins, not even elderly parents left alive to bother him the way they bothered other people. Christmas made him wonder what the purpose of his life was, just as he was now wondering what purpose Darren Evans had ever had in his life.

Nobody appeared to care about him. No trace could be found of a single relative; there was nobody to claim the body, and no one was sorry he was no more. A few expressions of shock in Stibbington at his passing, but mostly prurient questions as to the manner of it. But somebody had wanted him dead, or was it the work of some unhinged lunatic and Darren had just been unlucky? Steve Grayson had checked with the mental health authorities, and no one was missing from their care in the community programme, which was just as well. Nothing was guaranteed to get the media and politicians more excited than a mental patient on the loose who then committed a crime. If the escaped patient perished quietly in a hedge somewhere, from cold or starvation, no one was particularly worried, but if they harmed a member of the public that was quite a different matter.

No, at the moment there were no leads, no motive for the killing, and in a strange way it seemed appropriate to Maguire. No motive for death just as there appeared to be no motive for Darren's life. There'd be no trace of him once his mortal remains were disposed of. Even snails, thought Maguire, leave an opaque trail when they pass, but it looked as if Darren would leave nothing but questions.

'What is it, Adam?' Phineas peered across the table, his round, pink face creased with concern.

Adam shook himself, relinquished the reverie, and came back to the present. 'Nothing, Phineas. I was just being self-indulgent.' He looked across at Phineas and marvelled for the umpteenth time at the contradictions in the man. It was difficult not to be affected by Phineas's concern, and for the first time in more than twenty-four hours Adam felt warmth stealing over him. *Enough to warm the cockles of your heart.* That was something his mother had always said when something nice happened, and Adam surprised himself by remembering it. He smiled across at Phineas, 'It's just Christmas, making me sentimental,' he said.

'Glad to hear it,' said Phineas. 'There's far too little *real* sentimentality in the world today. Cynicism is the order of the day.' Tess turned round in her place in front of the fire, coughed and lay down to toast her other flank, and Phineas returned to the material plane and looked at the menu again. 'What shall we have? Venison steak, salad, and fries?'

'Sounds good to me.'

'I'll get it. You stay with the dog.' Phineas made his way across to the bar where food had to be ordered.

Adam leaned down and absentmindedly pulled at Tess's silky ears. 'What would I do without you, old girl,' he said softly.

'Excuse me, but may I have a word?' It was Major Brockett-Smythe. Not a man Adam cared for much. Uninvited, he plonked himself down on the seat just vacated by Phineas. He came straight to the point. 'Is it true, the rumour circulating in Stibbington this morning, that Darren Evans is dead?'

Why should he, Major Brockett-Smythe, be interested in a dropout like Darren Evans? Adam stopped pulling the dog's ears, outwardly still relaxed, but imperceptibly tensed, and alert. 'Did you know him?'

'You haven't answered my question,' said the Major.

'The answer is yes.'

'Accident or murder?'

'Murder, I'm afraid,' said Adam. 'And you haven't answered *my* question. Did you know him?'

'In a manner of speaking, yes.'

Adam leaned forward. 'And what exactly does that mean?'

Major Brockett-Smythe gestured behind him, and his wife, a small, timid-looking woman darted forward like an obedient whippet. 'It's true, my dear,' he said. 'Darren is dead. Been murdered, according to Detective Maguire here.'

'Detective Chief Inspector Maguire,' said Adam. Old Brockett-Smythe always insisted on being called 'Major', so why the hell couldn't he address him by his correct title? He fixed them both with a stern stare. 'Perhaps you'd better tell me what Darren Evans's death has got to do with you.'

'Oh, he used to come, he used to . . . ' Mrs Brockett-Smythe petered into silence beneath her husband's gaze.

'He use to come on a regular basis and do the garden for us,' interrupted the major.

'Oh, yes, yes. Do the garden,' echoed his wife.

Adam didn't believe a word. They were lying. A less convincing couple would have been hard to find. 'Really! I wasn't aware that Darren Evans did *any* work. He hardly looked strong enough.'

'But he was wiry, looks can be deceptive,' said the major quickly. 'He was very helpful to us, not that we asked him to do anything difficult, you understand. He just kept things tidy. When you get to our age it's difficult to manage on your own, and every little helps. And now that Melinda is ill we don't have that much time.'

'Of course.' Adam remembered hearing talk that they had a daughter who had a mental illness of some kind.

Major Brockett-Smythe stood up. His wife flitted nervously to his side and held his hand. Almost as if I was going to attack her, thought Maguire; the woman's a nervous wreck. The major coughed, then said quickly, 'If no one comes forward to claim Darren, you know, arrange for his funeral etc., Mary and I will be glad to do it.'

'That's very kind of you. But the state usually sees to things in cases like this.'

'We'd like to do it. Wouldn't we, Mary?' he turned to his wife, who nodded violently. 'Darren was very good to us.'

'Very,' said the timid little woman. 'I don't know what we'll do without him.'

'Then I'll make certain the appropriate authorities know,' said Adam. There was something bizarre about Major and Mrs Brockett-Smythe having a connection with Darren Evans. Something that needed further investigation. 'I'll need to call on you. Just routine inquiries. The last time Darren did any gardening for you, if he came regularly. You know, that sort of thing.'

It seemed to Maguire that they both took a mental step backwards in fear, although perhaps that was his own heightened senses. Then the major said, 'No we don't know. We've never been involved in a murder case before.'

'You're not exactly *involved* now. But you must understand that I need to take statements from everyone who knew the deceased. As I said, it's just routine, nothing to worry about.'

The major's normal bluff pomposity returned. 'Of course,' he said brusquely. 'But please ring Brockett Hall before you come to make certain it's convenient.'

Shepherding his wife before him he left just as Phineas returned. 'I've got us a pint of bitter each. Not on duty, I hope.' He took a sip. Adam shook his head and reached for his glass. Phineas stared after the departing couple. 'What did they want?'

'Among other things to pay for the funeral of Darren Evans.'

Phineas snorted into the froth on the top of his beer. 'Curiouser and curiouser as Alice said to the . . . who did she say it to?'

'No idea,' said Adam. 'You're the intellectual one, not me. But it is odd. They said he did the garden for them.'

Phineas raised his eyebrows. 'One thing that boy did not have, and that was a gardener's hands. Soft as any woman's they were; the heaviest thing he'd picked up recently was a syringe.'

Adam mused out loud. 'What on earth can they have to do with the murder victim?'

'Murder?' Phineas put his glass down on the table and looked serious. 'Don't jump to conclusions, Adam. I didn't put that in my report. I merely said that the skull was too badly shattered to be able to tell for certain. I only said that it *might* have been caused by a bullet. But that cannot be confirmed by the evidence; there wasn't enough skin left to do a proper test for gunshot wounds. The head might as well have been put in a liquidizer.'

'It's murder all right, Phineas. I should have told you, but I'm surprised you don't know. Everyone else in Stibbington seems to. The forensic boys picked out a bullet from the garage wall covered in Darren's blood. A nine-millimetre hand gun was the weapon.' Phineas whistled. 'Now,' said Adam, 'all I've got to do is to find out why on earth anyone would want to shoot a loner like Darren Evans. It's not as if he meant anything to anyone, apart from the Brockett-Smythes.'

'And they're hardly likely to shoot him for doing a bad job of the garden,' said Phineas. 'Although I have my doubts about the gardening bit, in view of his lily-white hands.'

'I agree,' said Adam thoughtfully. 'The Brockett-Smythes need a bit of investigation. Although I can't see either of them as murderers. That would be a bit extreme.'

'But Darren had obviously annoyed someone,' said Phineas. 'Enough to get himself killed. Ah! The steaks.'

Melanie, the landlord's daughter placed two steaming plates on the table. 'I'm just back to the kitchen for the fries and some more redcurrant sauce,' she said.

Tess sat up and nudged Adam's knee with her nose. 'Well, maybe just a small piece,' said Adam to the slavering dog. 'Too much will play havoc with your digestive system.'

'Don't forget that extra portion of fries I ordered,' Phineas called after Melanie. She gave him the thumbs up sign and disappeared into the kitchen. He turned to Adam. 'Stop talking to that dog as if she's human,' he ordered, 'and tell me what you know about Darren Evans.'

'Precious little at the moment,' answered Maguire.

CHAPTER SIX

TARQUIN GIRLING PRESENTED himself for duty at Lizzie's cottage early Saturday afternoon. He was tall, very thin – to the point of looking anorexic – pale, with faded blue eyes which peered at the world from behind trendy round, gold-rimmed glasses. At least, thought Lizzie, they would have been trendy on almost anyone else, but they did absolutely nothing for Tarquin. He was clad in rather grubby jeans and a torn leather bomber jacket, neither of which could disguise his thinness, and Lizzie wondered about his physical capability of actually doing any gardening let alone taming the jungle which surrounded Silver Cottage. However, it was his hair which really caught her attention. A glowing mane of reddish gold, it was clean, shiny, and quite beautiful. It was the colour most women would kill for, and it most certainly did not come from a bottle. It hung almost to his waist, and that afternoon was tied back loosely with a piece of string into a pony tail. The beautiful hair seemed at odds with the rest of him.

'Mum said to come because you might have some work,' he said, in a surprisingly well educated and cultured voice. His mother and younger brother Wayne had the soft, slow drawl of the area; the long vowel sounds, typical of a Hampshire accent. Tarquin, on the other hand, sounded as if he'd had elocution lessons.

'It's only gardening, I'm afraid,' said Lizzie. 'You won't earn a fortune.'

The semblance of a smile fluttered momentarily across Tarquin's features. 'I gave up any hope of earning a fortune years ago,' he said, in a resigned tone of voice. 'But I like gardening, and anyway, it's the only thing I can do. I'm not much use at anything else.'

Lizzie led the way through the cottage to the back where the garden stretched down to a small stream, which formed the bottom boundary of her property. They stood in silence for a moment regarding the wilderness. Then Lizzie spoke. 'I have to confess,' she told him, 'that the only gardening I've ever done is buy plants every spring from a garden centre, put them in pots around a paved area, and then try to remember to water them at regular intervals. My house in London didn't have much of a garden.'

Tarquin stood, hands in jean pockets. A cold northerly wind blew and Lizzie shivered, pulling her jacket more tightly around her. Tarquin, however, seemed oblivious. Then he said, 'This house used to have a lovely garden years ago when the Walshes lived here.'

The remark puzzled Lizzie. 'I thought a Mrs Burnett lived here until she died recently, and that you used to tidy the garden for her.'

'I did. But the Walshes lived here before her. It was then that the garden was lovely. Sometimes Niall and I used to help a bit, but mostly we played tennis.' He waved a hand in the direction of the field at the side of the cottage behind the privet hedge. 'That was a tennis court in those days.' He took a few steps and peered over the hedge into the empty field. 'All overgrown now. Nothing left to remind anyone of what it used to be like. Even the gate through the hedge has gone. Grown over by privet.'

'That field doesn't belong to me,' said Lizzie.

Tarquin sighed. 'No. Mrs Burnett sold it to Towles Farm but they've done nothing with it and now it'll never be a tennis court again.'

He sounded wistful, and Lizzie watched him as he stood moodily surveying the scene. There was something about him. He didn't fit in with the family she'd seen at Candover House. But it was more than that. There was a mantle of melancholy hanging over him. She shivered again.

'Who was Niall?' she asked, tucking her hands into the sleeves of her jacket.

'The Walshes' son. We were at school together. His dad paid my fees at Willhampton Private Grammar.' So that's how he acquired the educated accent, thought Lizzie. 'I was company for Niall.'

'And Niall was company for you,' said Lizzie.

Tarquin was silent. He seemed lost in thoughts of the past. Then he said softly, 'Yes. We were inseparable until. . . .' He stopped, took a deep breath, took both his hands out of his pockets, looked uncomfortable, and scuffed about in the grass with his feet. It was as if he had suddenly realized who he was talking to, and regretted his confidence.

'Yes, until?' prompted Lizzie, curiosity aroused.

'Until he moved away,' said Tarquin abruptly. The shuttered expression on his face told her that he would say no more.

'Well, let's get back to the subject of the garden,' she said briskly. 'Is there anything you can do at the moment, or is it the wrong time of year?'

'I can do a bit of clearing, and I can cut the hedge back. Best get that done before the birds start nesting in the spring. But the main part will have to be left until later next year.' He looked over at the greenhouse, which stood a little way back from the cottage with a shed beside it. 'Last time I was here that was in pretty good shape. If you get some oil, I'll light the heater and get some plants going in there. Then they'll be ready for bedding out in the spring.'

'You're on,' said Lizzie. 'I'll get the paraffin tomorrow morning from the garage.' She held out her hand. 'I'll give you seven pounds an hour, cash in hand. Is that okay?'

Tarquin held out his hand and grasped Lizzie's. 'Done, as long as you promise you won't shop me to the benefit people.'

'I promise. But whatever makes you think I'd do that?'

'You're a doctor. You're part of the "establishment", and establishment figures always stick to the letter of the law.'

'Not when they desperately need a gardener, they don't,' said Lizzie. 'Cash in hand it is, and mum's the word.'

'Thanks, I appreciate it.'

They walked slowly back into the house, or rather Tarquin walked slowly. It seemed to Lizzie that he was almost reluctant to leave the garden and its memories. 'Would you like a cup of tea?' she heard herself offering against her better judgement. What was the matter with her? She had plenty of things to do, without inviting a dejected young man in for tea. Half of her belongings were still in boxes stacked on the floor. She should be unpacking.

'Thanks,' he said again, then lapsed back into silence as he followed her into the kitchen.

Lizzie put the kettle on and got down two mugs from the dresser. The letter box on the front door clattered announcing the arrival of the evening paper. Lizzie retrieved it and put it on the table. She was finding

Tarquin's mournful silence rather unnerving. 'Have a look at the paper if you want,' she said, 'while I make the tea.'

She turned away and poured the boiling water into the pot. Behind her a strangled cry echoed through the kitchen. It was Tarquin. If she'd thought he was pale before it was nothing compared to the colour of his face now. He was a ghastly slate grey.

'Darren!' he croaked. 'Darren's been murdered.' Lizzie saw the newspaper spread out on the table. It was the headline in the *Stibbington Times*: *Local Man Murdered In His Own Home – No Motive – Who Will Be Next?*

Pulling out a kitchen chair she forced a trembling Tarquin to sit down. 'I'm sorry,' she said. 'Was he a friend of yours?'

'Yes . . . no. We were all. . . .' His voice tailed off into silence. Then he said in a dull voice. 'He wasn't a close friend. We went to school together, me, Niall, and Darren.'

For someone who wasn't a close friend, Lizzie thought, Tarquin had reacted very violently. In fact, quite unnaturally. She chose her words carefully. 'In a small place like this, where everyone knows everyone else, it's bound to be a shock when something horrible happens on your own doorstep.' How well had Tarquin really known Darren Evans? Well enough to be shaken to the core by his death, that much was plain to see.

'Yes,' he said slowly, 'it's a shock. Darren and I were not what you would call really good friends, but we still saw each other quite often, although we kept ourselves to ourselves. I never knew what he was thinking, and I don't suppose he even guessed at my thoughts.' He turned his pale face to Lizzie. 'It's true everyone does know everyone else, but at the same time no one truly knows anyone. You know, sometimes I think we are all living on our own separate little planets. We're surrounded by people and yet we're completely alone. Darren was alone. I'm alone. Sometimes it seems to me that there's no point in living at all. Why do we do it? Why are we even born?'

Lizzie regarded the young man before her. In her professional opinion he seemed to be perilously close to suffering full blown clinical depression. He was so young, and yet was obviously appallingly lonely and depressed. Everyone, including herself, suffered bouts of depression sometimes, but being swamped by a sense of hopelessness, and questioning life itself was different.

'Have you ever talked to anyone about the way you feel?' she asked carefully.

The shuttered look closed over Tarquin's face again. 'No. And I don't propose to. What I think is my business. Nothing to do with anyone else.'

'Yes, I suppose ...' Lizzie searched for words. She was unprepared. He wasn't a patient, or a friend. She'd only met him a few moments ago, and didn't know enough about him to offer words of advice or comfort. So what could she say? In the end she did what millions of other English men and women have done before in times of crisis, she poured a cup of tea. 'Here,' she said, pushing it across the kitchen table towards him. 'Drink this.'

The front door tweeted, and began playing a tinny version of the *Bluebells of Scotland.* 'Oh! I must get that damned doorbell changed before it drives me mad,' she said. A musical-box door bell might have suited Mrs Burnett's personality, but it was definitely not for Lizzie.

The effect on Tarquin was immediate. He jumped up as if an electric shock had just shot through the chair. 'You've got another visitor. You didn't say.'

Lizzie remembered the meeting with Adam Maguire. 'It's only the policeman in charge of the investigation into the murder. He's come to take a statement because ... ' she had been about to say 'because I discovered the body,' but Tarquin had already gone.

'I'll let myself out through the gate at the bottom of the garden, down by the stream,' he shouted over his shoulder. 'I know the way.' He disappeared through the utility room at the back of the house.

Lizzie heard the outside door slam and then there was silence for a moment until the front door tweeted again and this time started on *There's No Place like Home.* 'Damn,' said Lizzie and went to answer the door.

'Love the door bell,' said Maguire. He looked quite cheerful.

Lizzie looked at him suspiciously. Was he serious? 'I don't,' she said. 'I inherited it with the house, and it's being ripped out the moment I've got a minute to spare.'

'You've had a visitor, and he or she has just left by the back gate,' said Maguire. 'Why?'

'Presumably because he or she didn't want to meet you,' replied Lizzie sharply. 'Do you always snoop on people?'

'I'm afraid so. It comes with the job.' Maguire looked at her. She was hostile again. Was the respectable new lady doctor entertaining a man friend that she didn't want anyone to know about? And why shouldn't she? He'd heard she was divorced and on her own. She could do as she pleased. Have an orgy – although she didn't look the type – if she so minded. 'I'm not an ogre,' he said. 'Your friends have no need to run from me unless they have something to hide.'

Lizzie led the way into the kitchen feeling slightly ashamed for being so acerbic. Of course he was absolutely right. There was no point in being secretive when she had nothing to hide. 'For your information my visitor was Tarquin Girling. He's going to help me in the garden. And I think he may well think you *are* an ogre. From my brief acquaintance with Tarquin I have the feeling that he views anyone in authority with suspicion.' She took Tarquin's mug of tea and poured it down the sink, then got another clean mug and put it on the table. 'Would you like a cup of tea? I've only just made it.'

Maguire hesitated. The warmth of the kitchen was tempting, but he had Tess to think of. 'I can't be long. I've got Tess in the car.'

'Tess?'

'My dog. She's very old. I don't like to leave her too long on her own.'

'Bring her in. I like dogs.'

So Adam brought her in and Tess settled down happily on the rag mat in front of the gas boiler. The atmosphere almost visibly thawed. Adam looked around the kitchen. It was clean but untidy, not at all like his own clinically clean kitchen. There were stacks of books and medical magazines on the floor. The blank eye of an opened lap top computer stared at him from a small table in the corner.

Lizzie saw him looking at it. 'My work station. I can access patients' records at the surgery. At least, I'm supposed to be able to, but the whole system isn't up and running properly yet,' she said. 'Sorry about the muddle, but I prefer to work in the kitchen, that way I can always nibble on a biscuit when I feel like it. Now, tell me. What do you want to know?'

Maguire hauled a large manila envelope from his raincoat pocket, and took out a notepad. 'I need to know everything, and I do mean everything, that happened from the moment you first passed Darren's bungalow.'

'You mean even before Mrs Matthews flagged me down?' Lizzie poured the tea and passed a mug to Maguire.

'Anything you saw or heard might be useful.'

The whole process took about half an hour. Maguire meticulously recorded everything Lizzie told him, which wasn't a great deal. 'I'm sorry there's nothing new to tell you,' she said at last, 'but I was only involved on the periphery.'

Maguire snapped the notebook shut. Nothing she'd told him had moved the investigation on, but he said, 'every little helps. We've not got much to go on so far. At the moment, it's a question of racking our brains, and waiting for a lead.'

Lizzie raised her eyebrows. 'I thought everything was fed into a computer nowadays and the name of a suspect popped up at the click of a mouse.'

Maguire snorted. 'Computers! I hate the things. Computers don't have intuition; they only react to the data put in, and in this case there's not much of that. Trouble is the public seem to think that all we have to do is press a few keys and we've got the murderer. And an even bigger trouble is that some of the younger coppers are beginning to think that way as well.'

His vehement reaction amused Lizzie. She was already hooked on computers, and used them whenever possible. She'd suggested that the Honeywell Health Centre upgrade its computers, and that all the partners have compatible laptops, like her own, which could link into the main system. With a new system, and compatible laptops, the aim would be for a paperless practice. Lizzie's argument that this would save time and money had been greeted with scepticism by the other three partners, and a noticeable lack of enthusiasm by Tara Murphy, acting practice manager, and the rest of the office staff. But as yet, they were not to know that she had a reputation for stubbornness, and was determined to win them over. Mistakenly, they thought she had accepted defeat graciously, when in fact she'd made arrangements for new computers to be demonstrated the following week.

'What data have you got?' she asked. 'Or is that a state secret?'

'No, most of what we've got is common knowledge. Darren Evans was a drug addict. Registered at your own health centre, as you know, where Dr Jamieson prescribed him methadone, although he wasn't as rigorous with his check-ups as he should have been. If he'd checked more thoroughly he would have known that Darren was topping up his fix by mainlining heroin as well.'

'I expect Dick knew. Most addicts do that and there's not a lot you can do about it. But,' Lizzie frowned, 'do you think that had anything to do with his murder?'

'Who knows? He was almost certainly selling the stuff, although we don't know who to. He also had masses of cannabis drying in his upstairs bedroom, but there were no signs of fresh plants. So we'd like to know where the dried stuff came from.'

'I see. More questions than answers at the moment,' she said. 'And I suppose you must be thinking the motive was something to do with drugs.'

Maguire finished his tea with a gulp, stood, and picked his raincoat up from the back of the chair. 'It seems the most likely scenario. I can't think of any other reason why someone should want to pick off a no hoper like Darren Evans. His life was an uncomplicated, drug-fuelled mess. He had no purpose in life at all other than to obtain the next fix. And as far as we can make out, he had no friends either. Other than Major Brockett-Smythe, who he gardened for and who wants to pay for his funeral.'

'That's odd,' said Lizzie. 'I'm not sure I'd pay for my gardener's funeral.'

'My sentiments exactly. But as they say, there's nowt as queer as folk.' He bent down and prodded the sleeping dog. 'Come on, Tess. It's time we were on our way.'

The phone rang and Lizzie picked it up. It was Dick Jamieson. 'I know it's short notice, but Stephen is ill.'

'Not again,' said Lizzie. 'He's already had half a day off this week.'

'I know.' Dick sounded apologetic. 'But apparently it's some virulent stomach bug; both his kids have got it as well. Peter has gone away for the weekend to his in-laws, and I'm due at BMA dinner in London tonight. Tom has left his answerphone on and hasn't got a mobile, sensible man, so—'

'Can I do the late visits this evening?' Lizzie finished the sentence for him.

'Yes. There are two lined up already. Our old friend Mrs Matthews claims she's having panic attacks and is short of breath. Apparently, she's nervous about living so close to the scene of the murder, and is afraid the murderer will come back. I should think a few words over the phone will probably sort her out, and then there's Mr Hargreaves.

He had a stroke some time ago and his daughter has rung in to say he's unwell. She's not a time-waster so I think they ought to have a visit. Maybe the old chap has had another little stroke. Stibbington and the environs are usually pretty quiet on a Saturday evening so I think you'll be okay, but there's always Mike Hamilton at Stibbington Infirmary to call on if you get stuck.'

'I think I can manage without calling in Mike Hamilton,' said Lizzie wryly. The said Mike, fifteen years younger than herself, was still wet behind the ears in her opinion. She scribbled down the two messages. 'Okay, I'll do it. Just make sure that my mobile number is the one patients get put through to.'

Dick chuckled. 'I've already have done that. I didn't think you'd let us down. And there's no need to get touchy about calling in Mike. Everyone needs advice at some time.'

'Not *his* advice,' said Lizzie sharply. 'If I want advice it will be from someone older and wiser.' She put the phone down and immediately felt guilty for snapping Dick's head off.

'Problems?' asked Maguire.

'The main problem is being unattached,' said Lizzie. 'It's something I'm just beginning to find out. People expect you to step in whenever there's a gap to be filled. They assume that I've got no other plans.'

Maguire clipped on Tess's lead. 'You'll have to find yourself another man.'

'No thanks.' Lizzie shot the answer back quickly. A stab of irritation flashed through her. Why did men always think that women needed them? The irritation was short lived. She looked at her scribbled notes. 'Mrs Matthews, of the House by the Hard, is worrying that the murderer might come back and get her. Do you think she needs to worry?'

Maguire shook his head. 'No. I've got nothing to prove it yet, but I'm pretty certain that Darren's killing was drug related, not random. The world of drugs is a nasty one. Darren probably hadn't paid his dues.'

'Well, poor little devil, he's certainly paid them now,' said Lizzie. 'In the ultimate way.' She peered out of the window. It was already very dark, and from the light spilling out into the garden she could see that it was raining again. Shrugging herself into an old raincoat, as her other one was still soaking wet, she fished her medical bag out from beneath the table, snapped the lap top shut, and stood the two side by side ready to take with her.

Maguire frowned. 'Are there drugs in that?' He gestured towards the bag.

'Of course. My emergency supplies.'

'You ought to keep it in a safer place. Under the kitchen table is not particularly secure.'

Lizzie bristled. 'It's safe enough with me. I've carried drugs around with me for twenty years in London and never had them stolen yet.'

'There's always a first time.' Maguire looked about him slowly. 'You know this is a very lonely house. You ought to get a burglar alarm, or a dog. Preferably both. Don't forget there's a murderer somewhere on the loose in Stibbington.'

'Thanks a bundle, Chief Inspector. I shall sleep a whole lot easier in my bed tonight because of your words of comfort.' Lizzie ushered him towards the door. 'And now I must be on my way. By the way, don't worry about me. I've got a candlestick.'

Maguire looked puzzled. 'What for?'

'Hitting anyone who comes into my bedroom firmly on the head.'

Maguire looked at her expression and gave a slow grin. 'My sympathy would be all on the side of the intruder,' he said.

It seemed most logical to visit Mr Hargreaves and his daughter first. It was the furthest away. The house was in East Stibbington, and as the water-splash was still flooded the journey necessitated driving the long way round through the forest. The route lay through narrow lanes, which twisted and turned. The wind and heavy rain had wreaked more havoc out in the open countryside than it had in Stibbington. Broken branches lay across the road in many places, and great swathes of brambles snatched at the Alfa like hungry black fingers as Lizzie drove past.

Cursing Stephen and his stomach bug she squinted out into the darkened lanes. It was difficult to see, and she was just thinking that it was merciful there was no other traffic about when, on a sharp bend, she almost hit a motorcyclist. He was driving without any lights, at least, none worth mentioning. Only a feeble beam shone from the front of the bike, and it was going much too fast. By dint of jamming her foot down hard on the brake pedal Lizzie managed to bring the Alfa to a slithering halt, but she ended up at an angle, one wheel in the ditch. The motorcyclist hesitated, but only momentarily, then roared off into the night.

'Menace!' shouted Lizzie, lapsing into momentary road rage. Then she slowly edged the car forward. Mike had laughed when she'd bought a four-wheel drive Alfa. 'Trying to recapture the wild youth you never had,' he'd sneered. 'A sporty Alfa doesn't suit you.' Now, Lizzie was glad of it. There was no light to be seen in the darkness for miles around, and she didn't fancy trying to walk and find help. Now, the four-wheel drive came into its own, and she successfully extricated herself from the ditch, eventually arriving at the Hargreaves' house.

It was only as she sheltered in the porch from the rain, waiting for the front door to be opened, that Lizzie remembered the motorcyclist charging down the lane the afternoon Darren Evans had been murdered. It almost certainly had nothing whatsoever to do with the events of that afternoon, but she'd forgotten to mention it. And Adam Maguire had said he wanted to know *everything*. However, she couldn't believe it was either significant or urgent, but it was something to tell him when their paths next crossed.

CHAPTER SEVEN

'I'M SO GLAD you've come, Doctor. I just don't know what to do with him.' A small dark-haired woman practically dragged Lizzie over the soggy mat on the doorstep and into the house.

The house was small, the front door opening into a narrow hall. Lizzie presumed the woman was Peg Hargreaves, daughter of Len Hargreaves, and followed her leaving a trail of wet footprints into a claustrophobically small living room lit by a single light bulb hanging from the centre of the ceiling. There was no shade on the bulb and beside it dangled a spiral of sticky fly paper encrusted with black corpses. Through the door she could see into a tiny kitchen with two doors side by side. One was half open and Lizzie could see that inside was a lean-to bathroom tacked on to the back of the house. Cold and damp by the look of it, she thought, but better than a privy at the bottom of the garden, which had probably been the original feature.

Doing a quick recce was second nature to Lizzie after twenty years in general practice. A doctor could tell more about a patient's family by looking around than by asking questions. The interior of this house shrieked misery. It was the house of people who cared nothing for the outside world and not much for themselves. There were no books, not even a newspaper or a magazine in the living room, nor a television or video recorder, items which were mandatory in most modern homes no matter how cash-strapped the occupants might be. The decor had obviously not seen a lick of paint for thirty years or more, and was dark and depressive. The house felt cold and dank, worse in fact than the lane outside, and there was a faint, peculiarly, sweet smell which Lizzie recognized but couldn't place.

'Have you always lived here with your father, Miss Hargreaves?'

'Not always. I did when I was a child, of course. Mum died when I was ten and I stayed until I was sixteen, then I got away to Southampton as soon as it was legal to go. Dad couldn't stop me then. I could do as I pleased. But when he had his stroke six years ago, the social worker said that as there was no one else to do it I had to give up my job at the supermarket and come and look after him.' She paused a moment, then continued rather wistfully, 'I liked that job. I really did. I had a nice little council flat, and lots of girlfriends. But now I'm back in Stibbington again, stuck out here in this godforsaken place, and there's no one to be friendly with. I hate it.' She paused for breath, looked Lizzie straight in the eye and said, 'I hate him too. I've always hated him.'

'So why did you come back?'

She shrugged. 'I told you. Someone had to look after him, and there was no one else. He is my father, despite everything. So I came. I thought that once he'd had the stroke he couldn't do me no more harm. And he can't, but that doesn't stop me hating him. Sometimes I think I'll murder him one of these days.' She stared at Lizzie fiercely. 'I suppose you think I'm mad.'

Lizzie shook her head. Six years stuck out here in the sticks with a dependent old man was enough to drive anyone insane. In her opinion the social workers had been quite wrong to ask a young woman to sacrifice her freedom in order to be a full-time unpaid nurse. Sometimes the system was very cruel. 'No, I don't think you're mad,' she said gently. 'Anyone in your circumstances would feel the same. What we need to do is organize some help so that you can get away for a bit.'

Peg Hargreaves's face lit up, and Lizzie mentally crossed her fingers and prayed that social services would be able to find the necessary money from the community coffers to fund a period of respite care. 'Will you really speak to someone?' she exclaimed. 'Oh, you don't know how much I'd love to see a bit of telly.'

Lizzie thought it an odd remark. Watching television was not exactly getting away. 'I mean that you should leave this house,' she said. 'Go away for a few days. You could watch TV here.'

'Oh no I can't do that. Dad won't have it in the house. He says it's the evil eye. It can see into your soul and corrupt you. And believe me he knows all about corruption and evil.' She must have seen Lizzie's surprised expression because she added, 'Before his stroke he was a preacher at the Forest Saints Gospel Church. Every Sunday, twice a day, he preached about evil. Of course, he can't go there now. But he's still dead against the telly.'

'You could insist that you have one,' said Lizzie.

It was Peg's turn to look surprised. 'No I couldn't. This is his house. And besides, he gets very nasty when he's crossed.' She led the way upstairs. 'He's in his bedroom. Oh, and I better warn you,' she added, 'he's got no clothes on. Says I haven't washed them properly.'

She threw open the door to reveal a tall, scraggy, wild-eyed old man standing by the window clutching a tin biscuit box to his emaciated chest. Not for the first time Lizzie reflected that there was nothing beautiful about some people's old age. In the nude Len Hargreaves looked as if he were wearing an ill-fitting brownish crepe garment; only the angular bones of his shoulders and hips emphasized that it was skin and not material. Everything else hung limply. Everything, that is, apart from his genitals, and to Lizzie's dismay she saw he had a sturdy erection. 'Has he got a dressing gown?' she asked.

'Yes, although he won't put it on. But don't worry; he can't move fast enough to poke that thing into anyone now.' Peg waved at the offending organ dismissively. 'Time was, though,' she added on a bitter note, 'when he could and did.'

Lizzie glanced from demented father to depressed daughter, and realized she was looking at an abuser and the abused. How long had he used his daughter to satisfy his perverted sexual needs? Almost certainly until she'd escaped to her safe little council flat to live alone. Was it courage or weakness, Lizzie wondered, that had made Peg come back?

'He *will* wear the dressing gown,' she said firmly, fixing the shuffling old man with a stern stare. 'I've come to have a little chat and I don't want you getting a cold while we're talking. Colds can turn into pneumonia and then you'll end up in hospital.' It was unfair, she knew, unethical even, blackmailing an old man into submission, but from his hostile, wild-eyed stare Lizzie deduced that there was no alternative.

His flabby lower lip jutted forward in a childish pout. 'Don't want to go to hospital,' he whined. 'Not leaving here. Don't want to go nowhere.'

'If you put the dressing gown on then you won't have to go to hospital.'

Peg hurried over to the wardrobe and withdrew a voluminous

blue and red check dressing gown and handed it to her father. Lizzie noticed how she avoided actually touching him and didn't blame her. The dressing gown had the appearance of having been made from a horse blanket, and was much too large, but to her relief he obediently shrugged his way into it, although he never once let go of his biscuit tin.

'Sorry,' said Peg, indicating her father.

'Don't be. It's not your fault, my dear.'

'Shall I stay?' asked Peg.

'Yes please.' The experience of twenty odd years counts for nothing, thought Lizzie ruefully. I still find the thought of being left alone with this crazed old man with a gigantic erection disturbing. She silently cursed Stephen Walters. He should have been here, not me. But now I am here, what to do? Contending with dementia of any kind was not easy, not even with the modern range of drugs now available. 'Has he got worse recently?' she asked.

Peg nodded. 'Yes, he had a funny turn two days ago. It's since then he's refused to get dressed. He's more feeble now, lost his strength, but he's still aggressive.' She shivered and glowered at her father. 'Of course, he was always aggressive, all his life. But at least he hasn't been able to do anything these last few days. Not now that he can't hold his stick.'

'He's been hitting you?' Peg nodded. Lizzie sighed. Human nature could still surprise and horrify her.

Lizzie tapped in some notes on her laptop, then steeled herself, and made a physical examination of the old man, doing all the things a doctor should do: listening to his heart and chest, taking his blood pressure, checking his reflexes, looking into the wild, staring eyes, and all the time thinking what a nasty old man Len Hargreaves was, and at the same time mentally chiding herself for not being able to be the consummate professional she always prided herself on being.

Once she'd finished examining him she told Peg that, in her opinion, her father had probably had another small stroke. 'It doesn't happen to everyone, but unfortunately it does to some people.'

During their conversation Len Hargreaves sat on the edge of his bed and stared fixedly out of the window, muttering, 'Not going to hospital. Not going. Not going.'

Lizzie opened her case. 'Now, Mr Hargreaves.' She used the same brisk tone she'd used before. 'You will not be going to hospital if you promise me you will take this medicine.' He didn't face her, merely looked at her slyly out of the corner of his eyes, rocking his head from side to side. Lizzie went back to the blackmail. 'If you don't take the tablet I'm going to give you then I will have to send you to hospital.'

'I don't care if he doesn't take it.' Peg hovering by anxiously, sounded hopeful. 'I'd quite like him to go to hospital.'

Lizzie wished for Peg's sake that it was possible to ship him off to hospital for a few days, but he wasn't really a hospital case. And besides, it was a cold wet December, and Lizzie knew that Stibbington Infirmary was already full of elderly patients with chest infections.

'Take one now,' she said to Len Hargreaves, and popped a tablet from the bubble pack. She held it forward expecting him to take it in his hand, but he didn't, he stuck his tongue out instead. There was nothing to do but put the pill on the protruding leathery tongue, which she did, after a moment's hesitation, at the same time trying not to flinch. The thought crossed her mind that maybe she should give up medicine; it was coming to something when she could hardly bring herself to touch an old man. But, she consoled herself, there were old men and old men, and this one was particularly disgusting. Not only was he dirty, but a lascivious leer hovered around his slack mouth, and, much as she tried to, she couldn't avoid seeing the pink shaft of his penis still poking through the folds of his dressing gown. Resolutely ignoring it she scribbled out a prescription.

Peg led the way downstairs. 'What will that pill do?'

'Quieten him down,' said Lizzie. 'Here's a pack of six which I can give you now. Give him one tomorrow morning and one in the evening. Here's the prescription. There's a month's supply there, but don't hesitate to call the practice if they don't work, or if things get worse. In the meantime I'll see what I can do about getting you some help.'

'Thanks.' Peg peered at the sample pack. 'What are they, some kind of tranquillizer?'

Lizzie nodded affirmation. 'Yes. They should do the trick.'

'A friend told me that if I gave him some cannabis that would quieten him.'

It suddenly clicked. That familiar sweetish smell she noticed when she'd first entered the house. 'And have you tried it?' Lizzie asked.

'Oh no,' said Peg, adding hastily, 'I haven't got any.'

Not true, thought Lizzie, but didn't say so. 'I wouldn't advise you to get any or try it on him. It might have unwanted effects. Besides, it's against the law. You must know that.'

'Yes,' said Peg, then added, 'but you're a doctor. You could get it.'

'No I can't. It's against the law for me as well. I couldn't prescribe it even if I thought it might do some good, which, as a matter of fact, I don't. I know there's a lot of talk about it, but there's no real evidence that it has any proven medical uses. What made you think about using it?'

Peg shuffled her feet about and avoided Lizzie's gaze. 'I only mentioned it because, Darren Evans, you know the one who was murdered, well, he said cannabis was good for calming people.' She opened the front door and stood back as Lizzie passed. 'Thanks for coming out tonight. I appreciate it.'

Lizzie stepped outside. The wind had risen, shrieking through the bare branches like so many banshees. As the weather man had forecast, it was a force eight gale blowing straight in from the sea. The salt in the air stung her lips. 'It's my job to visit patients,' she said. 'And Peg, please don't even think of using cannabis for your father.' She paused and added, 'Or yourself.'

Her words were taken and tossed to the elements. And even if Peg had heard them, which Lizzie doubted, she knew that she was wasting her breath. There was cannabis in the house and one or the other, or both of them, were using it. Had Darren Evans supplied it? Was Peg Hargreaves worried now that he was dead because the supply was cut off? Was that why she'd called a doctor? A bit far-fetched, Lizzie decided, but both Peg and her father were strange. However, patients' confidentiality prohibited the mentioning of it to anyone, except to one of the other partners. Lizzie resolved to speak to Dick Jamieson about the Hargreaves father and daughter after the weekend.

Emmy Matthews felt restless. What was the point of having a paying guest, if she never saw hide nor hair of her? The policeman on duty at Stibbington Station had told her not to worry about the murder. 'Your house may be isolated,' he'd said, 'but at least you are not alone. You have a guest. There are two of you there.'

'Not alone,' sniffed Emmy to herself, and decided to make yet another cup of tea. 'But I might as well be alone, for all that I see of that woman. Talk about being anti-social. Doesn't want her evening meal! Doesn't want this, doesn't want that! Never lets me in her room. Anyone would think she's got a man in there.'

The kettle boiled. Emmy put two bags in the pot – she liked her tea strong – and poured in the hot water. And where was the doctor? Her chest was tight with worry. All she could think of was Darren Evans, poor boy, lying there in all that blood. It was enough to turn one's brain. She'd *told* the surgery it was an emergency. She needed something strong to make her sleep. What with this wind and rain battering the house, and being all alone, apart from Mrs Smithson, who didn't count, she just knew she'd never sleep a wink unless she had a tablet.

She stirred the tea and poured a cup. Then had a brainwave. It was almost nine o'clock. Surely, if she took Mrs Smithson along a cup of tea she would open the door. She couldn't ignore such a good-natured gesture, and they could have a little chat. But to Emmy's frustration she *was* ignored. Classic FM was being played loudly on the radio. It was Wagner. Emmy's knowledge of classical music was limited, but she knew what it was because the announcer had just introduced the piece. She knocked and waited. There was no response.

'Well, you can be unfriendly if you want,' muttered Emmy, 'but no one can accuse me of not doing my best to be a good hostess.' She put the cup down outside the door, carefully placing the saucer on the top so that the tea would stay warm for a while, then made her way back to the kitchen. Above the whistle of the wind she suddenly heard a lower sound – the roar of a car engine. Thank God, the doctor at last.

The tide was high and the waters of the Stib lashed the foreshore of the gravel hard, the waves splashing right over the road in some places. Lizzie cursed Mrs Matthews and her panic attacks but reluctantly admitted that all this was her own fault. She shouldn't be so damned conscientious. She should have phoned as Dick had suggested.

The House by the Hard, although two storeys, was a low house. What it lacked in height, though, it made up for in length, and it stretched away into the darkness at the far end of the shore.

As Lizzie drew up she noticed that only the nearest portion of the house was lit; the front porch had a lamp in it, and several windows either side had lights shining behind closed curtains. The rest of the house appeared to be in darkness, apart from one window at the far end where there was a light on. As Lizzie parked the car a sudden movement attracted her eye. It was the curtains of the far lighted window. Caught by the wind they were billowing out into the night. The sash window was pushed up about a foot. Someone must be very fond of fresh air, thought Lizzie, and shivered. Personally, she was having too much fresh air tonight for her liking; to be at home in front of a log fire with a gin and tonic would be preferable by far.

She rang the front door bell and wondered what she could accurately or even inaccurately call Mrs Matthews' panic attack when writing up her notes. That was one problem with computerized records: a coded nomenclature was required. Lizzie was finding her way through the system and becoming relatively expert; Dick Jamieson on the other hand was always having his diagnoses spat back at him by the computer as *Error – not recognized*.

Emmy Matthews opened the front door. 'Oh, Doctor,' she said. 'You don't know how pleased I am to see you. It will be lovely to talk to someone.'

'I'm not on call to come out and talk to people,' said Lizzie sharply. 'But to try to cure patients of their ailments. What is wrong with you, Mrs Matthews?'

Much later that night, after she'd handed over at eleven o'clock to the Medicare Duty Doctor, and when she was finally sitting down with a drink, Lizzie felt ashamed of her acerbic outburst. But some patients would try the patience of a saint, and Lizzie accepted the fact that she was no saint. The trouble was that patients did not fit into diagnostic categories, or very rarely did. But then, she thought wearily, no member of the human race fitted neatly into any sort of category. Just when you thought you'd pigeon-holed someone they developed another, totally unexpected characteristic.

The central heating had switched itself off and she was chilly. She switched it back on but still felt shivery, and looked longingly at the empty grate. A log fire would have been lovely, but it was too late for that now. She'd have to make do with a hot water bottle instead.

The phone rang. It was Louise. 'Hi. How are you, Mum?'

'Tired,' said Lizzie. 'How are you? It sounds as if you are at a party.' A tremendous racket was ricocheting down the phone line. 'It sounds as if someone is having a plate-smashing session.'

'I'm in a sushi bar. We decided to come here after the private view. It was a fascinating show. All constructivist art.'

'Don't tell me,' said Lizzie. 'Used urinals, beat-up bicycles and piles of dog crap.'

'Mother!' Louise sounded put out. 'You really ought to have a more open mind. It's the way you look at things that matters, not what they are. Anyway, what are you sounding so grumpy about?'

'I've been charging around the countryside tonight in a howling gale and pouring rain seeing patients.'

'What kind of patients? Are they very different to your London ones?'

'Too soon to tell, although I doubt it. People are similar the world over. But tonight I had one lecherous old man, and one silly elderly woman.'

'Lecherous!' Louise laughed. 'I knew men would be making passes at you as soon as you were on your own. Even Ben (Ben was the latest boyfriend) says you are a very attractive woman, for your age. Of course, it's difficult for me to appreciate it because you're my mother.'

'Tell Ben thanks,' said Lizzie dryly. She wasn't at all sure she wanted to be approved of by Ben, who she considered a lazy layabout. He was so laid back Lizzie thought it a marvel that he managed to take a breath. 'Anyway, this letch didn't make a pass at me in particular, anyone would have done.'

'How do you know?'Louise sounded puzzled, and Lizzie reflected that for all her daughter's sophisticated lifestyle, she was still an innocent concerning the nastier side of human behaviour.

'Let me just say that this was one patient who certainly didn't need viagra.'

'Oh. You mean he had a—'

'Yes, a very noticeable one,' said Lizzie. 'Now, Louise, much as I would like to have a natter, I'm tired and to make matters worse the house is cold so I think I'm going to take my gin and go up to bed.'

'Oh.' Louise sounded disappointed. 'I wish you were still here in London. I know I didn't see you that often, but at least I knew you were near. You didn't have to go running off into the depths of the country. You could have stayed. You didn't have to run that far from Dad.'

'Louise,' Lizzie felt irritated. 'I am not running away from anything or anyone. I wanted a new life, and this is the one I have chosen. In fact, were it not for your father, I would have left London years ago. When we split up it was the ideal opportunity. I like living in the country.' Outside an extra fierce gust of wind buffeted Silver Cottage, closely followed by a crashing sound somewhere in the depths of the garden. 'It's so peaceful,' said Lizzie, mentally raising her eyebrows. 'And now I'm going to bed. I'll ring you in the morning.'

'Okay. But not before lunch time, please. You know I need to get some beauty sleep.'

Lizzie knew and disapproved of her daughter's lifestyle. Maybe it was being old-fashioned, but she couldn't help thinking it a waste of time spending most of the day in bed, and most of the night partying. Louise was twenty-three years old now. Surely it was time she grew up? When she was that age she'd been practising in Whitechapel, was married and had a child, Louise. There'd been no time for fun in those days.

'After lunch, I promise,' she said, and put down the phone.

Once upstairs, she slotted *Concerto De Aranjuez* into the CD player, then with the hot water bottle and a refilled glass she tried to settle down for half an hour's read. It was a crime novel, but after coming across two gory murders within the space of the first ten pages, Lizzie closed the book. Murder was too close to home for comfort at the moment. Besides, there were things preying on her mind now that she was at home and alone. That motorcyclist for one thing. Who was he, and why did he not use lights? Common sense told her that the lights were probably broken and he'd not bothered to get them fixed. No one seemed to bother unduly about rules and regulations in Stibbington, except the police, and they were in the minority.

Eventually, exhaustion, the gin, and the warmth of the hot water bottle combined to send her drifting into sleep. The last thing she thought of was the open window at the House on the Hard. Now she realized that it had been closed when she'd left, although the light was still on. That was strange. Who had closed it? The paying guest? Must have done it very quietly, for there'd been no sound, and the windows of the House on the Hard were of the old fashioned, heavy sash variety. The type that slid down and chopped off your fingers if you were not careful. Anyway, why had it been open in the first place on such a terrible night?

Her mind slid between sleep and consciousness. Of course, Mrs Matthews must have closed it as she was getting into the car. It had to be her. Neurotic Mrs Matthews had discovered it, and shut it tightly when she was locking the house up for the night. She'd said she was going to check every lock in the house before going to bed, and then she was going to take the pill Lizzie, very reluctantly, had given her.

Lizzie reached out in the dark and closed her fingers around the comforting cold shape of the brass candlestick. She was all right. Silver Cottage was just as safe, safer in fact, than her old home in Blackheath. A million demons might be on the loose outside in the wild darkness of the night, but she was locked in *and* had a weapon.

CHAPTER EIGHT

A DAM MAGUIRE WORKED most of the weekend with Tess as his sole companion. Not that working all those extra hours progressed the case much further. By the time Monday morning came he felt tired, stale, had a headache, and was beginning to think the mystery of Darren Evans's death was one which would remain unsolved. It was unlike him to be so defeatist, and he felt angry with himself.

Steve Grayson coming bouncing into the office, full of good health and general bonhomie did nothing for Maguire's temper or headache. He fished out a large brown bottle from his bottom drawer, extracted two paracetamol, and swallowed them.

'You ought to take those with water or tea,' said Grayson.

'That's your first job. Get me some tea,' growled Maguire.

His sergeant disappeared cheerfully, and Maguire felt remorseful for being so churlish. He'd been the one who'd allowed Grayson to go home on Sunday to be with his pregnant wife, and while there, thought Maguire enviously, he'd almost certainly had some good home-cooked meals, whereas he'd made do with pasties and sandwiches from the only shop in Stibbington to remain open on a Sunday, the *STOP 'N SHOP*. Seven days a week twenty-four hour shopping en masse had yet to arrive in Stibbington, and if the local shopkeepers had their way it never would.

The sandwiches were his own fault, of course. He could have gone to any one of the numerous pubs which abounded in the area, but chose not to. Sundays were family days. Everywhere was full of families, although in the winter it wasn't quite so bad, at least then he didn't have to slink past pub gardens with bouncy castles full of excited tiny tots. But even so he still felt very conspicuous. A lone man and a dog, amidst a sea of people was a pathetic sight, and the last thing he wanted was pity. He had enough of that lugubrious emotion swishing about in the dark reaches of his own soul; other people's was not welcome. Therefore, Sunday outings were to be avoided.

Grayson came back with a cup of tea. 'Well?' he demanded, 'solved the murder mystery?'

'Don't be bloody facetious,' said Maguire.

Grayson put a plastic sandwich box on the desk in front of Maguire. 'Ann sent you this. It's a piece of game pie. It's made to a proper old-fashioned recipe, hot water crust pastry. Ann's trying it out. She's going to enter the pie competition in next summer's New Forest Show.'

Maguire opened the lid. 'Smells delicious. But won't it be off by next summer?'

'That's not the pie, she's just trying . . . oh, you're joking.'

'Yes.' Maguire pulled a wry face. 'You've just confirmed my suspicions. I'll never be able to earn my living as a comic.' His sergeant looked confused, as well he might. Grayson was not blessed with an acute sense of humour, and needed warning of a joke, time to get his brain into the right gear. But never mind, Maguire reminded himself, he was a good lad, good at his job. One couldn't ask for miracles. 'Thanks for the pie. I'll have it tonight with a jacket potato. I'm quite good at doing those in the microwave.'

Grayson hung his raincoat on the peg behind the door and reached into the pocket. 'And here's a bone for Tess.' He handed over a brown paper bag wrapped in plastic.

'Thanks.' Maguire took the parcel. 'But put your raincoat back on. I feel like a breath of fresh air. I think we'll visit the Brockett-Smythes and find out why they're so keen to pay for Darren Evans's funeral.'

Grayson shrugged himself back into the garment he'd just hung up. 'Do you think it's suspicious?'

'Let's just say it's pretty bloody strange.' Maguire put his own coat on. 'You're more local than me. Do you know anything about the Brockett-Smythes?'

Grayson pulled a face. 'Not much. Although they have lived here for ages. They bought the big house, and then, so Ann says, renamed it Brockett Hall. Used to be called Fox Hill House.' Grayson sniffed. 'Brockett Hall! Pretentious rubbish. Got fancy ideas if you ask me. Not that it's done them much good. They've got a daughter with some mental illness. She used to be okay, went to the local primary school, but no one ever sees her now. Gossip has it that she howls in the night. Never heard it myself, but then I never go over that way.'

'Howls in the night?' said Maguire irritably. 'What is she, some kind of werewolf?'

'I'm only repeating what I've heard, sir.'

'Huh!' Maguire picked up the sandwich box and the parcel containing the bone. He would pop in and let Tess out on the way back, he decided. 'It sounds as if the local inhabitants have been watching too many horror movies.' He threw a bunch of keys at Grayson, who fielded them. 'You can drive,' he said. 'I want to think.'

Tarquin Girling got up early on Monday morning, as soon as it was light. Nine o'clock, maybe not early for most people, but it was very early for him.

His mother was in the kitchen, still wearing the same wrap-over pinny she'd been wearing the previous week. She was standing at the stove stirring a grey mass in a dented saucepan. 'Want any porridge?' she asked.

Tarquin looked in the pot. The porridge was lumpy. 'No thanks. I'll just have tea.'

'It's no use,' said his mother. 'I can't cook on an electric stove. I shall never get used to it.'

Tarquin let out a breath of exasperation. Sometimes he wanted to shake his mother, she was so useless. 'You've been cooking on that stove for the last twenty odd years, ever since we moved into this house.'

'Yes, and I shall never get used to it,' his mother replied stubbornly. 'When we lived in Stibbington I had gas. My cooking was all right then.'

Tarquin didn't argue. There was no point. He couldn't remember what his mother's cooking had been like when they'd lived in Stibbington, but he couldn't help thinking that twenty years was long enough to learn how to master an electric stove. But that was her problem. She'd never mastered anything. Never mastered finding herself a husband for one thing. She was the epitome of the perennial downtrodden woman and single mother. Neither he nor Wayne knew who their fathers were. He felt bitter. He'd had a good education thanks to the Walshes, and would have gone on to university if things had turned out differently. But one thing. That was all it had taken. Just one thing, one moment of madness, and everything had been ruined. And now here he was, stuck with his mother and younger brother; his brother who was permanently ill. It never occurred to Tarquin that the instrument for change might be himself, or just occasionally if it did, he soon rejected the thought. Initiating change took discipline and determination, and Tarquin was sadly lacking in both. It was much easier to do nothing, blame others and wallow in self-pity. One thing, yes that was all it had been. His mind ricocheted off the thought; one thing, plus the fact that he was different. But he didn't allow himself to think about that these days. It frightened him. He couldn't cope with not knowing who or what he was. Much safer to live in his own little world of self-imposed sterility.

He poured himself a cup of tea, dark reddish brown, very strong, and put in three heaped spoonfuls of sugar. 'I'm going out,' he announced. 'All day.'

'I was going to ask you to get us fish and chips for our dinner.' Mrs Girling's voice took on a plaintive whine. 'With Wayne being ill I've got nothing in the house except bread and baked beans.'

'Have those at dinner time then,' said Tarquin. 'I'll bring in the fish and chips for tonight. What do you want? Cod or haddock?'

'The cheapest,' said his mother. 'Just for you and me, and get some frizzits for Wayne. He can have those instead of chips, and I'll give him a bit of my fish.' The local fish and chip shop sold frizzits, the small pieces of fried batter which dropped off the fish into the fat, a few pence for a big bag. A bag of pure, unadulterated, cholesterol-raising rubbish thought Tarquin, but Wayne liked them, and his mother didn't care about healthy eating.

Tarquin drank the rest of his tea. 'Okay,' he said. 'See you this evening.'

'Where are you going?' Mrs Girling poured a molten mass of grey, lumpy porridge into a chipped bowl.

'To do Dr Browne's garden amongst other things.'

'What other things?'

'Never you mind. Just things I've got to do.'

The first thing he did was load up the car with boxes of plants. Dr Browne had said he could use her conservatory for his own plants as well as hers, and he intended to. The weather had been so bad lately that his plants all needed more light, and they certainly needed some warmth. Not something available at Candover House, where the seed-lings struggled for survival in a dimly lit shed at the bottom of the garden. Once loaded, it proved difficult for Tarquin to get his ancient estate car going on such a wet and windy morning. It only started after he'd taken out the plugs and wire brushed them, then wiped and sprayed the plug leads with WD40. When it finally spluttered into grudging life he drove out past the chickens, still pecking about looking for something eat, and was followed up the lane for about a hundred yards by Rover who'd bitten through his leash yet again and was on the loose.

Once on the road he felt more cheerful. Anything was better than being stuck in that dismal house with his mother and Wayne. As soon as he was in the conservatory at Silver Cottage he'd be all right. There was nothing he liked better than pricking out his seedlings. He felt almost light-headed. Pricking out was a therapeutic occupation. But before he could start on that he had the Brockett-Smythes to visit. They weren't expecting him, but he was pretty sure they'd be pleased to see him.

It was an inauspicious start. The major regarded Tarquin's long hair with distrust. 'Are you some kind of poofter?' he asked bluntly, staring at the golden tresses.

'If you mean, am I gay? The answer is it's none of your business,' said Tarquin firmly. 'It's nothing to do with you.'

'Why have you come? I don't know you, do I?'

'Not now. But once you did, very briefly. I went to school with your daughter and we have a mutual friend. Or rather we did have. Darren Evans. My name is Tarquin Girling.'

The cultured accent helped put the major at ease, and the name Darren Evans turned the key. Tarquin Girling. Yes, he remembered now. How could he forget? But it was difficult to equate the Tarquin Girling of ten years ago with the strange-looking young man standing before him now. He let him in despite still having doubts about that long hair. In the major's opinion it wasn't right that a man should have better hair than a woman.

He led the way through the spacious hall into the drawing room, which he pronounced 'droin room' when he let him in. The hall floor was tiled in black and white, like a large chess board, and was totally empty apart from a couple of huge, dark wooden cupboards, which were big enough to sleep in.

The 'droin room' was shabby but comfortable. A large red rug, which had seen better days, covered the polished wooden floor, a selection of chairs and escritoires with spindly legs stood around the room close to the windows, and near the open fire were two large sofas, the stuffing spilling out at the ends where generations of cats and dogs had clawed them. On one sofa lay a large black and white greyhound, flat on its back with its legs in the air, 'showing everything,' as Mrs Girling would have said.

'Move, yer bugger,' said the major, and sat down on the sofa beside the greyhound. He indicated that Tarquin should sit on the other sofa. 'Now what's this about Darren Evans?'

Tarquin came straight to the point. 'I know you did business with him because I supplied the raw material. Now he's gone I can carry on with it, if you still need it. But I need a store. Previously, I used Darren's cottage, but that's off limits now.'

Major Brockett-Smythe was silent for a moment. He'd been worried sick since Darren's death. How were they going to manage? Trouble was he didn't know if he could trust this Tarquin. Would he keep his mouth shut the way Darren had always done? He made a decision. Not that he had much choice. He'd have to trust him. But he had to ask him something first.

'You didn't kill him, did you?'

Tarquin shook his head violently. 'Of course I didn't. Why should I? But if I did do it, I'm hardly likely to be telling you, am I.'

That made sense. Damn silly question to ask now he thought of it. 'S'pose not.' The major gave a curt nod of agreement.

'In fact,' said Tarquin slowly, 'I can't think why anyone would want to kill Darren. He wasn't harming anyone. I know he mainlined, but he'd been on heroin for years. Never had any problems getting or paying for the stuff. I suppose you saw to that.'

'I paid him for services rendered, yes,' the major admitted reluctantly. That had been worrying him too. Had he, inadvertently, been responsible for Darren's death? Without his money Darren wouldn't have been able to indulge his habit quite so freely, but on the other hand, as Darren had often told him, he'd have stolen if necessary, so his money had at least avoided that criminal activity. He leaned forward and fixed Tarquin with a stare. 'Are you on the hard stuff as well?' Tarquin shook his head. The major breathed a sigh of relief. 'Good,' he said, 'because I can't help wondering if Darren's murder was something to do with that. I don't want to be involved with big-time drug pushers. I've got my reputation to think of. Besides, I don't want you to be murdered as well.'

'Neither do I,' said Tarquin. 'Shall we do business?'

The major wondered who had murdered Darren but decided there was no point in worrying. The police would find out who did it, they were paid to do that sort of thing. He put the thoughts from his mind and stood up. 'Follow me,' he said. 'I think I've got just the place you can use as a store.'

Monday morning was busy in the surgery. It had always been busy in the London practice, and Lizzie, forlornly as it turned out, had hoped for somewhat quieter mornings in Stibbington. But the customary melee ensued with the usual type of cases presenting. A smattering of sore throats, which, according to the patients, definitely needed to be zapped with the strongest antibiotic on the market, preferably the latest one they'd just read about in the tabloid press and which, according to the media pundits, was a miracle cure. Lizzie went into the familiar routine, which she knew by heart, of explaining that such a condition was self-limiting and would go away of its own accord in time if left alone. Her words generated the standard response of incredulity as the patient sitting before her realized that she was not going to write a prescription. Lizzie guessed her popularity rating in Stibbington was plummeting by the minute as patient after patient left in disgruntled fashion without that magic piece of paper: the prescription.

It was a snatched coffee break that morning. Stephen Walters was still off sick, which necessitated his patients being divided up between the other three.

'D and V, that's what Stephen Walters has,' reported Tara Murphy with relish, 'and all his kids as well.'

'Where's your pity, girl?' asked Dick Jamieson. 'It could be you.'

'Pity is a luxury I can't afford. And it couldn't be me because I'm always very healthy,' said Tara airily. 'Never had a day off school, nor,' she wagged a finger at him, 'nor a day off sick since I've worked here.' She slammed a filing cabinet drawer shut. 'And if you doctors had any sense, you would doctor yourselves up *before* you got ill.'

'Is she really as tough as she sounds?' asked Lizzie as Tara left the office-cum-coffee room to make her way back to the front reception desk.

'Tougher,' said Dick, 'but she's wonderful on reception. Frightens many a malingerer away.'

'Huh! She didn't do such a good job this morning,' grumbled Lizzie. 'Besides the usual coughs and colds, I had a, *Gran is getting on our wick and it's time someone, eg, me the doctor, did something about it. My boss is driving me insane and I need a four-day anti-suicidal break so tell me I'm ill and give me time off.* And, the best one, *United are playing live on Sky TV and I need a 'my breathing is wheezy' certificate.*' Lizzie paused for breath.

Dick laughed. 'Are you happy in your work?

Lizzie grinned. 'Yes, don't take any notice of me. I just need a caffeine drip to get me going. But I must say Stibbington appears to have more than its fair share of malingerers.'

'That's because they are all trying out the new doctor,' said Dick. He poured himself another coffee. 'By the way, thanks for stepping in Saturday night. How did it go?'

'Okay,' said Lizzie. 'But that reminds me. There was something I wanted to ask you. What do you know about Len Hargreaves and his daughter?'

'Not a lot,' said Dick. 'But I've heard the gossip, of course.'

'What sort of gossip?'

'Oh the usual incest thing. Father and daughter sleeping together. Have done for years. Since she was a child, or so they say.'

'I'd hardly put that in the usual category.' Lizzie was shocked at Dick's casual attitude. 'Why weren't the social services put on the case?'

'Because nobody complained. The daughter never complained, and the old man certainly didn't, not when he was getting what he wanted. Of course, he wouldn't have been old when it started. Then he was a lusty man in mid-life.'

'He still is lusty,' said Lizzie, and told Dick of her encounter with the naked Len Hargreaves. She thought about the cowed woman she'd seen in the house. 'What a life Peg Hargreaves must have had,' she said slowly. 'I still can't understand why something wasn't done about it years ago, when she was a child. Her life must have been ghastly.'

Dick agreed but was more pragmatic. 'These things have always happened. You must know that, Lizzie. Even now it happens, but there's a limit to how much one can interfere in other people's lives. If we did, we'd need a social worker dedicated to almost every family in the land.'

'Good God, Dick. Do you think every family is dysfunctional?'

'Probably. In one way or another,' said Dick, cheerfully. He looked at Lizzie's outraged face, and said seriously, 'We can't put right every wrong we come across. We can only try when we're asked to help. But, of course, if I'd known about this when Peg was a little girl, I would certainly have done something about it. But I wasn't practising in Stibbington then, and when I arrived the pattern was set in stone.'

Lizzie thought of Peg, alone with her depraved father in that depressing, nasty little house. The best thing that could happen for her would be for her father to die. 'She hates him, you know,' she said.

'Of course she does,' said Dick equably. 'But she'll look after him to the end, and I doubt she'll accept much help. These old country families tend to prefer to cope with their own troubles.'

'We'll see about that,' said Lizzie. 'I'm going to organize her some assistance through social services. She seemed quite keen on the idea.'

'When you've organized the help she'll refuse it. They like keeping themselves to themselves. I doubt that she'll want anyone poking around that house.'

Lizzie remembered the smell of cannabis. Perhaps Dick was right. But nothing ventured, nothing gained. 'Well, Dick,' she said, 'you might be content to let people muddle along; I prefer to get them sorted out.'

Dick smiled benignly. 'Perhaps you ought to do your visits on a white charger, then everyone would know you'd come to save them from themselves.'

Lizzie snorted. 'Laugh if you like, but I can't help the way I am.'

Dick was suddenly serious. 'I know. But in a small place like this one has to tread carefully. This isn't a shifting population; the majority of families have been in this area for hundreds of years. They're a close lot. Keep themselves to themselves, and don't like interference from strangers.'

'Meaning me,' said Lizzie.

'Meaning all of us medics,' Dick said wryly. 'We're all strangers. None of us have got great-grandparents buried in the local churchyard.'

'About time this place took a step into the twenty-first century,' muttered Lizzie.

'Maybe they will when it's the twenty-second.'

Lizzie didn't answer. There was nothing to say. She was going to mention the cannabis but then decided against it for the time being. Dick would probably say, "So what?" Instead, she sipped her coffee and looked through the pile of notes Tara Murphy, and her assistant Sharon, had prepared for her that morning. Laptops and main terminal computers were pie in the sky as far as Tara and Sharon were concerned; Honeywell Practice still sent its doctors out with a wad of patients' notes a mile high. The sooner the information was computerized the better, but the two girls were not the fastest workers when it came to working on the computer. However, there was nothing she could do about that other than nag occasionally, and hope that they'd all be fired with enthusiasm once they saw the new computers being demonstrated. It was as she was stuffing the notes in her bag ready for the morning visits that she remembered the motorcyclist.

'Who rides motorcycles around here?'

Peter Lee, one of the other partners came into the coffee room along with Maddy the practice nurse.

'All the local lads ride bikes,' Maddy told Lizzie. 'The casualty officer at Stibbington Infirmary would much rather they didn't, especially in this weather. They're always skidding on wet leaves and turning up to have knees and elbows patched up.'

'Why do you ask?' Peter poured himself a coffee from the filter machine and wrinkled his nose. 'God, this stuff smells stale.'

'I'll make some more.' Maddy emptied the dark brown liquid down the sink.

Maddy was the same age as Lizzie's daughter, Louise, but the difference between the two girls could not have been more stark. Louise, stick thin, pale, and glamorous, was resolutely refusing to grow up. Maddy, plump, with a ruddy complexion from riding her bike in all weathers – Lizzie doubted whether her face had ever been near a jar of moisturizer – was middle-aged long before her time. But she was uncomplicated and friendly. She grinned at Lizzie. 'Thinking of riding a motorbike yourself, then?'

'Good idea,' piped up Dick. 'Keep the practice costs down. That would be almost as good as a white charger.'

'Oh, shut up,' said Lizzie good-naturedly. It was impossible to stay cross with Dick for long. 'The reason I mentioned motorbikes is because twice I've nearly had a head-on collision with some mad man who rides without lights.'

'Oh, that'll be Spud Murphy from out at East End Farm,' said Maddy. 'He never bothers with lights. One of these days he'll get himself killed.'

Notes safely in her case, Lizzie snapped it shut. 'If I ever meet him, I shall have words to say to this Spud Murphy,' she said. So that was that. Mystery solved. It was one of the local lads; an irresponsible youth at that. 'See you at surgery this evening. After I've done my visits this morning I'm going home. Tarquin Girling is coming round to do a bit of tidying up in the garden for me. I want to make sure he does what I want and gets on with it.' She tapped her pocket. 'You can get me on my mobile.'

CHAPTER NINE

BUSINESS WITH THE major concluded to his satisfaction, Tarquin bowled happily along in his ramshackle estate car heading towards Silver Cottage.

At the top of the High Street he pulled into a parking bay at the side of the post office. On the opposite side of the road was a small general store and newsagent. Harris News had once been a thriving shop-cum-post office, but now most of their business had been poached by the new post office with its state of the art counters, electronic queuing boards, and stainless steel rail guards, which herded customers into narrow lines like so many cattle waiting to go to the slaughter. Unlike most young people Tarquin preferred things as they used to be, and consequently gave what little business he had to Mr and Mrs Harris in their down-at-heel shop.

He entered the shop, the doorbell clanging behind him. Mr Harris came shuffling out from the back room as fast as his chronic arthritis would allow. His progress was painful to watch. No justice in this world, thought Tarquin, watching him approach. He shouldn't be working, but the poor old devil probably can't sell the business for enough money to fund a decent retirement.

'Morning, young man.' That was another thing Tarquin liked about the Harris shop. They were old-fashioned, always polite and friendly, and never hurried their customers. Unlike the girls in the new post office who always had one finger on the mouse of their computer, never looked you in the eye, and were always in a hurry. No, the Harrises never hurried anyone. Never needed to. Time was the one thing they had in plenty.

'Hello, Mr Harris. I'll have a Cornish pasty please.'

Mr Harris nodded towards a glass case, which housed a solitary pasty. 'I'm afraid that's the only one we've got, and it's yesterday's. If you like you can have it for half price.'

'Thanks.' Tarquin dug deep into the pocket of his jeans for some change.

Mr Harris wrapped the pasty in a plastic bag and handed it over. 'Did you know that the Walshes have come back?'

Tarquin stopped looking for change. His head jerked up and he stared at Mr Harris. Another world leapt into his mind. A kaleidoscope of sights and sounds. Tennis in the summer, the sound of laughter, the sweet smell of freshly mown grass, piano music, and an overwhelming sense of happy security. A lifetime in a split second, but a world away from the present. 'The Walshes,' he whispered.

Mr Harris peered at him with pale, rheumy eyes. 'Thought you'd like to know,' he said kindly.

'All of them? Have they all come back?'

'No. Just Mr and Mrs Walsh. Apparently, they missed Stibbington. Of course, they're older now like the rest of us. Not so active. They've bought one of those flats at Forest Court down near the quay. Luxurious they are, so I'm told, and very expensive. But then,' he added with a hint of wistfulness, 'the Walshes always did have plenty of money.'

'I wonder what happened to Niall. I've often wondered.' Tarquin was hardly aware that he was speaking out loud; so many thoughts and memories were crowding in on him. He got a handful of change from his pocket and sorted out the right money, still in a dream.

'Niall will be here at Christmas. He's a solicitor now with a good practice in London, apparently, and married with a wife and son of his own. They're going to stay for Christmas at the House on the Hard because there's no room in the flat. I know because Mr Walsh told me so himself. He gets his paper from me. Every day he walks up the hill from the quay to our shop and gets his paper, the *Telegraph*, says it's his constitutional.' After such a long speech Mr Harris was puffed, and sucked his breath in sharply, making a faint whistling sound.

Tarquin was silent. He could see that Mr Harris was disappointed when he paid for the pasty and left without saying another word. But he couldn't stay and talk. The news that the Walshes had returned after so many years was unexpected, but he could cope with that. Would *have* to cope with it if they were going to be permanent residents. But the chance of meeting up with Niall again was a different matter. If he'd been called upon to give a definition of what he was feeling at that moment, he could not have formed any coherent answer, so muddled and confused were his feelings. And Niall qualified as a solicitor! Well, perhaps he shouldn't be so surprised at that. Niall had always applied his mind to whatever he'd undertaken, and he'd always been clever. So Niall was a success. That wasn't so surprising either. But Niall happily married and with a child of his own, a son, his own flesh and blood. That was hard to think about. Especially when compared to the barren emptiness of his own life. No job, no money, no prospects and no family of his own, unless he counted his mother and Wayne, which he didn't most of the time. Sometimes they felt as alien to him as the rest of the world. Ten years since he'd seen Niall. To Tarquin it seemed a lifetime. He felt guilty, and wondered if Niall felt the same. Probably not, he decided. Not now, because his life had moved on. It must be easy to forget the past in another place surrounded by different people. Whereas I, thought Tarquin morosely, am still in the same damned place, surrounded by the same damned people and yet nothing is really the same. At this point he stopped thinking because, as usual when he did think, he started going round and round in circles and getting nowhere.

He moved automatically, got into his car, and drove off, feeling more alone than ever. Alone and useless, and he wished Mr Harris hadn't told him about the Walshes.

He drove up the hill and out of Stibbington until Silver Cottage loomed into view through the trees. Despite trying not to, he was still thinking of Niall, and he saw for a brief moment Silver Cottage as it had once been in summer, surrounded by trees in translucent green leaf, the garden bright with flowers, and the lawn, freshly mown, the grass like crushed green velvet. Suddenly his feeling of gloom began to lift. Here was something he *could* do. He could regenerate this garden. Not for Dr Browne, although she was employing him, but for himself, because once he had been happy here. He could live again through the garden. He would recreate it exactly as it had been all those years before.

As Tarquin unloaded the boxes of plants and his garden tools, he began to hum Beethoven's Pastoral, one of his favourite pieces. It seemed appropriate and cheered him.

He set the boxes on the wooden benches in the greenhouse. The plants needed pricking out, but that would have to be done later in the day. First thing was to get the old paraffin heating system working. Dr Browne, true to her word, had left a can of paraffin in the shed, and he started work. To his surprise it didn't take long. Once he'd given the heater a thorough clean and a new wick then filled it with paraffin, it lit first time. He sat back on his heels and breathed in the smell of the burning oil, feeling the air move with the first tentative stirring of heat in the long-disused greenhouse. He was happy here in the musty house of glass, shut away from the world outside. The world to which he had no wish to belong.

The glass insulated him from sound. He couldn't hear the passing traffic, and he didn't hear the sound of footsteps along the quarry tiles set in the lawn, stepping stones leading down the garden to the greenhouse. The faint click of the door opening caught his attention. He stood up. Turned around. Caught his breath. Made as if to move. But too late. The bullet hit him square between the eyes. For one second he saw a blinding flash of brilliant white. Then darkness. Without a sound he fell backwards, as the door to the green house clicked shut.

The newly filled paraffin heater toppled beneath the weight of his body as he fell, spilling its load of fuel around his inert form and spreading across the concrete floor. For a few moments all remained silent, then with a sudden 'woof' fire engulfed the greenhouse. Golden flames, matching the gold of Tarquin's hair, caressed each strand in turn before consuming it. Within minutes the silent figure on the floor became a glowing torch.

The dead leaves and branches of the trees and bushes in the farthest reaches of the darkening garden leapt into flickering life as the fire gained momentum. Tarquin lay at its centre, a still, blackened effigy, unable to see the ghastly beauty of the fire. For him, all was merciful darkness.

CHAPTER TEN

THE SAME MONDAY morning that Tarquin had set off for Brockett Hall, Niall Walsh was being regarded with increasing exasperation by his wife Christina.

'Niall, I really don't see what you've got against going to Stibbington for Christmas.' She wiped a dribble of rusk from baby Tom's chin. 'Think about me for a change. It will be lovely to leave London. I've been looking forward to it. No cooking, no housework, only Tom to look after. And, anyway,' she concluded in a tone of voice that Niall knew meant she had made up her mind, 'it's really too late to cancel now. Your parents want us to go.'

Niall felt tired. Life seemed to be one continual battle lately. No sooner than he'd overcome one hurdle than another presented itself. He was tired, dispirited, and frightened, which was stupid, because he had nothing to fear. He could say no. But that was another problem. He couldn't, not really. He'd never been good at decisions. And now, inexorably, against his will, he was being drawn back to the place he'd thought he would never see again.

Sometimes he thought it was a conspiracy by Christina and his parents to destroy him. But that was being ridiculous. He knew he had to rein in such panicky thoughts. Why should they want to destroy him? The answer, of course, was that they did not. It was just his own pathetic fear, which was wreaking havoc with his peace of mind. A peace that had been forged with painstaking care but which, despite all his efforts, still remained a fragile substance. In his mind's eye he could see it, his own life, lying around him, like so many shards of a broken eggshell. He watched Christina fussing over Tom. She wanted an answer. He had to give it.

'I don't want to go to Stibbington,' he said, knowing he sounded childish and petulant, but unable to think of anything else to say. 'I don't want to stay in that cheap little guest house down by the hard.'

'It's not *that* cheap, for God's sake, and your parents wouldn't have chosen it for us if it were bad. Goodness knows they're fussy enough.' Christina's temper, kept in check so far, now flared. She regarded her husband with undisguised fury. 'Really, Niall, I don't know what's got into you recently. We never do anything I want to do. Sometimes I think you wish you'd never married me.'

Niall looked out of the window of their London house, a Georgian town house in Primrose Hill, overlooking the actual hill itself. Four storeys including the basement with a walled garden to the front and rear. It had cost a fortune, and the mortgage repayments made Niall shudder every time he looked at the bank statement. But he'd bought the house to please Christina, although God knows why I ever needed to do that, he thought moodily. It hasn't pleased her. She's never pleased.

He said, 'How can you say that? I've been as good a husband as I know how.'

Christina finished giving a reluctant Tom his breakfast. It had been a struggle as the baby was more interested in turning his dish upside down and banging the spoon loudly on the tray of his high chair than eating. 'I know you have,' she said, sounding more conciliatory. Suddenly she turned to look at Niall. 'But sometimes I feel that you don't like me. That you are keeping your distance.' Niall didn't answer, so she continued. 'And if you really want to know, although I don't suppose you do, I've felt that way ever since we've been married.'

Niall felt himself flushing guiltily. He was surprised and more than a little disconcerted. He hadn't realized that Christina was so perceptive. He'd always prided himself on being the perfect husband. He was considerate and affectionate, or as affectionate as he knew how to be to someone he didn't truly love. But what was true love? Once he'd discovered a week or so after their marriage that he didn't love Christina, at least not in the way she wanted, he'd given up trying to fathom out that puzzle. Instead he'd concentrated on providing all the outward trappings necessary for a successful young couple.

'I've given you everything you've ever wanted,' he said quietly, not wanting another quarrel, which seemed to erupt with increasing frequency these days. 'We have this house. We have a lovely son. What else do you want?'

'You could let me come close to that part of yourself you always withhold,' said Christina. 'I want to feel close to you. To know what you are really thinking sometimes.'

Niall turned away. An abrupt movement of abhorrence. Why were some people so demanding? The thought made him feel physically sick. His father was the same, always demanding that he fit into the mould he designed for him, never seeing that he didn't fit, would never fit. It was his idea that they go to Stibbington, he knew it was. His mother was different; he felt an affinity with her, they were alike in many ways. Her life hadn't been easy. He remembered her saying once that things would have been so different if she'd been free. At the time he'd wondered what she'd meant. Later he thought he knew, but had never dared ask. There was a barrier of reticence ingrained into the Walsh family. No one ever articulated their thoughts on personal matters. Those things were hugged close to one's self, a burden too heavy ever to be released for a moment. He thought of his wife and felt bitter. Christina was never content to take what he could give, was always demanding more.

But he'd had love and friendship once. Known that it was possible to be in tune with someone and yet at the same time be totally independent. Exist side by side. Have parallel but separate lives, and yet remain in complete harmony. Then he thought of his life back in Stibbington. Not something he had allowed himself to do for years. If they went back to Stibbington he might meet Tarquin again if he was still living there. He wondered what he was doing now. What would they say to each other after all this time? Would the tragedy they had survived, but which had left a ghastly mountain of guilt, be insurmountable? The guilt. He shivered. It was always there. A dark shadow in his life, day and night, and would be until he drew his final breath. He wondered if it were the same for the others. Did they battle to keep it at bay all the time? But now there was something else. Supposing he did meet Tarquin again, or the others, would he then be able to continue with his present life? Questions, questions, questions. So many questions. But not one single answer.

He turned and walked towards the door. 'I've got work to do.'

'You always have,' said Christina bitterly. 'You've never got time for Tom and me. Maybe I should go down to Stibbington without you.'

Niall knew he would eventually lose the battle, he always did, and the knowledge caused him to lose his temper. 'This is what it's all about isn't it,' he shouted, forgetting that he hadn't wanted an argument. 'All this deep, pseudo-psycho analytical stuff, which you glean from women's magazines, about not being able to get close to me, is a load of rubbish. What you really mean is you want to go to Stibbington for a holiday, rather than stay in your own beautiful house and have Christmas here. Well, all right. We'll go to Stibbington. We'll stay in the bloody House by the Hard with that horror of a Matthews woman; we'll sit through long and boring meals with my parents, and it will probably piss with rain all the time and Tom will catch a cold.'

He flung himself out of the room, slamming the door behind him with such force that the whole house reverberated. He knew Christina would be smiling, pleased that she had at last precipitated him into giving her an answer.

Christina *was* smiling. Left alone, she disentangled Tom from his reins, and carried him over to the window. Together they looked out on to the park. Children were flying kites, wrapped up like tiny Siberian peasants against the bitter cold wind. She kissed Tom on the side of his small pink cheek. 'We're going to Stibbington tomorrow for the whole of Christmas,' she said, enjoying her small victory. 'And Daddy *will* enjoy it. Even if it kills him.'

Then she phoned Louise Browne and made arrangements to meet her when they'd both be down in Stibbington for Christmas.

Adam Maguire and Steve Grayson saw Tarquin Girling leaving Brockett Hall as they arrived. 'Tarquin,' muttered Steve. 'God knows why his mother gave him such an outlandish name, and what's he doing prowling around here?'

'Huh! The Brockett-Smythes seem to keep peculiar company, and they probably like the name! But we'll ask later, when it's appropriate.'

Steve grinned. 'Is that a polite way of telling me to keep my mouth shut, sir?' he said.

'Got it in one,' said Maguire. 'Softly, softly, catchee monkey, as the saying goes.'

'Why have we come to see the major? And what or who do you think we might catch? You don't think the major has anything to do with the murder, do you?'

Maguire shook his head, but in puzzlement rather than in a gesture of affirmation. 'All questions, Steve, to which there appear to be no satisfactory answers. But we'll stick with Darren's funeral for starters, and see where that leads. We're feeling our way in the dark here. At the moment we've got absolutely nothing positive to go on. No forensic links with anyone, no real clues. Nothing.'

Steve pulled the car to a crunching halt in the sodden wet gravel in front of Brockett Hall. 'Well, we wanted an exciting case. And we've got one.'

'It will only be exciting when we get something that leads us somewhere. Unsolved crimes are not exciting. Unless you can call getting the top brass coming down on you like a ton of bricks exciting,' growled Maguire. 'And that's what will be happening if we don't start coming up with something soon.' He was still feeling irritable and very weary. Sitting in the car and thinking had done no good at all; not one single spark of inspiration had come. Maybe he should let Steve Grayson have his way, and blurt out the first questions that popped into his young head. One thing Maguire was certain of, and that was that he didn't know where to start with the Brockett-Smythes. So much for the subconscious intuition of a detective honed to a fine skill after years of experience, he thought morosely. This morning he would have given his eye teeth for a spark of such divine inspiration.

It was just after one o'clock in the afternoon when Lizzie pulled the Alfa Romeo out of her slot in the Honeywell Practice car park. Late again, she thought, shoving the car into gear and speeding off down the lane that joined the main road towards Stibbington. If she didn't get a move on she'd never be in time to go back to the cottage before it was time to start evening surgery again. Her stomach rumbled, reminding her that, apart from a cup of Tara's unpalatable coffee and a biscuit, she'd had nothing to eat since breakfast. Life in the country was proving to be just as hectic, if not more so, than life in London.

Her mobile rang. It was Louise. 'Hi.' She sounded cheerful. She always did. 'I'm back from Valencia. Just thought I'd ring and see how you are.'

'I'm fine.' As Lizzie had just begun the approach to Stibbington High Street she pulled into a parking bay by the side of the main post office. 'Look, I'm out on my visits, it's just luck that I've found somewhere to park so that I can speak to you. If I'd been in one of the lanes around here I'd never have found anywhere.'

'Oh, Mother!' Louise sounded exasperated. 'I *know* you're not *supposed* to talk on the phone when driving. But everyone does.'

'Not everyone,' said Lizzie firmly. 'I'm new here, and doing my best to appear a pillar of the establishment. I have to set an example. Now, why have you rung? What do you want?' She loved her daughter dearly but recognized her for the human being she truly was, sometimes despairing of the fact that she always seemed to take, rarely giving back. Although, to be fair, she had to admit that every now and then she astounded her with acts of generosity that left her speechless. Her unwavering devotion to both herself and Mike when they'd announced they were splitting up had made her feel very humble. True, she and Louise had argued a little about where she should go and where she should live, but once Lizzie had made the decision Louise had been one hundred per cent behind her. Her support had made the divorce that much more bearable, and she supposed Mike must feel the same way. Not that they'd ever discussed it. Their relationship had disintegrated to the extent that nothing could be discussed by the time they decided to split. Or to be more precise, by the time Mike had decided to leave.

'Well ...' Louise slid into a wheedling tone. Lizzie smiled, held her breath, and waited for the request. 'Can I come down tomorrow? The gallery has given me some extra time off, and a married friend of mine, Christina, is going down to Stibbington with her husband for Christmas. They're going down early, and she's asked me to see her tomorrow evening. This would suit me fine, because I could see you and her. By the way, I'm going skiing at Christmas. I did tell you, didn't I?'

'Yes, you did. And there's no need to feel guilty about going away at Christmas. I shall enjoy having a little time off on my own, and having the chance to sort the house out. I'll be all right.'

'I know you will. But the important thing is can I come down tomorrow?'

'Of course you can come. But is that all? You mean you don't want me to lend you any money for your skiing holiday?'

'Mother! Do I ever ask you for money?'

'Frequently.' This was true. The gallery job, although exciting, did not pay well. 'But you've never asked to stay before.'

Louise laughed. 'Don't worry. I'm solvent at the moment. But you've never lived in the country before. So now I've got two reasons to visit. No, three reasons. You, the new house, and Christina.'

Lizzie smiled. 'One thing I'll say for you and that is you take after me. Subtlety is not your forte.'

'Then I can come?'

'Of course. Would I say no to my own daughter? The spare bedroom is a bit of a tip, but you're very welcome. I'll enjoy the company, always assuming you've got time to spare for me, although I must warn you I've got surgeries morning and evening, and visits during the day.'

'That doesn't matter. I'm going to see Christina tomorrow evening anyway. Perhaps we can go out together for dinner on Thursday night before I go back. Book up somewhere nice. See you tomorrow. I'll catch the 5.30 train from Waterloo. And don't worry about picking me up; I'll get a taxi.' Louise rattled off her instructions without pausing for breath and then rang off.

So the country and the old school friend was the attraction. But Lizzie was pretty certain that Louise wouldn't have visited if she'd still been living with Mike. Louise had given the parental home a miss these last few years, preferring to share apartments and be in the company of their friends. Nothing had ever been mentioned and only now, with hindsight, did Lizzie realize that the atmosphere between her and Mike had been brittle for some time. But nothing comes from nothing, Lizzie reflected now, and if the break-up brought her closer to Louise then so much the better. Her company would be a nice change. Silver Cottage was a little lonely. Strange how when she was in London she'd always hated the ever-present roar of traffic, but now she was in the country she found the silence rather disturbing.

Her stomach reminded her again that it was empty. From her parking spot she could see the swinging sign of Antonio's Delicatessen. It was just the place to buy a snack for now, and something for supper. Locking the car she hurried towards it.

House visits that afternoon were carried out between bites of a stilton and broccoli pasty; crumbs brushed off each time before hauling the laptop and black bag out of the Alfa and trudging up the path to the next patient. The ailments were various and mostly minor, causing Lizzie to become increasingly disgruntled as the afternoon wore on. Practically all the patients could easily have come to the surgery, instead of calling out a doctor for a visit. But she bit her tongue, dealt with them efficiently, if rather brusquely, politely informing them that visiting the surgery enabled doctors to see more people, more quickly, which saved time and money and was better for everyone.

The weak winter sun, which had struggled through the ever-threatening rain clouds, began to sink down, and a glance at her watch told Lizzie that she'd have to get a move on if she was to get back in time to see Tarquin and give him instructions about the garden.

One visit to go: Furzey Cottage. It would have to be a quick visit as she was now way behind schedule, but she couldn't find it on the sat nav. However, she eventually managed to find it on her large-scale Ordnance Survey map; it appeared to be in the middle of the forest at the end of a dirt track.

The map was quite correct. It was in the middle of a particularly dense patch of the New Forest and the track was gravel, heavily overgrown with moss, indicating that not much traffic passed that way.

Parking the car outside the house, which was wooden and painted dark brown, Lizzie fished out the patient's notes. They informed her that a Mrs Mills lived here alone, and that she was eighty-seven.

All thoughts of making it a quick visit vanished when she saw Mrs Mills. Riddled with arthritis, the old woman had shuffled, with the help of a Zimmer frame, to answer the door. Wizened and bent double by age and arthritis, she had the appearance of a witch straight out of one of Grimms' fairy tales. But the smile, which beamed from ear to ear when she saw Lizzie, transformed her face into that of a vulnerable child.

'Dick Jamieson told me he'd send me the new lady doctor,' she said, 'so I've made some fresh bread and a fruit cake especially. Come in, come in.' She waved a mittened hand in welcome. 'Sit by the fire and have a cup of tea. It's a miserable day out there. These dark winter days seem to go on for ever and ever.'

So Lizzie sat by the open log fire watching the flames leap orange and red, and gave up trying to hurry. How did an old woman manage to exist in such a remote part of the forest? She couldn't throw the old lady's hospitality back in her face. Watching her bent figure struggle back into the kitchen Lizzie could only guess at the determination and will power which gave her the strength to make bread and cakes, and keep the cottage as clean and bright as it was. Outside, the towering trees crowded in on the little house, but inside the brass ornaments sparkled, and the lace doilies on the sideboard were starched a stiff snowy white.

Mrs Mills re-entered after a few minutes, having discarded her Zimmer frame for a wooden trolley, the top of which was laden with a teapot, milk jug, cups and saucers. The bottom level had plates of fruit cake and thick cut slices of bread and jam.

Thinking it best to dispense with the medical problems before the tea, Lizzie said, 'Before we relax perhaps you'd better tell me why you needed a visit, Mrs Mills. What is the problem?'

Mrs Mills nodded towards the wedge of notes on Lizzie's lap. 'As you can see I'm the proverbial creaking gate post,' she said. 'But it's none of those things written down there, except that I could do with some stronger pain killers for the arthritis if you will prescribe them. But nothing that makes me constipated, mind. I don't want that. No, this time, it's this.' She held out a leg, which was bandaged and clad in a stocking cut off at the knee and held up by an elastic band. 'I've looked in my medical book and I've come to the conclusion that I've got a varicose ulcer.'

After peeling her way through layers of stocking and bandage Lizzie looked. It was a very nasty ulcer. She dressed it and said, 'I think we'd better get the district nurse to come in every day to dress it for you until it has healed.'

Mrs Mills' smile positively glistened with delight. 'Someone to visit every day! Oh, that'll be nice. I do like a bit of company.'

Later over a cup of tea, and bread and butter spread thickly with home-made blackberry jam, Lizzie learned that Mrs Mills had been headmistress at Stibbington's one and only primary school.

'You've lived here for a long time, then.'

'Born here,' said Mrs Mills. 'Went away to train as a teacher but came back, got married, and stayed ever since. I can't tell you how much I miss my days at school. Harry and I never had any children of our own, but there was a time when I knew every child in Stibbington by name, and they all knew me. I taught that boy Darren Evans, you know. The one they found dead, poor lamb.'

Lizzie thought it unlikely that anyone else would have called Darren Evans a lamb. She accepted another cup of tea and progressed to the fruit cake. Rich, dark, and sticky, she munched her way through it, ignoring all thoughts of the calories. It tasted delicious. 'How long have you been here on your own?' she asked, surreptitiously dropping a few crumbs for the ancient cairn sitting by the fire and looking up at her with imploring eyes.

'Oh, for nigh on ten years now. I lost my Harry one December night. A night such as this it was.'

For one wild moment Lizzie imagined the said Mr Mills wandering off into the forest all alone and never returning, then reined in her recalcitrant thoughts. The different ways in which people referred to death was something she'd never got used to. According to her patients their loved ones rarely died. They *passed over, got lost, passed away, popped their clogs*, but never actually died or were dead.

But it was Mrs Mills' words, 'a night such as this,' that made her cast an instinctive glance out of the window. One look confirmed she was late. Very late. She looked at her watch. If she hurried she might catch Tarquin. He could still be working in the greenhouse potting out the plants he was bringing; it was a possibility as he'd be able to see because of the outside light on the wall at the end of the cottage.

Leaving Mrs Mills with a promise of coming again soon, which she meant to keep, and that a district nurse would be arranged for the next day, Lizzie put the Alfa in gear and roared off down the gravel track at a speed which would have earned her pole position on the starting grid of any Grand Prix.

Leaving the denseness of Mrs Mills' particular patch of forest, she rejoined a tarmac road and drove around the outskirts of Stibbington towards Silver Cottage. It was when all other signs of civilization were behind her and the darkness was again almost total that Lizzie saw a strange glow in the sky. Not constant, but flickering. A worrying premonition lodged cold and hard in her throat. Speeding towards it, she rounded the last corner of the bend in the lane and saw the fire. Scarlet and golden flames were shooting skywards, clothing the sides of Silver Cottage in a coat of brilliant colours. For one split second she thought it was the house itself on fire, then realized it was the greenhouse and the wooden shed that stood beside it. Her first thought was that Tarquin had lit the heater, and then gone and left it before making certain it was safe. Silly boy. Lucky for him it wasn't the house burning.

Without even realizing that she had actually done it, Lizzie punched out the emergency number on her mobile phone, then stood waiting until a high-pitched wail announced the arrival of the fire engine.

It didn't take the fire team long to douse the flames. The chief fire officer walked towards her, illuminated against the steaming smoke still spiralling towards the night sky by the powerful lights on the fire appliance.

'Thank you,' said Lizzie. 'I was afraid the cottage might go up as well. I suppose I ought to offer you a cup of tea or something. I've never had a fire before; I'm not sure what to do next.'

The chief fire officer, a man of considerable bulk and middle years named George Beeson, took off his helmet. 'What we've got to do next, Dr Browne,' he said, 'is wait for the police and ambulance.'

'Wait for the police and ambulance,' repeated Lizzie.

'Yes. There's a charred body in there. Any idea as to who it might be?'

'Oh no.' Lizzie felt sick. 'It can't be him. Surely not.' She started to run towards the blackened ruins of the greenhouse, and on reaching it knelt, oblivious of the mess, by the body. The clothes had been burned away; just sticky remnants remained clinging to the charred remains. The smell of burnt flesh made her gag, but she had to do it. She reached out and felt in vain for any sign of life.

'Can't be who?' Out of breath, George Beeson caught up and stood over her.

Lizzie looked up. For a moment she couldn't speak. Mouth dry. Heart hammering. All she could think of was that a man had died on her property.

'Can't be who? George Beeson repeated.

'Tarquin Girling. He was working in my garden this afternoon.'

But her words were lost in the dual scream of sirens as, with blue lights flashing and engines revving, the ambulance and police car arrived almost simultaneously at the scene.

CHAPTER ELEVEN

THE CALL CAME through late Monday afternoon. Another body found in suspicious circumstances. Maguire didn't know whether to be glad or sorry that matters at Stibbington police station had suddenly taken another dramatic turn. This time, according to the fire officer, George Beeson, the body was burned beyond recognition, and had been found at the new doctor's cottage. Maguire reflected wryly that Dr Browne was certainly coming in for more than her fair share of excitement since moving to Stibbington.

When the call came he had been going through what they'd got on Darren Evans, trying to tie in something with the Brockett-Smythes but without much success. A gut feeling that there was something made Maguire persist; although the major was insisting that Darren Evans had merely helped out in the garden and done a few other odd jobs, Maguire did not believe him. There was something weird about their connection. Darren Evans was not the type the major would normally have employed for any odd jobs. Why hadn't he chosen any one of the number of retired men who did such work? There were plenty of adverts in the local paper; all respectable elderly men; the type of man the major would naturally gravitate towards. What was more, Phineas had stated quite categorically that Darren's hands were not those of a man who did manual labour. And everyone else who'd had dealings with Darren all confirmed that he had expended as little physical effort as possible for as long as anyone could remember. He was the archetypal dropout.

At least the visit to Brockett Hall had solved the mystery of Melinda Brockett-Smythe, the daughter. Nothing sinister there, just a tragedy. She, apparently, was suffering from a severe mental illness, and needed constant care and medication for relief of her symptoms, which consisted of aggressive and anti-social behaviour. Maguire felt sorry for the Brockett-Smythes. It was at times like this that he told himself it was a blessing not to have children. At least he had nothing and no one to worry about. The major and his wife, his second wife it transpired during the conversation, his first having died before the daughter developed the illness, cared for Melinda on their own, apart from two mornings a week when a local woman, Ivy James, came in to care for her to enable them to take a break. It was then that they usually went to the Royal Oak for lunch, where they had met Maguire.

Maguire now thought he knew why Mrs Brockett-Smythe looked so drained and exhausted. She was being dragged down by caring for a child who was not even her own. Maguire wondered how he'd feel in that situation. Was it worse because the child was not your own, or would you feel the same if it were your own flesh and blood?

Switching off the computer, he closed the slim folder containing his notes. He still recorded everything by hand as well as logging it on the computer. Somehow he couldn't entirely trust computers, and was resisting becoming paperless as County Headquarters had instructed. He shoved the notes in the bottom drawer of his desk.

'Come on, Steve,' he called across to Grayson. 'We've got another body on our hands.'

Grayson, who'd been playing with a pile of paper clips and counting the minutes to when he could reasonable ask Maguire if he could leave to go home to Ann and the son they were expecting, groaned. The scan had clearly shown it was a boy, and Steve was longing to tell Maguire. He'd told everyone else in the station who was willing to listen, but as Maguire had never enquired, he'd kept silent. You could never be sure with Maguire; he might say congratulations, or he might bite his head off and tell him to concentrate on his work. Something which Steve was finding very difficult to do this particular afternoon. The trail to and from Darren Evans had petered out, and with it so had his enthusiasm. Normally, he would have been thrilled with the thought of additional excitement, but another body to be investigated late on Monday, which would inevitably spill over into the evening, had not featured in his plans, and failed to enthuse him.

'Where is it, sir?' he said, trying to sound alert.

'At Dr Browne's place. Silver Cottage in Deer Leap Lane.'

Steve sat up and whistled. 'Perhaps she's our murderer.'

Maguire snorted. 'Don't be bloody ridiculous. Let's get going. I'll drive tonight.'

As they ploughed through the darkness Steve worried about Ann. She'd been expecting him back for supper, a casserole, she'd said. He'd have to ask Maguire if he could phone her in a moment and tell her he'd be late. But not now. One glance at Maguire's profile told him this would not be an appropriate moment. He tried texting by holding the phone down between his knees, but Maguire glanced over as soon as the faint light shone from the keyboard. He switched it off. He'd have to wait, and so would Ann.

Maguire thought about Tess. She'd been left alone since lunch time. A long time for an old dog. He hoped her bladder and bowels lasted, and there wouldn't be a mess to clear up. It had never been a problem when Rosemary had been alive. Then she had walked the dog when he'd been delayed, and Tess had never made a mess. It wasn't fair keeping a dog when one lived alone, but, and for a moment his expression softened, he wouldn't be without her. Life would be unbearably lonely.

At Silver Cottage Lizzie stood in numb disbelief watching the nightmarish scene unfold. Maguire and Grayson arrived, siren wailing. Hardly necessary, thought Lizzie, they were too late to help whoever it was lying in the remains of the greenhouse. She was refusing to let herself think it was Tarquin. She had to keep the body anonymous in her mind for as long as possible. The ambulance arrived, sirens screeching, blue lights flashing. Why hadn't someone told them he, *it*, was dead. Dead! There was no need to make a noise. The ambulance decanted two paramedics glowing eerily in their white and green jackets. They rushed across to the greenhouse carrying with them a box of resuscitation equipment. You won't need that, thought Lizzie grimly, but said nothing.

More and more people arrived, arc lights were set up. The cottage and garden was fenced off from prying eyes by blue and white plastic tape, and a tarpaulin was erected over the debris of the greenhouse to protect the human remains. The paramedics packed up their box of tricks, hung about for a few minutes and chatted, then went off, hopefully to find a more rewarding customer who might respond to their administrations. Maguire walked back to where Lizzie was standing. 'Did you touch the body?'

She swallowed. 'I had to.' The memory of the repulsive feel of the seared flesh against her fingertips and the sickly smell was still vivid. It hadn't seemed like a human being at all, more like a piece of barbecued meat. She swallowed again. 'As a doctor it was my duty to feel for any vital signs, although common sense told me there would be none.'

'I shall need a statement, as you were the first doctor on the scene. You can pronounce him dead.'

'Yes, I suppose so.'

'What do you mean, "suppose so"?'

Phineas Merryweather arrived looking robustly cheerful as ever, and waved at Maguire, who raised a hand in reply. The forensic photographer trailed along behind Phineas, looking anything but cheerful.

'I can't pronounce *him* dead,' said Lizzie. 'The body is too badly burned to be recognizable, and I didn't investigate *that* closely. All I can say is that it is the body of an adult, weighing approximately sixty kilos, and I am unable to determine the sex.'

'I was told that you thought it was Tarquin Girling.' Maguire felt irritated. Did she have to be so pedantic?

'I said that he was going to start clearing my garden this afternoon, and he said he would be potting out some plants in the greenhouse. That's why I thought perhaps . . .' her voice tailed away.

'But you don't know for certain whether he came or not.'

Lizzie shook her head, trying to obliterate a sense of guilt. It was *her* greenhouse, *her* ancient paraffin heater. And if it were Tarquin lying beneath the tarpaulin, it was *her* fault for not ensuring that the heater was safe. She should have checked it when she bought the paraffin. For surely it was the heater that had caused the fire. It must have exploded. 'He said he would come, and I intended to be here to see him. But I got delayed with my visits and when I got back the fire had already taken hold.'

'Thanks.' Maguire made a move towards the tarpaulin. 'I'd better go and see how Phineas and the photographer are getting on. You are free to go into the house now if you wish.'

Free to go into the house. His words shook Lizzie into a realization of the time. Everything, since she had arrived and seen the fire, had seemed to move with lightning speed and yet at the same time stand still. Now she was acutely aware that she was late for surgery. Her patients would be waiting. 'I've got an evening clinic to do at the practice. I'm late already. Am I free to go back into Stibbington?'

'Of course.' Maguire nodded his assent and moved off across the tangled mass of dead vegetation in the garden. Lizzie stood watching him for a moment, then turned towards the drive and her car. As she turned she thought she saw a movement in the bushes at the side of the garden, the side where Tarquin had said that once there'd been a tennis court. The lights from the scene of the incident spilled over raggedly into that part of the garden, probing fingers of light into the darkness. She couldn't be sure, because it was so indistinct, but Lizzie could have sworn she saw the shadowy figure of a man. But the figure faded into oblivion before she had the chance to reinforce her suspicion, leaving nothing but bushes and the hedgerow, matted with last summer's tangled mass of Old Man's Beard, waving slightly in the wind.

She walked back to the car trying to calm her jangling nerves. Imagination. Of course it was. She was overwrought. It was time to get back to the familiar world of the surgery, and the never-ending queue of patients with their reassuringly familiar ailments, most of which were never serious. It was as the central locking system of the car beeped and clicked the door open that she heard the distant sound of a motorbike in the adjoining lane. A chill ran up her spine but not for long. She gave herself a mental shake. What was the matter with her? Coincidence, of course it was. Plenty of people owned motorbikes in the Stibbington area. But it reminded her that she had forgotten to tell Adam Maguire about the motorcyclist riding away from the scene of Darren's death. She'd tell him tomorrow when she gave her statement.

Emmy Matthews was agitated. She made herself a cup of camomile tea to sooth her nerves, and sat down in her green and white kitchen to drink it. Normally, camomile tea worked wonders for both her indigestion and her state of mind. And if that failed, the kitchen, all twenty thousand pounds of the best matching green coloured laminate that money could buy, and which had only been installed six months ago, gave her a smug satisfaction. Not that she was usually too worried about anything. Despite her continual visits to the doctor complaining of her nerves, Emmy Matthews, as Dick Jamieson often observed, had nerves of steel and the hide of a rhinoceros. But tonight those nerves were distinctly frayed. And it was her guest, Mrs Smithson, who'd done the fraying.

Emmy always prided herself on not being a nosy landlady. Not like some of the guest house landladies in Stibbington, tut-tutting when a couple shared a room and gave different names, but taking the money just the same. Emmy always called a spade a spade and was not afraid to say so.

'What people get up to in their private moments is no business of mine,' she told the other landladies rather primly. There was friendly competition between them as they compared their best and worst guests. 'And these days hardly anybody is married,' said Emmy. 'Even families with several children have parents who are not married. Who am I to pass comment? And what I see when I'm cleaning the rooms is no business of mine, no matter how weird it might be.'

Weird was one thing. Emmy had seen sexual aids that practically gave her hair a spontaneous permanent wave. She had never mentioned those to her fellow landladies, not wanting anyone to think she ran a 'loose' establishment, and besides, as she was so fond of saying, it was none of her business. But what was her business? Was something suspicious her business? Especially when she couldn't be really certain what she had seen?

The problem had arisen with the cleaning of Mrs Smithson's room. Finally, on Monday afternoon, Emmy lost patience. It was all right waiting to be given permission, but pride would not allow her to let a guest's room go uncleaned for more than four days. Mrs Smithson had been in residence since Thursday evening; it was now Monday afternoon, and time the room had a good 'do through' to use Emmy's favourite expression.

It was dark; nearly five o'clock by the time Emmy was nearly finished. The sheets had been changed, the bed remade, the bathroom cleaned with the latest cleaner, which killed, cleaned, and sparkled all in one go. And not until her own distorted reflection looked back at her from the bathroom taps and shower head was she satisfied.

She was just about to leave the room when she remembered she hadn't polished the top of the white melamine wardrobe. It had a fancy gilt edged scroll running around the top which left a hollow in the middle. The hollow collected dust. Or it would have done if Emmy ever allowed it to, which she never did.

Clambering on to a chair she reached into the hollow, tin of polish in one hand and duster in the other, only to find a large cardboard box wedged on the top. Lifting it out and climbing down, holding the box with both hands, proved to be difficult, and just as her foot touched the floor, the door to the room opened, and in strode Mrs Smithson.

Emmy fell flat on her face. The box shot across the room, the lid flying off in the process. To her amazement the box was full of wigs, each one identical. There was also a small plastic packet, which was full of brass colour things, which at first she thought were bullets, but must have been packets of hairgrips. But she only had a fleeting glance so she couldn't be sure. Mrs Smithson slammed the lid back on the box before she had a chance to take a closer look. Then she turned back to Emmy, who was still on the floor, with an expression of fury on her face, which made her shiver.

'How dare you snoop in my room.' Mrs Smithson's voice was low, and there was no disguising the menace in it. Emmy was too frightened to think. She tried to scrabble across the floor towards the door on her hands and knees but Mrs Smithson stood in her way. 'How dare you pry amongst my things,' she said, towering above her.

'I wasn't prying,' Emmy gasped. 'I came in to clean. I was polishing the top of the wardrobe. You made me jump and I dropped the box.' She scrambled to her feet intending to make a speedy exit but Mrs Smithson barred her way again.

'I don't want my private possessions gossiped about.'

'Of course not. I'm sorry I saw your wigs if you didn't want me to.' The words tumbled one over the other in her terror. 'Lot's of women wear wigs, it's nothing—'

'Get out!' The words were spat at her.

Emmy scuttled in a sideways crab-like movement to reach the door without having to go too near her frightening guest. 'Yes, I won't clean again. Not if you don't want me to.' She heard her voice, breathless, squeaky, and so faint she doubted that Mrs Smithson even heard her.

With a sharp movement, which nearly caused Emmy to have a heart attack there and then, Mrs Smithson picked up the tin of polish and the duster and threw them after Emmy.

'Take your bloody polish with you.'

The tin of polish hit the wall opposite, ricocheting back into Emmy. She couldn't get out fast enough, only stopping momentarily to pick up the polish and the duster. She was hardly through the door when it slammed shut behind her leaving her trembling in the corridor outside.

Now she sat sipping her camomile tea, and wondered whether she ought to ring the police. After all, ordinary women didn't carry bullets about with them, and there had been a murder recently. A shooting, in fact. And then the next moment she told herself that the bullets were a product of her overwrought imagination. She couldn't be sure of anything and Mrs Smithson must need a lot of grips to cope with all those wigs. Bullets were just too far-fetched. It must have been hairgrips. She had just convinced herself that this was the most likely explanation when there was a knock on the door.

It was Mrs Smithson. All smiles and apologetic. 'I must apologize for my unforgivable behaviour,' she said. 'I've been feeling a bit edgy lately. My book hasn't been going at all well.'

If that's what writing a book does to you, thought Emmy grimly, then it's best left well alone. Waste of time, anyway. How many people had time to read a book? She certainly didn't. Magazines with plenty of pictures was what she liked. But she took the proffered peace offering and said. 'That's all right. It was my fault too. I should have asked you first, not gone in and done it while you were out.'

'No, no. It's my fault.' Mrs Smithson was insistent. 'I shouldn't have been so difficult. Please go in and clean every day, if you wish. But I'd be glad if you didn't disturb my papers.'

'Of course not,' said Emmy, feeling an immense sense of relief. She had been worrying about nothing. 'Would you like a cup of camomile tea? I always find it very soothing. It's supposed to be good for the nerves.'

'I'd love one.' Mrs Smithson perched herself rather awkwardly on one of the shiny green-topped stools beside the breakfast bar. 'Anything that would sooth the nerves would do me good.' She watched Emmy plug the kettle in and get out another cup and a camomile tea bag, then said, 'That's why I wear the wigs, you know. Nerves.'

'Oh! Really?' Emmy wasn't sure she saw the connection.

'Yes. I suffer from alopecia. A baldness caused by a nervous condition. So it's either wear wigs or a headscarf. I prefer wigs. But I don't like people to know. I know it's silly pride, but I can't help it.'

'Oh, you poor thing,' said Emmy, pouring hot water onto the tea bag. She settled herself comfortably opposite Mrs Smithson, ready for a cosy, woman-to-woman, chat. She patted her own rigidly permed and lacquered hair. A visit to Snippets once a week ensured that never a hair was out of place. A brush and comb were hardly necessary, just a push in with the fingers was all that was required. 'It must be terrible to have to wear wigs all the time,' she said. 'But don't worry. I'll never breathe a word to anyone.'

How Lizzie got through that evening's surgery she never knew. To each patient their ailment, no matter how trivial, was of immense importance to them. She knew this and tried to concentrate on the sore throats, painful knees, chesty coughs, and other winter maladies. But all the time she was waiting for news, hoping against hope that the body would not be identified as that of Tarquin Girling.

Her worst fears began to materialize towards the end of surgery, just before the last two patients were to be seen.

Tara Murphy knocked on her door and came in. 'Sorry to interrupt,' she said in her most efficient, surgery receptionist manner, 'but I've got Mrs Girling on the phone. She says is Tarquin still working at your place? Because if he is, he should hurry up and come home with the fish and chips he promised. She and Wayne are waiting for their supper.'

Lizzie shook her head. The only people she had mentioned the fire to were Dick and Peter, the two partners present that evening; Stephen still being absent due to the turbulence of his large intestine. 'Tell Mrs Girling that he is not at my house, and that I have no idea where he might be.' For a moment she toyed with the idea of suggesting Mrs Girling might ring the police, but then thought better of it. No need to raise the alarm and cause distress unnecessarily. Far better to wait until a positive identification had been made.

'I'll tell her,' said Tara pertly. 'I thought she had a cheek ringing anyway. I nearly didn't ask you.'

'You were right to ask. It's only natural for a mother to worry about her children.'

'He isn't a child,' said Tara. 'He's twenty-seven if he's a day. Practically thirty.' Her tone implied that being practically thirty was having one foot in the grave. Wonder what she thinks about being over forty, thought Lizzie wryly, buzzing for the next patient to come in.

CHAPTER TWELVE

Mᴿˢ Gɪʀʟɪɴɢ ᴅɪᴅɴ'ᴛ ask Adam Maguire into the house when he arrived that Monday evening. She stood, one hand on the thin lurcher, the other holding her small son's hand. The child was coughing, had a runny nose, and was clinging hold of her hand and apron as if his life depended on it. All three regarded him apprehensively.

Maguire took the initiative. 'I think I'd better come in, and you'd better sit down, Mrs Girling,' he said gently.

This was something he hated doing. There was no easy way to deal with violent death, accidental or otherwise. As a young policeman he'd thought he'd get used to seeing the look on people's faces when they were told that someone close to them would not be coming home. But the years had taught him otherwise. The only constant emotion was his feeling of helpless ineffectuality. Every single person, every family, reacted differently. Some screamed wild cries of disbelief. The grief of others was quieter, but so raw it was almost tangible; others greeted the news with expressionless stony silence. The silence of the grave as Steve Grayson had once aptly put it. And as a policeman, when it was murder as it was in this case, it was his duty to try to interpret both the cries and the silences. What did it all mean? Did they know why it had happened? Were they involved in any way?

The grisly scene at the greenhouse had left him feeling physically exhausted. There was no doubt that the body was Tarquin Girling, and, according to Phineas, no doubt that he'd been murdered. He'd been wearing an identity bracelet, and that combined with the dental records – there were only two dentists in Stibbington and Phineas had checked with them both immediately – had given positive identification. Events were pressing in on him with claustrophobic speed. Two murders in less than a week. A new investigation, new suspects, if they were lucky. The whole slow process to be set in motion all over again. If he wasn't careful he'd have the upper echelons moving in from County Headquarters, taking over the case, inferring that he was incapable of dealing with it. I'm getting too old for this job, he thought, wearily. And there was Tess. He still hadn't got home. She was still waiting.

Without a word Mrs Girling led the way into the kitchen, sat the child on a small chair near the kitchen range, then sat herself on a wooden chair by the side of the table. 'Well?' she demanded.

She didn't offer him a chair but Maguire took one and sat on it anyway, not wanting to appear a figure of authority by towering over the woman. 'I've come about your son, Tarquin,' he said.

'He's late.' The child whined nasally. 'He said he'd bring us in fish and chips and I'm hungry.'

'What about Tarquin?' said Mrs Girling.

'I'm afraid he's not coming in with the fish and chips,' said Maguire.

Lizzie went back to Silver Cottage with mixed feelings. Both Dick and Peter had offered to put her up for the night, but Lizzie had said no.

'I've got to go back at some time,' she'd said, 'unless I up sticks and move out of the house altogether, and I've no intention of doing that. So tonight is as good a night as any. I've got to get used to the fact that a man died in the grounds of my property. There's no point in being frightened. Dead people can't harm the living.'

Dick Jamieson wasn't happy, but Lizzie was adamant.

When she arrived all was silent, but flapping blue and white tape still cut her house off from the outside world. A solitary policeman sat on guard in a police van. She parked the Alfa by the side of the garage and approached the van.

'Am I allowed in?' she asked.

The policeman unfolded his limbs; he was exceptionally tall, and emerged from the van touching his cap respectfully. She saw it was Kevin Harrison. Poor boy, he seemed to be permanently on duty at ghastly scenes. 'Yes, Dr Browne, you are allowed in,' he said. 'But Chief Inspector Maguire asked that you do not go into the remains of the greenhouse. Just in case forensics need to come back.'

'I wouldn't dream of going there.' Lizzie shuddered. 'And I can tell you this. As soon as I have the all clear from the police I shall have the place razed to the ground. There'll be no new greenhouse or shed. I shall have a rose garden or something. Anything to make me forget what happened here.'

Kevin nodded sympathetically. 'I think you're very brave. My mum wouldn't stay on alone in a house after a murder.'

Lizzie caught her breath, and put her black bag down with a heavy thump beside the car. She found she was trembling, but tried to keep her voice steady. 'A murder? Did you say a murder? I thought it was an accident. I thought the stove must have exploded.'

Kevin Harrison looked worried. 'Perhaps I wasn't supposed to say anything, but no one said not to.'

'Well, go on, now you've started,' said Lizzie. 'I'm entitled to know. It happened on my property.'

Kevin hesitated, then said, 'Apparently he was shot before the fire started. And the bullet was from the same gun as the one which killed Darren Evans.'

'I see,' said Lizzie, but she didn't. The whole thing was assuming nightmare proportions. Why would two individuals be shot in a sleepy backwater like Stibbington? It didn't make sense. It was such a quiet place.

'It doesn't make sense,' said Kevin echoing her thoughts. 'I don't know who this last victim was, but Darren Evans was a nonentity. Why would anyone kill him? He was hardly worth killing.'

Lizzie felt duty bound to stand up for Darren. 'All human life is always worth something,' she said.

'I know. I didn't mean it like that.' He shuffled about in the gravel of the path uncomfortably. 'What I meant was, well, why? Who would think . . . well! I mean to say. This isn't London or LA.'

'No. But if the crime figures go on at this rate Stibbington will soon be on a par with those cities,' said Lizzie sharply. It is important, she told herself, to keep a sense of balance, of equilibrium, and put things into their proper perspective. The police would solve the murders soon. She said as much to Kevin, who was now slapping his arms over his chest, and hopping from one boot to the other. An indication, she thought, that he would prefer to get back into the van. It had turned very cold.

'Oh, they'll be solved,' he said, climbing back into the van. 'Probably turn out to be the work of a madman on the loose,' he added cheerfully, slamming the van door shut.

Hardly the kind of remark to inspire confidence, reflected Lizzie, who'd been thinking along the same lines. She wished the darkness wasn't quite so dense and black. She found the thought of someone lurking about with a gun unnerving. Picking up her black bag, she started for the cottage, then remembering her laptop and the bag of food from Antonio's went back to the car. After retrieving them, she got herself and her luggage into the house. The first thing she did was switch on all the lights. Somehow the blazing lights were reassuring. Then she decided that a large malt whisky was in order, reasoning that should the murderer come back and shoot her she might as well die happy. But before a drop of the malt had passed her lips a sweep of headlights announced the arrival of another car.

The two of them were finishing up in the office. No point in hanging around now; there was nothing they could usefully do until the post-mortem results came through and Grayson was anxious to get home. But he felt he had to offer to visit Dr Browne. 'Of course,' he said, 'she'll never be there. Not after the murder.'

'She doesn't know it is murder yet,' Maguire replied. 'She thinks it was an accident.'

'Murder, accident. Someone has been killed at her place. It's enough to frighten any woman off. But I'll go over and see if she's there if you like.'

'No, I'll go. Silver Cottage is more in my direction than yours.'

Maguire was not surprised to find her at home. He guessed that she would be nervous – who wouldn't after finding a corpse on one's property – but he also guessed that the gritty single-mindedness he suspected she possessed would make her determined to stand her ground. Lizzie Browne was not the type to be frightened away, although even she, mused Maguire, might be more than a little perturbed at the thought of a serial killer on the loose. Well, he corrected his own thoughts, a potential serial killer. Two murders by the same gun, inevitably meant the same person, and two murders in such quick suc-cession was moving into serial type territory. Once the news got out the media would start a clamorous public demand that the killer be found. Such pressure, he knew from experience, hampered police efforts. It got in the way of the cool detachment needed to look at all the evidence, and tended to make rational decisions difficult. But he was keeping his fingers crossed on that score. At the moment the media were obsessed with unearthing sexual and financial improprieties of various cabinet ministers. And long may it go on, thought Maguire. The more dirt they discover in Westminster, the less notice anyone will take of what is going on in Stibbington.

When he arrived he stopped and spoke to Kevin Harrison. 'When do you finish?' Tess, who he'd picked up on the way, rustled about in the undergrowth at the side of the drive pursuing elusive scents.

'Ten o'clock, sir. Someone from Southampton's coming out to relieve me. We've run out of man hours at Stibbington.'

'I'm going in to talk to Dr Browne. I'll be some time. Keep your eyes peeled. It's very unlikely that the murderer will return to the scene of the crime, but it's not unknown.'

'Yes, sir.' Kevin surreptitiously slid the book he'd been reading down between the two front seats.

But Maguire had already seen the manual. 'I know you're studying for your exams, but if, while reading, someone slips past you and murders me and the local doctor, I doubt that you'd get promoted no matter how good your results!' Maguire called Tess and walked towards the front door. He noted all the lights blazing and guessed the reasoning behind it.

Lizzie pre-empted his knock and opened the door. 'I already know it was murder. He,' she nodded towards the police van, 'told me. But not who it was.'

Tess pushed her way past Maguire and made straight for the kitchen and the rag mat in front of the boiler. 'May I come in?'

'As your dog seems to have decided to visit me it's a little difficult to keep you standing on the doorstep. You'd better come in as well.' Lizzie indicated the route followed by Tess and followed Maguire through the narrow hall into the warmth of the kitchen where Tess was already snoring. Lizzie saw Maguire eyeing the generous tumbler of malt on the kitchen table. 'Laphroaig,' she said. 'Would you like some?'

'Well,' said Maguire slowly, 'I suppose I am off duty.'

'Enough said.' Lizzie poured another whisky and handed it to Maguire.

They both sipped slowly, Maguire savouring the fiery, peaty liquid. It was a long time since he'd had good malt. Mrs Clackett did his shopping, and always bought whatever happened to be on offer. To her whisky was whisky and the cheaper the better. He felt himself relaxing in the warmth. It was a long time since he'd sat in a warm kitchen. There was a lot to be said for having the central heating boiler in the kitchen. It was also pleasant to be sitting in a room that contained another human being instead of being alone with Tess. It seemed to him that the atmosphere was friendly. He looked across at Lizzie. She was watching him seriously over the top of her glass and he remembered why he had come. 'I'm sorry to have to tell you that the body has been identified as that of Tarquin Girling.'

Lizzie's hand trembled slightly, but her voice was steady. 'So he did come here. And the murderer found him. Have you told his mother?'

Maguire sighed at the memory. 'Yes, I have. And I've had her house and garden searched by forensics. She was not co-operative.'

'How could you expect her to be? What woman would be co-operative, as you put it, after just being told that her son had been murdered? She must be terribly upset.'

Maguire thought about Mrs Girling's impassive face. 'No,' he said slowly. 'You're wrong. She wasn't upset. In a strange way I felt she was almost relieved. It was as if a secret guilt had been lifted from her shoulders. She said the strangest thing. She told me that she'd lost Tarquin years ago.'

Lizzie frowned. 'What did she mean?'

Maguire shook his head. Sometimes he wished he lived and worked in a metropolis, where people were anonymous. Where everyone had secrets but where none of them were that important because there were so many. Secrets ceased to matter when nobody knew anybody else. Here, in Stibbington, it was different. Secrets were common knowledge to the privileged few; the local residents whose families had inhabited the place for generations. But that knowledge was closely guarded against newcomers like him. The infuriating part of it was that most of the people in authority in Stibbington – the police, the doctors, even most of the town councillors – had only lived in the area since the late 1980s when the town had started expanding. Life before that was a closed book to most of them, himself included.

'I don't know what she meant. I thought for a moment that she was going to tell me, but then she clammed up.' He shrugged his shoulders and took another swallow of the whisky. 'It's probably not relevant. Some family quarrel, I expect.'

Lizzie remembered she had intended to look up the existence of a Mr Girling but the first murder had driven it out of her head. 'Is there a Mr Girling? And if so, what did he say?'

Maguire shook his head. 'There's no Mr Girling. She's fended for herself for years. Never been married, as far as I know. Both her children have different fathers. A bit of a goer when she was younger, apparently, though you'd never think it now.'

Lizzie was silent for a moment, then leaned across the table towards Maguire. 'The real question is, why Tarquin?' she said. 'And before that, why Darren? What possible connection can these two young men, dropouts both of them, have with each other?'

It was something Maguire had been puzzling over himself and then forensics had found a link. The awkward thing was that it had happened in Lizzie's greenhouse and therefore linked her to the murders as well. He didn't relish having to quiz her, but it had to be done, and although he cursed the job, which made it necessary to interrogate people, it was the name of the game. Maybe, he thought ruefully, that was why Gilbert and Sullivan had written the song *A Policeman's Lot is Not a Happy One*.

'If I knew the answer to that I might be nearer to solving the crimes.' He looked at Lizzie before saying, 'But there is a link of some sort. One that you might be able to help me with.'

'Me?'

'Yes. The link is cannabis. Darren Evans had it in his house, and substantial remains of plants were found in the ashes of your greenhouse.'

'In *my* greenhouse?' Her voice rose, sounding indignant.

Maguire felt the relaxed atmosphere evaporating. 'I'm afraid so. And I have to ask you this. Have you any idea of how the plants came to be there?'

'Of course not. They must have been put there by Tarquin.'

That must indeed be the case. Common sense told Maguire so. The woman before him did not seem the type to smoke illicit substances. But he had to pursue the questioning nonetheless. 'There was nothing in his house. Not a single plant. We searched the whole place. House and garden. And, I'm afraid I'm going to have to ask you to allow the forensics team in here tomorrow morning. We need to search Silver Cottage as well.'

'Search wherever you want. You can search now if you want. You won't find any cannabis here.'

He was relieved. She hadn't flown off the handle, which was what he'd expected. 'Thanks. I'm sorry to have to do it, but we cannot leave any stone unturned. But no need to disturb you now; I'll send Grayson over in the morning.'

Lizzie put her elbows on the table and held the half-empty tumbler between her two hands. 'Tarquin did ask my permission to put some of his own plants in the greenhouse,' she said. 'I, of course, said yes. Why not? I had no plants of my own. I didn't intend to use the space. However, I must admit the thought that they might be cannabis didn't cross my mind.' She frowned. 'Are you absolutely sure?'

'The chaps in the lab are certain and I have to go on their word.' He felt he ought to try to put her mind at rest. Tell her that no one suspected her of anything. But he couldn't. At this stage he had to suspect everything and everyone. But he heard himself saying, 'It's a common enough substance. Although I've never been aware of a big drug problem in Stibbington, and anyway, according to the boys who work on the drug squad, cannabis hardly comes into that category nowadays.'

Lizzie raised her eyebrows. 'Really? I should have thought it would. It is an illegal substance.'

'It is, of course,' Maguire hastened to clarify his words. 'What I meant was that they are so used to dealing with heroin, cocaine, crack – the mix-it, shoot-it brigade – that they are pretty blasé about pot.' He drained the last of the malt and stood up. 'It's not strictly the done thing, but if you could draft out exactly what you saw and did when you arrived here this afternoon up until the time you found the body, I'll get it typed up and you can sign it.' It was a small peace offering and he hoped Lizzie would recognize it as such.

She must have done for she said, 'I can do better than that. I'll type it up on my laptop, sign it and give it to you before you go.' She paused and then scooped the two empty glasses towards her. 'You said you were off-duty.'

'If you're offering another drink I'll have to decline,' Maguire said reluctantly. 'The only solid thing that has passed my lips today has been half a rather dried-up ham sandwich. Another glass of that malt and the constable outside will arrest me for being drunk in charge of a dog.'

'I was thinking of something more substantial,' said Lizzie. 'How do you fancy some tortellini with mascarpone and ricotta cheese, served with a sage and butter sauce over the top?'

'Sounds delicious,' Maguire heard himself saying. He had no idea what it was; the only words he recognized for certain were sage and butter. His repasts were of the easily recognizable, very English variety. Rosemary had been a very good, plain cook, and he still stuck to the same kind of dishes. Shepherd's pie, sausage and mash or casserole of some sort if Mrs Clackett did it. But the thought of someone else preparing food, especially now when he was feeling so weary, was an offer he couldn't turn down. But an awkward thought occurred. 'Of course,' he said, feeling a little ill at ease, 'it would be sure to cause a certain amount of gossip. Kevin Harris is bound to mention it.'

'Gossip?' Lizzie turned back from the fridge where she'd been extracting the ingredients. 'What on earth do you mean?' Then she suddenly laughed. 'Oh, you mean about two middle-aged people of the opposite sex having supper together.'

'Exactly,' said Maguire. 'Although I don't like to think of myself as middle-aged.'

'You may not like to think it, but that is precisely what you are, and so am I,' replied Lizzie briskly. Maguire suddenly had a picture of how she was when dealing with her patients. She would have a brisk, no-nonsense, practical manner. She'd be kind but call a spade a spade. 'Now, if you are going to stay,' she continued, 'you can make yourself useful and get down those two pots from the top shelf behind you. No! Not those two. The other two. The large one and the small one. And here is a bottle of red wine. Open that for me so that it has a chance to breathe.'

Obediently, Maguire began to follow her instructions, and reflected that life was full of ambiguities. Here he was feeling almost happy, just because unexpected domesticity had suddenly been thrust upon him.

Supper finished, the report typed out and put in Maguire's pocket, they sat in silence either side of the table, Lizzie indulging in another glass of wine. She hated admitting it, and certainly would not have divulged it to Adam Maguire, but the truth was she hadn't wanted him to leave. It wasn't an overwhelming desire for his company which made her invite him to supper, but an overwhelming desire not to be on her own. She had never before considered herself to be of a nervous disposition, but since living in Stibbington she'd begun to doubt whether she was as strong and self-sufficient as she liked to think. Two murders in less than a week were proving to be more than a little daunting even though she'd lived with, and amongst, violence in an inner-city district, and it had never bothered her. Somehow the violence there had seemed quite separate from her life. Something that happened to other people because of the company they kept. She only became involved on the periphery, helping to pick up the pieces when necessary. But in Stibbington the murders assumed a menace, which reached out and touched the whole community. The very quietness of the place caused the deaths to appear sinister. Now it was time for Maguire to leave and she was feeling apprehensive again.

It seemed that perhaps he was aware of her fears for as he was shrugging his broad shoulders into his overcoat, he said, 'The policeman outside will remain on guard the rest of the night.'

Lizzie managed what she hoped was a confident smile. 'I'm not nervous,' she lied. 'After all, I remember you telling Mrs Matthews that murderers rarely return to the scene of their crime.'

'True,' agreed Maguire. 'Why should they? Once something is done it's done. They move on, just the same as the rest of us.' He buttoned up the overcoat, adding, rather grimly, thought Lizzie, 'That is what makes them so bloody difficult to catch.' He bent down and roused a very sleepy Tess, who'd thought she was in for a good night's sleep in front of the boiler. 'I'd offer to leave you Tess. But she'd be no use. She's deaf and too arthritic to catch a cold, let alone an intruder.'

'I'm not nervous,' Lizzie repeated, then added, 'anyway, don't forget I've got an enormous brass candlestick by the side of my bed. As I told you, if uninvited guests arrive I shall clout them first and ask questions later.'

'And the intruder will probably prosecute you for grievous bodily harm with intent,' said Maguire.

'Not for defending my own property and person, surely.'

'Huh!' Maguire snorted. 'You can't count on that for defence these days. There are some bloody clever Dick lawyers about. I tell you it's a minefield out there sometimes. People sue at the drop of a hat.'

His melancholy tone of voice made Lizzie smile. 'Sounds a bit like medicine,' she said. 'Nowadays one treats the patient and worries about their litigious intent at the same time.'

Maguire opened the front door and started off down the path. 'I'll check with forensics, but I'm pretty certain that we'll be out of your garden and leave you in peace by tomorrow afternoon. And once Grayson and company have gone over the house, you'll be on your own again.'

Lizzie bit her lip. Damn. She had forgotten. 'How long will they be in the house?'

Maguire paused. 'They should be all finished by lunchtime at the latest. You'll be left in peace after that.'

Lizzie breathed a sigh of relief. 'Good. My daughter's coming down to Stibbington tomorrow for a few days. It will be her first visit and I'd prefer us not to be hedged in by police tape and large policemen.'

She'd been wondering how to explain the police presence to Louise. She now decided that if they'd finished and were gone before Louise arrived, she'd not mention the murder. At least, not at first; no need to worry her unnecessarily.

CHAPTER THIRTEEN

JOAN WALSH SLID the silver drop earrings into place and screwed on the butterfly backs. She looked at her husband's reflection in the mirror. He was in a bad mood. Nothing new there. She needed to go shopping to prepare for Niall and Christina's Christmas visit. He wanted to play golf, but the course was waterlogged so it was closed. Now he had no excuse to refuse to give her a lift to the supermarket.

But Geoffrey Walsh was impatient. 'Hurry up, woman, for God's sake. The shops will be crowded and you know I hate crowds.'

Joan rammed a hat on her head, but said nothing as she followed him out to the car. She took one last fleeting glance at her reflection in the hall mirror as they left their small apartment. A faded woman, with no distinguishing features at all. I'm weak, she thought miserably.

If only they had stayed away from Stibbington. When Geoffrey had decided that they should leave after the accident, it was the one thing with which she was in wholehearted agreement. But then he changed his mind and they came back, and now old ghosts had returned to haunt her. Long suppressed memories were beginning to intrude upon her consciousness ever more frequently, reminding her that she could have broken free when the tragedy happened. But she'd missed that opportunity.

She thought about Niall and Christina. She and Geoffrey should be going to London and staying with Niall and his family for Christmas. But, as usual, Geoffrey's will had prevailed, and they were coming to Stibbington. Sometimes Joan wondered if he took a sadistic pleasure in tormenting his son.

Now she prayed. Let it be a happy Christmas, and don't let Niall be upset by coming back, and don't let him meet any of his old friends again.

'We shall need to get something for today's lunch,' she said once they were outside. 'I spoke to Christina yesterday; they're coming to us for a lunchtime sandwich before checking into The House on the Hard, and then coming back for supper tonight.'

To her surprise Geoffrey's mood changed; he seemed quite jovial. 'Let's cancel the supermarket for today,' he suggested. 'Let's go to the farm shop at the end of Deer Leap Lane. Get some of that nice ham on the bone, some fresh bread, and their home-made pickles. Nothing like a good ploughman's for lunch, I always say.'

Joan would much rather have not gone to Deer Leap Lane, but said nothing as they drove down the High Street, along which the Christmas lights had been switched on. All the shops had Christmas trees outside; the whole scene was festive, and Joan began to relax. Perhaps Christmas wouldn't be so bad after all. Niall would be with them all the time. After all, he had his wife and baby Tom to think about; he wouldn't dwell on the past.

At the bottom of the High Street they turned left onto a small cobbled lane leading to the quayside and harbour, then followed a wide road with ships' chandlers lining each side. Now in winter Stibbington was quiet, but in summer it was thronged with sailors of all nationalities from the marina in the River Stib. Row after row of serried masts stretched out as far as the eye could see, jostling for space in the sheltered waters of the Stib, until the salt marshes stopped their progress, and after that the waters of the Solent swelled across towards the Isle of Wight and the jagged rocks of The Needles.

Deer Leap Lane, small and narrow, led away from Stibbington, upwards towards higher ground, a mixture of farmland and forest. There were few houses, but both knew the road well. Joan glanced sideways at her husband. They were near. She knew she'd hardly be able to bring herself to look at Silver Cottage, where she'd known both happiness and misery. What was he thinking? Did he care? Suddenly she heard a sharp intake of breath.

'Good God,' said Geoffrey.

Silver Cottage was now right in front of them; fenced off with the distinctive blue and white plastic tape of the police. A police car and two policemen were standing at the gate. Geoffrey drew the car drew to a halt opposite the policemen.

Joan wound down her window. 'Has there been an accident?'

One of the policemen bent down and leaned on the car windowsill. 'No, madam.'

'What is it then?' Geoffrey leaned across. 'Something must have happened.'

The policeman looked at his watch. 'Nearly time for the news on Radio Solent,' he said. 'Officially, I can't tell you, but if you listen I think you'll find out.'

Without a word Joan reached forward and turned on the radio. The announcer was still on the local weather forecast; more rain and high winds. Then the news started. 'The body found in the fire at a cottage near Stibbington has now been identified as that of Tarquin Girling, a local man. The police are treating the death as suspicious.'

With a sudden movement Geoffrey switched off the radio, but apart from that abrupt motion, and a twitching muscle in the side of his cheek, Joan noticed that he showed no emotion. For herself, she felt like weeping. Although she hadn't seen Tarquin for years, she'd always felt guilty about leaving him to fend for himself when they'd moved away after the accident. And now in a strange way she felt relieved. At least Niall wouldn't be meeting him.

She glanced sideways. What, if anything, would Geoffrey say? But he remained expressionless as he started the car, put it in gear and drove on towards the farm shop with his usual careful precision. Not a word was said.

Emmy Matthews hurried to the supermarket which was situated halfway down the High Street. She was going to buy extra bacon, eggs, tomatoes, and mushrooms for the Walsh family, who were arriving later on in the day. She might even buy some black pudding to fry up at tomorrow's breakfast, Mrs Smithson had confessed a liking for that, and Emmy wanted to please her.

The Christmas lights were on and she felt cheerful. In fact, she had been feeling surprisingly cheerful ever since her little tête-à-tête with Mrs Smithson. It was amazing how much more secure she felt now, knowing that there was another, sympathetic, woman living in the house. There might be a murderer lurking about in Stibbington, but she and Mrs Smithson were quite safe. No one would dare to attack the two of them.

Pushing her trolley down the aisles, to the accompaniment of *Rudolf the Red-Nosed Reindeer*, she met Amy Cameron and Freda Smee. 'Have you heard the news?' they chorused.

Emmy said she hadn't.

'Tarquin Girling has been murdered now.' Freda imparted the news with relish. 'I always said no good would come to that boy. His mother was no better than she should have been, and besides, it wasn't natural having all that hair hanging down his back. I knew something like this would happen.'

Amy Cameron was more pragmatic. 'Don't talk such rubbish, Freda. The boy was shot by the same gun as the one which killed Darren Evans. I know that because my girl Melanie works in the offices of the *Stibbington Times*, and she told me. Danny Bayley, the editor, is furious that it's happened today, because he won't get a chance to get it in his paper until the paper comes out on Saturday. By then it'll be old news. Unless,' she added, 'the killer strikes again and there's another body. Which, of course, is a possibility,' she said, adding, 'apparently Danny Bayley has a theory. He thinks there's a serial killer loose in Stibbington.'

Emmy shivered, and was even more glad she had company in her lonely house. 'Newspaper talk,' she said briskly, trying to convince herself.

'Probably,' agreed Amy, and changed the subject. 'What are you doing shopping here on a Tuesday morning, Emmy? It's not your usual day.'

'I need more provisions, but not enough to warrant going to the Cash and Carry in Southampton, so I came here. I've got Niall Walsh, his wife, and their baby son coming to stay. They're with me from today until after Christmas. Only bed and breakfast. Geoffrey Walsh and his wife haven't got room for them in their new flat down by the quay, you see.'

'Niall Walsh,' said Freda slowly. 'Wasn't he friendly with Tarquin Girling?'

'And Darren Evans.' Amy screwed her face up trying to remember. 'Yes, and the Brockett-Smythe's daughter, Melinda. Of course, that was before—' She broke of suddenly, and looked guilty. 'Hello Mrs Brockett-Smythe. How are you?'

'I'm fine, thank you, Mrs Cameron.' Mrs Brockett-Smythe hurried past, and disappeared down between the aisles of canned vegetables.

'She looks anything but fine to me. Did you see that bruise over her right eye?' Emmy stared after her. 'The woman was as pale as a ghost.'

'And who wouldn't be,' said Amy. 'Having to look after a stepdaughter like Melinda would be enough to make anyone pale. As for the bruise, she probably had a tussle with the girl. Apparently she can be quite violent. It must be a terrible strain. And they don't have any help except Ivy James who goes in twice a week to keep an eye on the daughter while they go out together.'

'Excuse me, ladies.' A gangly youth, pushing a pallet laden with boxes of long life milk and tins of rice pudding, tried to manoeuvre past.

Emmy had the prime position on the end, and took the opportunity to escape. 'Must go, dears. Otherwise my guests will arrive and I'll still be out. Merry Christmas.'

She left the other two grid-locked with the youth and the pallet. From the way the trolley wheels were jammed it looked as if they might be there for some time.

Stephen Walters finally came back to the practice after his stomach bug had run its course.

'And about time too,' sniffed Tara, passing Lizzie her pile of notes for morning surgery. 'It's been terribly hard work for everyone else.'

Lizzie thought Tara was being rather hard. 'He couldn't help being ill,' she said mildly, flicking through the pile Tara had handed her and noting with a sinking heart that many of her regulars, the incurables, as she privately nicknamed them, were there.

'He was never sick before you arrived.'

Lizzie laughed. 'What's that supposed to mean? Do you think he's allergic to women?'

'Allergic to women doctors more like,' said Maddy picking up her own pile of notes. 'Mrs Shearing, please come through,' she called out to the assembled patients. She turned back to Lizzie. 'I'm not one to gossip, but watch your back where Stephen's concerned. He'll offload as much as he can on to you because you're a woman, and hope that you will break under the strain and throw in the towel.'

Lizzie frowned. 'Why should he do that? He appointed me, for goodness' sake.'

'Wrong. He was outvoted. He wanted a young male colleague.'

'Not a middle-aged has-been,' said Tara.

'Tara!' Maddy went bright red with embarrassment.

'I'm only repeating what Stephen said.' Tara started blushing too.

Maddy began retreating towards her clinic room. 'Sometimes, Tara, it is better to keep your mouth shut.'

'Oh dear. Dr Browne. Lizzie.' Tara's confusion was complete. 'I'm sorry. I didn't mean that I think that you are middle aged . . . or a has-been. I think that you are just—'

'I know. Don't tell me. You think that I am just *old*!' Lizzie swept from the room behind reception into her own private consulting room, and threw the notes down on the table. Bound together as they were with an elastic band they were heavy and landed with a resounding thump.

Dick Jamieson's voice crackled on the intercom. 'What's going on in there? You okay, Lizzie?'

Lizzie flicked the reply switch. 'Are you free for a moment, Dick?'

'I haven't started yet. Come in.' Dick's genial voice boomed through the intercom.

Lizzie burst into the room. 'Why didn't you tell me that Stephen Walters was against my appointment?'

'Because it wasn't important; he was outvoted, and accepted defeat gracefully. He may be young, you know, but over some issues he has the mentality of a man twice my age. Peter and I are counting on him going backwards as he gets older.' Dick looked quizzically at Lizzie. 'Who told you?'

'Tara and Maddy.'

Dick tutted irritably. 'Women! They drive me mad sometimes.'

'Not you as well,' said Lizzie.

'Look,' said Dick firmly. 'Don't start getting upset. Stephen is okay but he has rather a lot of troubles at the moment. A huge house and mortgage to pay off; four children and an irresponsible wife with expensive tastes; he never has enough money to go around.'

'Hardly my problem,' said Lizzie. 'As a recent divorcee I'm hardly flush with loot myself. If his damned house is too large, he should downsize as I've had to do. But anyway, that has nothing to do with the fact that he didn't want me.'

'It wasn't you he didn't want. He didn't want change. It has nothing to do with you personally,' said Dick. 'Believe me. Peter and I wouldn't have insisted on going ahead with your appointment if we'd thought Stephen's hostility would be a permanent feature.'

'How about his long period of sickness?' demanded Lizzie. 'According to Tara and Maddy that's never happened before.'

'A mixture of clinical and psychosomatic,' said Dick firmly. 'I'm certain it won't happen again.'

'You're damned right it won't,' said Lizzie. 'I'll go out and prescribe the treatment myself next time he's sick.'

Dick grinned. 'I tell him you've offered. I think that fact alone will be enough to keep him well for some time!'

Reluctantly, Lizzie grinned back. 'All right. I'll keep quiet. But I'm warning you. I shall be keeping my eye on him.'

'We all will,' said Dick.

CHAPTER FOURTEEN

Melinda Brockett-Smythe slowly unwrapped a cigarette paper from its small red cardboard container. Then she carefully shredded the last of a few brown fibres from the pouch beside it into the paper. It wasn't easy, but with a deliberate relish she rolled the flimsy paper, licked the edge, and regarded what was now a very knobbly-looking cigarette. Nowadays life was mostly dark and rather frightening, and somewhere in the turbulent recesses of her mind Melinda knew what was happening to her, but was unable to control events. Sometimes, on a good day, she could see her father's face quite clearly. It was loving and yet distant, as if he were afraid of her. She wanted to reach out and say, 'Don't be afraid. I'll never hurt you,' but when she tried, he shied away from her. So she was always alone. Alone and frightened in her increasingly indistinct world, with no boundaries, no edges, and no one but herself to fight the murky demons devouring her.

But smoking helped. For a few moments at least it released her from the dark depths into a kinder, softer place where the demons couldn't get her, and her body was still, sometimes even obeying her commands. Melinda needed to smoke. It was her last tenuous hold on some kind of sanity.

'That's all finished.' She indicated the empty pouch. She didn't look at her companion. 'Get me some more, as soon as you can.'

'I'm not sure that we can. There might not be any more.'

'No more?' Something inside of Melinda snapped. 'No more?' It was a scream more than words.

A blackness descended over Melinda obscuring the room and everything in it. She could feel her body spiralling out of control; feel herself sliding down into the dark slime at the bottom of the pit she feared so much. No more! No more! The wordless scream of anguish shattered her head with pain, splitting it into a million tiny pieces. But her eyes could still see her own head on the floor, so many shards of matter, out of reach, out of control. Then, before her horrified gaze each splintered piece assumed a life of its own; tiny black slithering snakes with hissing tongues and pinprick green eyes. They were coming towards her, and she knew what they wanted to do. They would devour her. But she'd always known this was going to happen and she was prepared. She had a knife ready for just such an emergency.

Through the darkening mist she could just see her desk on the other side of the room. That's where the knife was hidden away. That's where she had to get to. Crawling, falling, stumbling, and screaming all the while, she dragged herself towards the desk.

'Melinda. Melinda. What are you doing?'

She could hear the words but couldn't stop to reply. If she did the snakes would get her. With a roar of triumph she got to the desk, wrenched opened the drawer and grasped the knife. Now, she would cut them all into tiny pieces, every single snake, until there was nothing left and she would be safe. Stabbing wildly, she could feel strength, almost a divine power, surge into her arms, and began to laugh. She would win. She knew it. She would win.

'Melinda. Melinda.'

She heard the voice and in a split second saw herself in the mirror opposite. The knife was not in her hand now, it had been taken away, and someone else had got it. She lunged, grabbing the hand that held the knife, desperate to get it. The knife came up and slid in one single slicing movement across her throat. She felt herself falling. Falling down into the darkness she feared. She tried to scream but no sound came. Then pulsating warmth closed around her. It was peaceful. She let go. There was nothing.

Melinda lay on her back. Her eyes wide open staring sightlessly at the ceiling. She looked as if she was laughing. The open slit in her throat looked like an obscene grimace, the edges of the gap coruscating with globules of red blood and white droplets of fat. Blood was spilling out on to the floor, an ever-spreading pool of brilliant crimson.

After a moment or two, the knife was laid down gently beside her. Then the door to the room closed shut.

All was silent. There would be no more cries in the night.

CHAPTER FIFTEEN

RAIN HURLED ITSELF down from clouds so black that it seemed as if it were late evening instead of only midday. And although it was Tuesday the traffic on the motorway was heavy; Niall had hoped it would be lighter if they went down mid-week. But enormous lorries going down to Southampton docks terminal stretched along the motorway as far as the eye could see. The windscreen on the front of Niall's BMW became thick with mud and water, bringing the visibility down to nil every time they passed one. He was tired, concentration was difficult because of the road conditions, and because Tom was howling loudly. The baby, rebellious at being strapped in his buggy in the back seat, was puce in the face and struggling to get out. 'Can't you keep him quiet?'

'He wants a drink,' said Christina. 'We ought to stop.'

'We can't. We're on the M3. There's no stopping, you know that.'

'We could stop on the hard shoulder. You're allowed to do that in an emergency.'

'A thirsty baby is not an emergency.' He heard Christina's sharp intake of breath and knew she was annoyed. He compromised. 'We'll stop at the next service station.'

'Well, all right then,' Christina said grudgingly, adding, 'If we weren't running so late Tom wouldn't be fretful and thirsty. He's been very good up until now.'

'I know. But I'm not in control of the volume of traffic.' Niall was tempted to add that they could have been earlier, and missed some of the traffic, if she hadn't fiddled around so much at the last minute, but decided against mentioning it. Anything for peace and quiet.

'Thank God,' said Christina as the lights of the service station came into view through the gloom. 'I'm going to take Tom to the baby room, change his nappy, and give him a drink.'

'I'll come with you. I'll get an *Echo* and catch up with some local news. Should be out now it's nearly lunch time.'

Niall held the umbrella and sheltered Christina and Tom as they hurried across the car park towards the lights and warmth of the service station. It wouldn't be long before they arrived in Stibbington and Niall's thoughts wandered on to his old friends. Once it was all over his parents had always pretended that nothing had ever happened. Did they really think he had forgotten? Some things you could never forget, which was the reason he had not wanted to visit Stibbington again. But his father had insisted, and Christina thought it was a lovely idea. His mother had said nothing, so Niall remained silent too.

Once inside the service station entrance Christina turned. 'It will take me about fifteen minutes to sort Tom out. What will you do?'

'I'll get a paper, and sit over there.' Niall nodded towards a red metal bench. 'I'll wait for you.'

Christina took Tom, who had now stopped howling and was looking about with interest, and hurried off in the direction of the mother and baby room. Niall went into the shop in search of the local paper. They were located at the far end, past the cold counter laden with sandwiches in plastic containers, Cornish pasties and, as it was nearly Christmas, boxes of mince pies. The sight of all the food made him feel hungry, and he felt mean for not having been more sympathetic towards Tom and his needs. His expression softened as he thought of him. He was his son, his own flesh and blood, and he loved him.

He found the papers, but the local *Echo* was not there. Disappointed, he turned away to be confronted by a large youth, clad in bright yellow oilskins. In his arms was a pile of the newly issued *Echo*.

'Bit late today, mate,' he said to Niall, dumping down his load. 'They held the first page back because of the latest murder.'

Niall took the top copy. The headlines screamed *SECOND MURDER IN STIBBINGTON. Serial Killer at Large.* He paid at the counter and bought himself a small bar of chocolate, then had second thoughts and went back and bought another for Christina, went outside, sat on the red bench, bit off a piece of chocolate, and started to read.

When Christina came out with a clean and happily replete Tom she found Niall sitting staring into space, the half-wrapped chocolate bar still in his hand, his face ashen.

'What is the matter?' She sat beside him.

'There's been a murder. Two murders, in fact.' He pushed the paper towards her.

Christina handed Tom over to Niall. He took him in his arms and held him close. All he could think of was Tarquin. All he could see was the gold of Tarquin's hair. The same colour as Tom's. Darren and Tarquin. Both dead. He hadn't thought about Darren for years. Had difficulty in even visualizing him now after such a long time. But Tarquin was different. He had no difficulty in visualizing him; they'd been so close at school. Was it chance that the two of them had been murdered, or was there a connection? Surely it was too much of a coincidence? But why now after so long? A kaleidoscope of emotions swirled through his head, long suppressed memories and fears. The accident. It was horribly vivid, so real it could have happened only a few moments ago. Time could never erase some memories. He shuddered as the scream of tyres sounded in his head, the revving of an engine, the sickening crash and subsequent silence. He tried to stop it searing into his mind once more, but failed. It was there in all its terrifying reality. Without realizing it he tightened his hold on Tom, who began to cry.

Christina snatched the baby back. 'Don't hold him so tightly, Niall. He doesn't like it.' She dropped the paper on the floor. 'And what are you getting so uptight about? A couple of dropouts in Stibbington have been murdered. So what? It's nothing to do with us. We don't mix with people like that. There's no danger to us from the killer, whoever he might be.'

Niall picked up the paper. 'I suppose you're right.'

'Of course I'm right.' Christina smiled at him. 'What on earth made you so worried?'

'Well,' Niall hesitated. 'I suppose it's because I knew both of the victims. We all went to primary school together, and then Tarquin and I went to the same grammar school.' He left it at that. No need to tell her that his father had paid Tarquin's fees. No one else knew. Even his father thought that he, Niall, was in total ignorance of the fact. So it had never been mentioned, remaining yet another unspoken barrier between them.

Christina laid her hand on his and squeezed it. 'I'm sorry. I understand now. It must be sad to read about one's school friends like that.

But I don't expect you've seen them for years, and what has happened to them has nothing to do with you, has it?'

'No,' Niall agreed. 'It hasn't and it's true I haven't seen them for years. Come on. Let's get going.' He stood up and unfurled the umbrella. It was necessary to keep a tight rein on his imagination. He'd come this far, no point in breaking down now and letting the past catch up with him.

'I'm starving,' said Christina, once they were settled again in the car. 'Let's hurry. I hope your mother has got something nice to eat.'

'She's sure to have,' said Niall. He passed her the chocolate and wondered whether his parents knew of Tarquin's death yet. He wouldn't say anything about it, he decided. He'd wait and see.

'Oh, give me back the good old days.' Dick Jamieson sank down into the lumpy armchair, which was reserved for him in the coffee room at Honeywell Practice.

'What exactly do you mean by that?' Lizzie poured herself some coffee and took a biscuit from the communal tin. 'Were there any good old days?'

'I mean the days when I knew more than the patients about their illnesses. There was no internet to look it up on and then self-diagnose. These days most of them think they suffer from stress. Or else they present with a bewildering set of symptoms that have no physical manifestation, and then proceed to tell me they've got something that sounds as if it's been made up by an advertising agency.' He sniffed and took another biscuit. 'And probably has.'

Lizzie laughed.

Peter Lee came in, overheard Dick moaning, and laughed as well. 'You can blame all these tabloid newspaper and magazine doctors,' he said. 'Only last week my wife read an article in a woman's magazine advising readers to call their GP if they suspected they had poltergeist activity in their house.'

'Well, if they called me for that, I'd refer them on pretty smartly to a psychiatrist,' said Lizzie.

Maddy bustled in and snatched a cup of coffee. 'Can't stop,' she puffed. 'I'm just off to the AHA for a meeting of the PCG for the WH region. The whole thing has been set up by the NHPCC so it's important that I'm there.' She paused by Dick, gulped back her coffee, and said, 'Now, Dick, anything special you want me to bring up?' Dick shook his head, and Maddy dashed off, the door banging behind her.

'Was a time,' he said, still in nostalgic mood, 'when we used carbolic as a disinfectant, and I knew what nurses were talking about, and what's more, they called me Doctor, not Dick.'

Lizzie laughed, and Peter said, 'You've got to move with the times, man.'

The phone rang as Stephen came in for his coffee. He picked it up. 'House call. Now. Urgent.' He scribbled down an address. 'Okay, the duty doctor will get on to it.' He put the phone down, and turned to the room with one of his, Lizzie felt, carefully calculated, enchanting smiles. 'Who is the duty doctor today? I have a feeling it ought to be me.'

'It was you on the original rota,' said Lizzie pointedly, ignoring the smile. He *knew* who it was; she'd seen him looking at the new rota. What was he playing at? 'But Tara has changed everything. So today it's me.'

Stephen gave her the personal benefit of the smile which made him so popular with his patients. 'I don't mind taking an extra turn, Lizzie. After all, I've missed a few. I'll go.'

'No, I'll go. We don't want the rota messed up again,' said Lizzie forcefully. 'I've planned my social engagements around it now.' Not strictly true, but she wasn't going to admit that to anyone. She was being awkward and stubborn, and knew Dick thought so too. She could tell that from his frowning expression. But she wasn't ready to capitulate to Stephen's charm yet and be friendly. He'd have to work for it. Then, and only then, she might think about it.

Stephen shrugged and handed her the piece of paper. 'It's up at Brockett Hall. Ivy James the carer called. An emergency with Melinda Brockett-Smythe, she said. I didn't bother to inquire what kind of emergency. I expect it's the usual burst of anti social behaviour, although they hardly ever call us. If only they did, and allowed us to get her some treatment, these emergencies would never happen. But the Brockett-Smythes prefer to deal with her themselves.'

Dick levered himself from his chair. 'Perhaps I'd better go,' he said. 'Could be a difficult situation. You know what the major is like. '

Already on edge Lizzie exploded. 'For goodness' sake! Do you think I haven't dealt with difficult situations before? I've been working as an inner-city GP, remember. So I've probably had more difficult and hair-raising situations to deal with than you lot have had hot dinners.'

'But you're a woman,' said Peter, 'and the major is a man. A difficult man.'

'And what damned difference does that make? I can deal with difficult men.'

'Of course you can,' said Dick quietly.

Lizzie went, regretting her hasty words and her hot temper. Always a problem, it had got her into trouble on more than one occasion, usually concerning the same thing: men's attitude to women. She didn't think of herself as a rabid feminist, but saw no reason why women should ever be considered less able than men. Count to ten, her mother had always advised, then you will be easier to live with. But she had never counted. Maybe if she had, then she and Mike .... Lizzie shuttered her mind. No use in thinking about the past. All that was behind her. Those doors had closed and now others were opening. But she'd gone and put her big foot right in it. And all because Dick, kind man that he was, had offered to help. She'd have to apologize when she got back. But her first priority now was to find Brockett Hall and sort out Melinda Brockett-Smythe.

A distraught woman met her at the gate, flagging the Alfa down as Lizzie turned into the long gravel drive.

'I didn't know what to do. Perhaps I should have called the police. But I know Major Brockett-Smythe wouldn't like that. So I called a doctor instead. But there's nothing you can do. Nothing at all. Oh dear, and she was left in my care. I should have gone in straight away, instead of making myself a cup of tea and some toast in the kitchen. But with Mrs Brockett-Smythe calling me in today, so unexpected ... it's not my day, you know, I didn't have time to stop and have any breakfast at home, so I was hungry. And as all was quiet, I thought I'd have time for a spot to eat and drink before I went in to see her. But I shouldn't have done. I shouldn't have done. Oh dear. What will the major say?'

She ran out of breath and collapsed against the side of the car. Lizzie opened the door and literally had to haul the overwrought woman in. First things first, she thought, and asked, 'Who are you?'

'Ivy James. I come in and look after Melinda two mornings a week. But Mrs Brockett-Smythe asked me to come in today as she had some shopping to do. Today is not my usual day.'

'What days are your days?' Lizzie didn't think it important, but the woman was on the verge of hysteria. It was important to keep her talking.

'Wednesday and Saturdays. That's when they, Major and Mrs Brockett-Smythe, go out to the Royal Oak for lunch. They have a regular booking for those days.'

While she was talking Lizzie sped up the drive and pulled to a halt beside the Doric pillars flanking the portico behind which was the front door to Brockett Hall. It was a large Georgian mansion with a double row of white painted windows facing on to the drive, most of which had their blinds drawn, giving the house a sleepy look. It was beautiful, and so were the grounds. In fact, thought Lizzie, the whole set-up must be worth a small fortune. But money was no cushion against misfortune, and the Brockett-Smythe's only daughter apparently had a severe mental illness. Damn, in her rush Lizzie realized she hadn't bothered to pick up the notes on the girl. She'd have to ring back in for the medication list.

'You'd better take me to Melinda,' she said.

Without a word Ivy James opened the door, which was unlocked, and led the way upstairs towards a room at the back of the house. Brockett Hall was divided into two by a long corridor, which ran the length of the house. Melinda's room was in the far left hand corner of the house. Outside the door, Ivy James stood back and gestured with her hand. 'I can't go in there again,' she said. 'You'll have to go in alone.'

Lizzie opened the door. The sight that met her eyes was so horrific that for a moment she stood rooted to the spot. Nothing Ivy James had said had prepared her for this. Slowly, she edged her way around the dead girl. No need to search for vital signs; there was no doubt in her mind that Melinda was dead. Almost every drop of her blood had flooded out onto the carpet from the severed jugular. Lizzie bent down. She could even see the end of the artery, a tiny, now empty, little tube that had once contained the life-giving liquid now lying in a puddle beside the body. Already the blood was congealing, the edges a darker, richer colour, almost maroon, the inner pool still a light bright red. The gaping hole in the throat grimaced up at her and Lizzie shuddered. 'Why didn't you tell me she was dead?' she called.

Outside the door Ivy James began to sob. 'I meant to. I thought I did. Oh dear, what will the major say?'

Lizzie stepped out of the room, taking care not to touch anything or get the sticky blood on her shoes. Extracting her mobile phone from her pocket she punched out 999. 'Police,' she said. 'Brockett Hall. There's been another murder.' Then she turned to the sobbing woman and gently led her downstairs. 'I'll make us both a nice strong cup of tea,' she said. As they walked back slowly down the stairs Lizzie felt her own legs trembling. They hardly felt strong enough to support her, and as well as that she felt sick.

Beside her, a sagging Ivy James was only managing the stairs with difficulty. She was getting more and more agitated. 'What will the major say?' she kept moaning. 'What will the major say?'

Whatever the major says it will be pretty irrelevant, thought Lizzie grimly. Nothing is going to alter the fact that his daughter is dead. Murdered, by all appearances, by a person or persons unknown. Stibbington, Lizzie reflected, was becoming a dangerous place to live.

'In a way it's a blessed relief,' said the major.

Maguire and Grayson both looked at him with something akin to disbelief. Relief? thought Maguire. Relief, when his daughter had been slashed to death as she had. But the major hadn't seen her yet. They were downstairs in the kitchen now, while Phineas Merryweather was still up with the body. The photographer had been, and had departed looking greener about the gills than usual.

'That boy's in the wrong business,' Phineas had said with a snort. 'Should be doing society portraiture, not forensic photography.'

'Perhaps he's trying to break into that business by the back door,' said Grayson. 'Build up a reputation.'

Maguire thought the remark in poor taste. Phineas didn't, he laughed. 'One thing is for certain, he's accumulated an interesting port-folio, although not one to tempt your average punter.'

Maguire now concentrated on Major Brockett-Smythe. 'Can you think of anyone who would wish to harm your daughter?'

He shook his head. 'She's not been out of the house these last five years, and lately we've kept her locked in her room. When the symptoms first began she could still mix with people, but five years ago she began to get enormous mood swings, and become aggressive, and as the time has gone by she's become much worse. Uncontrollable, sometimes.'

'I'm sorry to have to ask you questions at a time like this. But it is necessary.'

The major nodded. 'I know. Go on.'

'Well, it doesn't appear that she put up any resistance,' said Maguire. 'Does that surprise you?'

He shook his head. 'Sometimes she was unaware of her surroundings, unaware of people about her. It was impossible to predict when she was going to be like that. We just had to try to cope with each episode as it occurred. It's quite likely that she didn't even realize that anyone was there.'

Maguire watched him carefully; he was always aware that statistics proved that very often a chat with the bereaved was also a chat with the murderer, although Major Brockett-Smythe was a most unlikely looking candidate for murder. 'We'll leave it there for the time being, Major. The room upstairs will have to remain sealed until forensics have finished. I will talk to your wife as soon as she comes in.'

Lizzie had insisted on making her statement as soon as possible, and also sat with Ivy James while she made her initial statement. Both their statements were taken down in laborious longhand by Steve Grayson. When she signed hers Lizzie noticed several glaring spelling errors, but said nothing. What was a spelling mistake when someone had just been murdered? Murder put everything into perspective; spelling was not high on the agenda.

'I intend to take Mrs James home now,' Lizzie told Maguire. 'She needs something to calm her down. She's had the most terrible shock.'

'What about you?' asked Maguire.

Lizzie was calm now, but her calmness was procured at a cost. She couldn't admit to Adam Maguire that she was constantly beating off the image of that grotesque body still lying upstairs. 'I must admit I was pretty nauseated when I first saw her. But I've got over it now. I didn't know her in life, so it's easier for me. But she,' she indicated a mute Ivy, 'knew and cared for her. It must be much worse when one knows the victim.'

'Yes,' said Maguire. 'It must be.' He looked at Lizzie. 'I'm sorry that the beginning of your life in Stibbington has had such a violent introduction.'

'It's not your fault,' said Lizzie. 'Just catch the killer. Catch him as soon as possible.'

'Him, or her,' said Maguire, adding, 'although I doubt that this is connected to the other two. She's not been shot.'

'True,' said Lizzie. She was thinking of the Brockett-Smythes, struggling to manage on their own. They should have had more help. Melinda should have been in a place where she could have had proper psychiatric nursing care. But she knew from conversation at the practice that the Brockett-Smythes were very secretive, and had not wanted people to see Melinda when she was ill. The tragedy was that by keeping her locked up, although they hadn't ill treated her, they had denied her medical treatment. A difficult situation, and one, which as far as she could ascertain, no one had tried to solve. More and more she was beginning to realize that the people of Stibbington, including it seemed some of her colleagues at the surgery, preferred to let sleeping dogs lie. But no one should die in such a ghastly fashion. It was a strange and tragic case. Lizzie helped Ivy James into her coat, then turned back to Adam Maguire. 'Do you ever have gut feelings?' she asked.

'Very rarely, and when I do they are even more rarely correct. They tend to put me off.'

'Maybe,' said Lizzie, and decided to tell him what was on her mind. 'I have a feeling about this murder. Do you realize that she was the same age as the other two? They probably all knew each other when they were younger. Before Melinda became ill. Perhaps these killings are connected in some way.'

'This is different,' said Maguire.

'But serial killers don't always use the same method, do they?'

'Not always. But often they do, because the killer wants you know that it is his work.'

'Or hers,' said Lizzie.

'Or hers,' agreed Maguire. 'And of course, I will look into a possible connection. We'll look at everything. But in the meantime . . . ' he hesitated.

'Yes?'

'Be careful,' said Maguire. 'But don't tell the press I said that. I want to keep all this as low key as possible.'

Lizzie raised her eyebrows. 'Something tells me you're going to find that very difficult. Three murders in one small town in one week! It's going to make the national news. I'm just surprised the TV crews aren't down here already.'

'That's what I'm afraid of,' said Maguire gloomily. 'I'm just praying that the political brouhaha going on up at Westminster continues to occupy them.' He turned and left the kitchen.

As Lizzie drove Ivy James home she thought of old Mrs Mills, Stibbington's retired headmistress. She had known Darren, and must have known Tarquin. So there was a good chance she'd known Melinda in the days when she appeared to be a normal little girl. Perhaps a clue to the connection might be there. But, she decided, it wasn't fair to unleash the police onto an old lady. She'd make a few discreet inquiries herself. She'd pay Mrs Mills another visit as soon as possible.

CHAPTER SIXTEEN

'WHEN ARE YOUR new guests arriving?'
Mrs Smithson came into the kitchen looking, Emmy thought, a little edgy. Anyone else might have thought the woman looked unwell, but Emmy, always obsessed with her own state of health, wasn't much given to noticing other people. To her, Mrs Smithson was merely edgy, and slightly bad tempered.

'I'm expecting them at about three o'clock this afternoon,' she replied warily, wondering where the conversation might lead.

'I see. I thought they were coming earlier.'

Emmy didn't think it was any of Mrs Smithson's business but didn't say so. Although she was all sweetness and light now, the episode in the bedroom had made Emmy very careful not to say anything that might upset her. 'They did intend checking in before lunch,' she said. No harm in telling her that, not that it was of any interest as far as she could see. 'But Niall rang me from his parents' house to say they were having lunch there and then coming on here.'

'Oh.' Mrs Smithson didn't leave the kitchen; instead she sat down rather heavily on one of the green plastic-covered stools. 'I wonder if I could have a spot of lunch.' She must have seen Emmy's surprised stare for she continued, 'I know I don't normally want anything, but I've been busy all this morning.' Emmy knew this because she'd heard her. It had sounded as if she was moving things about and she'd wondered what she was up to. She hoped that Mrs Smithson wasn't altering the arrangement of the furniture. Sometimes the guests did that and it always infuriated Emmy. 'And to tell you the truth,' she finished by saying, 'I'm feeling a bit off colour.'

'How about a cheese omelette, would that be all right?'

'That would be just perfect. Nothing too solid.'

She sounded breathless, causing Emmy to look a little closer. She thought that she did look rather dark around the eyes. Her make-up, which was always too heavy for Emmy's liking anyway, seemed even heavier, making it impossible to see whether or not she was pale, but the foundation couldn't disguise the skin around the eyes. Yes, Emmy concluded, she did look a bit poorly. She got the omelette pan from the cupboard, cracked two eggs in a bowl and began to whisk them. 'You should see a doctor,' she said. 'I'll call one for you if you like.'

'No!' The vehemence of the reply astounded Emmy.

'I only offered,' she said, offended, and a little unnerved by the violent reaction. Really, there was no telling with this woman what she'd do next. Not for the first time Emmy wished that she had a more normal guest. Although, if anyone had asked her what was *abnormal* about Mrs Smithson, apart from her volatile temperament, she'd have been hard pushed to say. 'I wouldn't dream of calling a doctor if you didn't want me to. It was just a suggestion.' Mrs Smithson made no reply, merely sat in rigid silence watching Emmy.

Her presence made Emmy feel uncomfortable, and to fill the awkward silence in the kitchen she switched on the radio. It was tuned into the local radio station, Radio Solent. Emmy always had it on that station. She felt she knew all the announcers personally, so familiar were their voices. It was like having your own family, once removed, actually in the room with you, she was fond of thinking. She put a knob of butter in the pan, watching it dissolve over the heat, swirling it around ready for the beaten egg, idly listening as the radio played the jingle which always announced the news. 'The one o'clock news,' the announcer said.

'The police have just issued a statement that the small town of Stibbington has had its third murder in a week. The victim has been named as Melinda Brockett-Smythe, aged twenty-seven, the only daughter of Major and Mrs Brockett-Smythe. No statement has been issued as to the manner of her death, but it is understood that no fire-arms were involved.'

'Aaah,' Emmy turned around just as Mrs Smithson swayed, and then slid from the stool.

Discarding the omelette pan, she rushed forward and just managed to catch her before she fell. Wedging her back against the wall, Emmy straightened her wig, then said, 'Mrs Smithson, I really do think I should call the doctor.'

But Mrs Smithson, although nearly unconscious, was adamantly opposed to the idea. 'I shall be all right,' she said. 'I'll just lie down for a few moments.' She tried to stand unaided, pushing Emmy away, but in doing so swayed again and came perilously close to falling.

Emmy held on to her, and pushed her back down on to the stool. Their faces were very close together, and Emmy noticed that Mrs Smithson's skin was peculiarly smooth and hairless. She could see now, that beneath the make-up the skin was shiny, that she had hardly any eyelashes, and that the eyebrows were not eyebrows at all, but cleverly pencilled lines. Perhaps that was all due to the alopecia. She'd look it up in her medical encyclopaedia later but for now she had to help the poor woman. 'I'll help you to your room,' she said firmly.

Mrs Smithson didn't object this time, but when they reached the end of the corridor she got out her key and inserted it in the lock herself. 'I shall be all right now,' she said.

The inference was quite clear. She had no intention of letting Emmy into her room. Emmy wondered about the lunch she was supposed to be cooking. 'Shall I bring your omelette along to your room?'

Mrs Smithson thought for a moment, then said, 'Yes, please. Just knock on the door and leave it outside.'

So she definitely wasn't going to let her in. Not even now, when she wasn't well. Oh well, that was her funeral. Emmy retraced her steps back to the kitchen. She'd make the omelette and leave it outside the room as requested, and if it got cold, then that was too bad. She could do no more.

She made the omelette, took it back, knocked the door as instructed and left it outside. 'I'm leaving your lunch.' She called as she knocked the door.

'Thank you.'

As she went back down the corridor she heard the door open, and the rattle of the plate on the tray as it was taken into the bedroom. Emmy breathed a sigh of relief. Mrs Smithson couldn't be too bad, then, not if she was going to eat her lunch. For a moment there, back in the kitchen, she'd thought Stibbington was about to acquire another corpse, this time at the House on the Hard. Another corpse! Her mind went back to the news broadcast just before Mrs Smithson's queer turn. So

Melinda Brockett-Smythe had been murdered. Emmy thought that very strange. Everyone knew that Melinda was a virtual prisoner at Brockett Hall these days. Mad as a hatter, so the gossip went. Apparently the major had given strict orders that she was not to be let out. Then Emmy remembered Mrs Brockett-Smythe; she'd seen her only that morning, poor thing. That must have been before the murder. She wouldn't have gone shopping afterwards. It stood to reason.

Emmy felt restless. Mrs Smithson's odd behaviour was beginning to get her down. The radio was playing Christmassy tunes and on impulse she went through into the lounge where she kept the drinks cabinet. Locked, of course, in case guests should think the drinks were meant for them. After pouring a generous measure of cream sherry, telling herself that she deserved it because she was feeling a bit shaky, and after all it was nearly Christmas, she took her drink back into the kitchen, intending to relax. It was then that she saw something lying beneath the stool Mrs Smithson had been sitting on. It was very small and thin, of a size that would slip easily into a pocket. On closer inspection it proved to be a booklet – thin paper sheets between a shiny, dark red cover. Strange thing was it was all stuck together. Emmy picked it up, turning it over and over in her hands. Peeling back the edge she thought she could see that it was headed SHAF something. But that was as far as she could read. With a huff of frustration Emmy regarded the cover. She was dying to read it, but daren't. If she did Mrs Smithson would probably fly at her again, and she couldn't risk that. Already she was feeling shaky herself, and her heart was hammering. Besides, she had obviously stuck it together for a reason, and she was so unpredictable. But the more Emmy thought about it the stranger it seemed. What was Mrs Smithson doing walking around with a sealed-up booklet? With a sigh she put it down; she'd give it back later. It was probably something to do with the woman's writing.

That Tuesday afternoon Peg Hargreaves rang the surgery and said she thought her father had suffered another stroke, and Lizzie, as duty doctor answered the call and went to the Hargreaves' forest cottage on the edge of Stibbington. Her conscience was troubling her. She'd managed to make arrangements for Mrs Mills' leg to be dressed the moment she'd returned to the practice, but no help had yet been forthcoming from social services to help Peg Hargreaves, and Lizzie regretted not pushing them a little harder. The social worker had been hostile and offhand, resenting being hassled. Lizzie, knowing how stretched the budget was, and how many cases of a similar nature the social worker was probably trying to cope with, had spent time sympathizing with her to the point of being quite friendly, but had still not achieved a visit for Peg. Now, she reflected, it was probably too late. Almost certainly Len Hargreaves would need to be hospitalized, at least for the time being, and then put into a nursing home. So Peg would be free, but it was no thanks to her.

Peg let her in silently. She led the way through to the dismal kitchen. The single light bulb was on; the fly-encrusted paper was still dangling from the ceiling, eddying round in slow circles in the warmth from the gas fire.

'I think he's gone,' she said.

'Gone? Do you mean dead?'

'I think so,' said Peg. 'He looks very dead to me.'

'Why on earth didn't you say so when you phoned? Or call an ambulance instead of a doctor?'

'Because I didn't want a circus coming out here. I know what happens when you call an ambulance. You get one with its sirens blaring and then a police car comes as well. We like our privacy, Dad and me. You can just pronounce him dead and then the undertakers can take him away. It will be nice and quiet. Nothing for anyone to gossip about. I don't want people talking about him now he's gone.'

She sounded defensive and forlorn. Strange, Lizzie reflected, but then perhaps not. Human nature never failed to surprise. Only last week Peg had been telling her that she hated her father, and couldn't wait to get away. Now she seemed to want to protect him.

Without another word she heaved the bag and laptop from the table where she'd deposited them only a second ago, and climbed the steep narrow stairs to Len Hargreaves' bedroom at the front of the house. Peg was right. He was dead.

'Dead as a dodo,' muttered Lizzie to herself and felt surprisingly cheerful. It was almost a pleasure to find someone who had died of natural causes. A nice change to find a cadaver lying tidily in bed, eyes closed, hands clasped, and blankets pulled up. She pulled the blankets back, and gave a wry smile. He was still hanging on to that blasted old tin box. Gently, she took it from his hands and heard Peg come into the room. 'When did this happen?'

'I don't know for sure. I put him to bed for his rest at about one o'clock this afternoon. After he'd had something to eat. And then I looked in on him at about three o'clock and he was like this.'

Lizzie felt him again. He was quite cold but rigor mortis had not yet begun. Death probably occurred soon after Peg had originally left him. 'A merciful release, Peg.' She heard herself using the old adage.

'Yes.' Peg sighed. 'For both of us.'

The sigh said so much, and yet nothing at all. What had this young woman suffered? Her youthful innocence despoiled, and then her chance of freedom and a normal life snatched away from her by events beyond her control. No one to help her. No friends or relatives, and the state, which had once boasted to care for its citizens from cradle to grave, had not been interested. Of course, it was unrealistic to expect that it should. The state had neither the time nor the resources to deal with every family crisis in the land. Only people like herself could help, and she and her colleagues had done nothing.

But now, belated though it was, Lizzie felt bound to try to reach out to her. 'Peg, if there's anything you want to talk about, now, or at any other time, don't be afraid to come to me.'

There was silence for a moment, then Peg said, 'No, there's nothing. It's finished now. Except. . . .'

'Yes?' said Lizzie.

'Except that I think I should tell you that I've been smoking cannabis. I know that's a crime and I shouldn't have done. But I did.'

Of all the things she could have told her, she chose this small misdemeanour, thought Lizzie. 'Yes,' she said gently, 'I know. I knew the first time I came to your house. I could smell it.'

Peg looked surprised. 'Why didn't you say something?'

'It was not my business. I came to see your father.'

Peg seemed to relax and little. A slow smiled crossed her face. 'I shan't need it now, which is just as well as I can't get any more.'

'You got it from Darren Evans?'

'Yes. He needed the money and I needed the smoke.' She walked over and looked down at her father. 'Now neither of us has needs any more. I shall be able to manage without my smoke, and Darren doesn't need money.' She picked up the tin box from the bed and put it on the chest of drawers.

Lizzie looked at the box. 'What was in there that was so important to him?'

Peg sniffed. 'Dirty pictures, that's what,' she said. 'Pathetic, really. Take a look if you don't believe me.' She opened the lid and passed the box across to Lizzie.

They were indeed dirty pictures, but of a very inoffensive kind. Not the kind that would get a policeman excited. No pornography or pae-dophilia. Merely tattered pieces of old newspapers, mostly page three type girls; big, buxom blondes with surgically enhanced breasts leapt out from the pages. Most of the papers were ten years old or more and were from the more lurid national tabloids. Some were local papers, the *Echo* and the *Stibbington Times*. Pictures of local beauty queens of years gone by parading in their swimsuits; it all looked so old-fashioned now. A pathetic little collection. The subject of an old man's fantasies. She folded the papers up and replaced them.

'Yes, I see what you mean.' On the point of closing the lid a name leapt up at her from the back of one of the faded pages from a copy of the *Stibbington Times*: Melinda Brockett-Smythe. She saw from the top of the page that the paper was ten years old. Slowly, she took it out, unfolded it, and scanned the text. Finally, she folded it again, and said to Peg, 'Would you mind if I kept this paper? There's an article in it that interests me.' She hoped Peg wouldn't ask what it was because it would be difficult to explain a hunch. Her hopes were realized. Peg Hargreaves was not interested.

'Keep it,' she said. 'Just give me a death certificate so that I can get on to the undertakers and get Dad moved out of here.'

Lizzie pocketed the newspaper cutting and duly obliged with the death certificate. No problem there; she'd seen the patient earlier in the week and had known his medical condition. She handed the certificate to Peg. 'There you are.'

Peg read it. 'What does myocardial infarction mean?'

'In other words his heart stopped,' said Lizzie.

'I thought everyone's heart stopped when they were dead.' Peg looked slightly puzzled.

'True. Everyone's heart does stop. But the law requires me to put it in more formal language.' Lizzie snapped the black bag shut. No need to finalize Len Hargreaves' notes on the laptop now. That could be done later at her leisure. Right now she wanted to get out and phone Adam

Maguire. She felt a mixture of triumph and fear. If her theory was right, there was one more murder to go.

Adam Maguire was surprised to receive Lizzie's phone call. She sounded excited and very mysterious. 'Can you come round this evening?' she asked, adding, 'I've got something to show you which I think links up your three murder victims.'

'Is that an invitation to supper as well?' Against his better judgement Maguire heard himself angling for the invitation. It was not that he saw Lizzie in any romantic light. Far from it. She was much too brisk and efficient for that. Frightened him a little, if truth be told. But she was an extremely good cook, and the meal he'd shared with her the previous evening had made him reluctant to munch his way through another microwaved dinner for one this evening. Although common sense told him that microwaved dinners were his lot in life for the foreseeable future, unless he galvanized himself into learning how to cook, and that possibility was about as remote as the proverbial pig flying.

'Oh!' She was surprised, he could tell that. 'I hadn't even thought about supper.' He cursed himself for being stupid. What was wrong with him? It was pathetic of him to be angling for an invitation. 'To tell you the truth,' Lizzie continued, 'I haven't had time to think about anything, I'm just about to start seeing patients. But now that I do think for a moment, I realize that as soon as I've finished here I shall have to scoot down the High Street to the supermarket and pray that it's still open. My daughter is arriving tonight, and apart from some breakfast cereal and a carton of milk I've absolutely nothing worth mentioning in the food cupboard.'

Maguire attempted to mitigate his previous faux pas with a joke. 'If you're really desperate I have some tins of dog food I can let you have.'

To his relief Lizzie seemed to see the joke. She laughed. 'If it comes to that,' she said. 'You are invited round to Chummy risotto, or whatever dog food is called these days.'

'Being quite serious for a moment,' said Maguire, 'I will come. But I have a hell of a lot to clear up here before I'll be free. So if it's all right with you, I'll come over at about 9.30 this evening. That should give you time to see your daughter, and for you to eat together, then you can settle down and tell me about this clue you've found.' He breathed a silent sigh of relief at having, skilfully, he thought, extricated himself from a potentially embarrassing situation.

'You don't sound very anxious to know.' To his ears he thought she sounded disappointed. 'I've always been under the impression that the police leapt on every clue, panting with anticipation. I can tell you some of it over the phone if you want.'

'No,' said Maguire, 'don't bother. Police procedure is to go through everything slowly and methodically, which, by the way, is how we came to be known as Mr Plods, I suppose. And the reason we do that is because, from bitter experience, we often find that clues have a nasty habit of leading us in the wrong direction. I can wait until this evening.'

'Ah well, have it your own way,' said Lizzie briskly. He heard the buzzer go and guessed she was signalling that she was ready for her first patient of the evening surgery. 'I'll expect you later this evening, then.'

Maguire put the phone down with a sigh. He'd miss out on supper, that was a pity, but probably sensible. Besides, he had more work to do on Melinda Brockett-Smythe's murder, which was different. He'd told Lizzie that gut feelings were rarely correct, but sometimes, not often, they did lead one in the right direction. And as far as this particular murder was concerned, he had a very strong gut feeling that it was contained within the family circle and had nothing to do with either of the other two murders. So far no one had been ruled out, or in. He suspected them all, and had told Grayson to do the same.

'Don't be afraid of noting any behaviour you think might be relevant, or pursuing any conversation no matter how informal, or even embarrassing, it might seem. Our task is to obtain and then evaluate. Sometimes it means asking questions we might prefer not to out of deference to the bereaved. But believe me; I think the answer lies at Brockett Hall.'

Grayson, however, had other ideas. He linked the murder to the other two. 'It's difficult to believe it could be anyone at the Hall, and surely it can't just be coincidence that three young people have been killed so soon after one another. They must be connected in some way.'

'Maybe that's what we're supposed to think,' said Maguire. Then he repeated what he'd told Lizzie earlier on. 'We'll look into any connection, of course. But I don't expect to find one.'

But suspecting the major, his wife, or even Ivy James was one thing; proving it would be the problem. With his lack of success in unearthing any leads in regard to the deaths of both Darren and Tarquin, Maguire found himself wondering whether people who committed crimes were getting more devious and clever, or whether maybe he was getting more thick-headed as the years went by. There'd already been ominous rumblings from County Headquarters, and there were a couple of officers from the Regional Crime Squad being drafted down to help. He knew that if they'd had the manpower they'd have sent someone more senior down to 'assist' him, which was polite speak for taking over the case because he was incompetent.

Then there was the press to worry about. So far so good. All the murders had been reported, of course, but there'd been no great hue and cry in the media. However, that couldn't go on for long. Sooner or later some newshound would get the bit between his teeth and then all hell would be let loose.

Maguire took a deep breath and mentally girded his loins. He'd talk to the major's wife again. He'd keep it very informal for the time being. She seemed the most nervous of all of them and was the most likely person to let something slip out. Something that might give some insight into why this particular murder had been committed and by whom.

Niall sat in silence watching his mother and father play happy families with Christina and Tom. He couldn't join in, although he sensed that Christina was trying to shame him into displaying some sort of filial and paternal devotion. But for Niall that was out of the question; two of his old school friends had been murdered. Why? Was it anything to do with him?

So he sat there in the flat, which reminded him of the living room of Silver Cottage. Everything was the same. The same pictures, hung in much the same places and at the same angles. The same sideboard, polished to an unnatural shine, with potted plants on lace doilies, all exactly in the middle as if they'd been placed there with the precision of a slide rule. He hated it. Hated all of it. The room was a symbol of his life. Everything in it, including himself, controlled to claustrophobic proportions. The only time it had been different was one summer when he was in his early teens. That summer he remembered seemingly endless days of playing tennis with Tarquin, Darren, and Melinda. The sun had always been shining, or so it seemed looking back on it; they had lived in the garden, lying chattering in the long grass scattered with buttercups beside the tennis court. It had been a golden summer with his friends, carefree, and full of laughter. Then, in a few split seconds it had all been ruined.

Watching his father, he wondered if he knew of the deaths. If he did, how could he act as if nothing had happened? No mention had been made of them. Geoffrey Walsh gave nothing away as he bounced Tom on his knee pretending that he was giving him a ride on a rocking horse. Tom squealed in delight; tiredness and tears forgotten now that he was safely on terra firma.

'I thought I'd do tonight's dinner at about 6.30,' said his mother. 'I know that's a little early, but I thought you'd want to settle Tom down fairly early after your long journey.'

'It's not that long a journey,' said Niall. He didn't relish spending time with his parents, but a long evening spent at the House on the Hard with nothing to do but watch television and listen to Christina's chatter was even worse. 'He can stay up later while we're down here.'

'No.' Christina was very firm. 'We won't disrupt Tom's bedtime tonight. Besides, I've made arrangements to meet an old school friend this evening. She's coming down to the House on the Hard after dinner.'

'I didn't know that you knew anyone here, dear,' said Joan. She liked Christina. Such a sensible girl. So neat and tidy with a good methodical approach to life. Joan liked that. A good regime meant stability to her, and stability was a measure of sanity. Without her strict routines Joan knew she would have gone under years ago. Stability was so essential for Niall as well. He needed that. He'd been lucky to find a girl like Christina.

Christina smiled at her mother-in-law. 'Louise is not from Stibbington. Her mother has recently come to work down here, and Louise is combining a visit to her with a visit to me. It will be fun to catch up with old gossip. I haven't seen her since Niall and I were married, so we've a lot of ground to cover.'

'What will you do, Niall? Watch television?' asked Joan. She didn't want him to go out in Stibbington. Not alone. He might meet someone he knew from the old days. He might find out about Darren and Tarquin. She was certain he didn't know anything because she'd watched him carefully. If he had, surely he'd have given some sign, or said something.

'Probably.'

Niall looked across at Tom. His hair, glinting gold in the light from the table lamp, reminded him of Tarquin again. But he'd already made up his mind. He wouldn't stay in; he'd ask Mrs Matthews to baby sit, and if she said yes, he'd go down to the Ship Inn on the quay. Someone there would know what had happened to Darren and Tarquin, and why. That was important. He needed to know why. The article in the paper had been sketchy on actual details other than the fact that they'd both been shot. Fear shuddered through him, gripping him in a strangle-hold. Perhaps it wasn't wise to ask questions, but he had to know. If he'd been able to talk to either one of his parents it would have helped, but that was impossible.

CHAPTER SEVENTEEN

WPC JONES CAME in from Stibbington Police Headquarters' general office and plonked a piece of paper on Steve Grayson's desk. 'Looks like you might be getting somewhere,' she said.

It was a report from the lab. The result of the forensic search of Melinda Brockett-Smythe's room. There were a lot of things of no particular note, but cannabis had also been found. From the evidence it appeared that she had been a regular smoker. Grayson raised his eyebrows. It was a link of sorts, but not something to get too excited about. He agreed with Maguire. Smoking pot was no big deal. And, in his opinion, the evidence in Melinda's room merely showed that the habit was more widespread in Stibbington than they'd realized. Maybe the major and his wife smoked as well, and perhaps Darren had been the supplier, or Tarquin Girling. Or perhaps they were both involved in it together. But none of that could really explain why the two of them had got themselves shot and Melinda's throat had been slit. Grayson shuddered at the thought of Melinda. What a sight. He hoped he wouldn't come across anything like that too often.

The phone rang. It was the girl manning the switchboard. 'It's your wife for you, Steve. Seems in a bit of a state.'

Grayson frowned; it was unlike Ann to phone him at work. She was not that kind of wife. She never usually bothered him. He heard her anxious voice. 'It's started, Steve. The baby, it's coming.'

'It can't be, Ann. He's not due for five months. You must have stomach cramp or something.'

At the other end of the phone he could tell Ann was near to tears. 'I'm telling you something is happening to the baby. I know it, Steve. You must come.'

He looked at the report he'd just received back from the forensic lab, and then stuffed it in his pocket. It could wait. It wasn't that important. 'All right, I'm on my way. But you'd better ring the doctor as well. If there is anything wrong I'm not likely to be of much help.'

Kevin Harrison came into Grayson and Maguire's cramped office. 'Anything new on the latest murder?' he asked cheerfully. For a moment Grayson envied him. A bachelor with no worries except whether or not he'd be selected to play football on Saturdays for Stibbington Wanderers. He didn't have a pregnant wife in premature labour.

'No,' he lied, the lab report burning a hole in his pocket. There *was* something new and he ought to pass it on even if he thought it wasn't that vital. And he would. But he'd do that later. Not now. 'Can you tell Maguire, if you see him, that I've had to go out. I'll be back as soon as I can.'

'Where is he? And where are you going?'

'If Maguire's left Brockett Hall then he's gone back to the Evans bungalow, or on to Silver Cottage. He said he was going back to look at both sites. Although God knows what he expects to find.'

'Inspiration,' said Kevin cheekily before withering beneath Grayson's angry stare. 'Sorry,' he muttered. 'But you don't seem to be getting very far and I heard the super on the phone saying that a load of traffic cops could do better than Stibbington CID.'

'Bloody cheek,' said Grayson, shrugging himself into his raincoat. 'I'd like to see them try.' He felt very guilty about the paper in his pocket. Bloody hell! What a dilemma. But he had to go. Ann needed him. Maguire would have gone if it had been his wife. He was certain of that.

'Anyway, you haven't told me where you're going in such a hurry,' Kevin persisted.

'None of your bloody business,' said Grayson, guilt making him angry with Kevin and himself. 'On second thoughts, don't say anything to Maguire. I won't be long.'

'Least said soonest mended,' said Kevin with a knowing smirk. 'A case of when the cat's away, eh?'

'You're asking for a punch on the nose.' Grayson pushed past violently, elbowing a grinning Kevin out of the way. 'Haven't you got anything useful to do?'

'Now, now.' WPC Jones hurried past. 'Don't fight, you two, or I shall arrest one of you for assaulting a police officer. I'm very surprised at you, Steve.'

'Shut up,' said Grayson bad-temperedly, and then to Kevin, 'go on, push off. What have you got to do next?'

'Night duty again.' Kevin was less cheerful as he said it. 'I never get any of the action. I seem to spend all my time lately standing around at the scene of the crime when everything interesting has been taken away.'

'Best place for you,' said Grayson. 'Action is for grown up cops, not those still wet behind the ears.' He left the building and a glowering Kevin. He'd sort Ann out. Well, to be more precise he'd get the doctor to sort her out. If necessary he'd take her to the infirmary himself; the doctors there would know what to do. Then after that he'd get straight back on the case. He would have to. Ann would understand.

At the House by the Hard Emmy Matthews was welcoming Niall, Christina, and baby Tom. She showed them up to their room. One of her best. One that fronted on to the river. In summer it had a beautiful view of the River Stib, the serene blue of the water stretching away to the distant saltings. But today, the view was threatening: grey sky, grey water, even the moored boats were all grey reflecting the water slapping beneath their hulls. The only colour to be seen was the occasional splash of dark green from the holly and yew trees dotted about on the opposite shore. Emmy drew the curtains against the scene, and switched on the wall lights, which illuminated the dark red curtains giving the room a cosy feel.

'I think you'll find this warm enough. I've put a cot over there near the bathroom door – the room is ensuite, of course – and the television is over there in the opposite corner so if you want to watch it, it shouldn't disturb the babe too much.'

'Thank you,' said Niall.

Emmy looked at him. So this was Niall now. He didn't remember her. Why should he? She was just an ordinary woman of Stibbington, one of the many people he'd left behind when the family had moved away. But he seemed to have grown up well enough, considering. A bit different from Darren and Tarquin, who'd never pulled themselves together afterwards. But then of course, he'd had a respectable family to help him on his way. The other two had not been so lucky, and there'd always been gossip about Tarquin. Of course Melinda would probably have been all right, too, if she hadn't become ill. She wondered if Niall knew about the murders. 'Have you been keeping up with news of Stibbington?' she asked tactfully.

'No,' said Niall. 'I haven't thought of Stibbington since I moved away.'

'That's true,' Christina piped up. She seemed very pleased, and had just finished inspecting the bathroom and Tom's cot. 'Do you know, Mrs Matthews, he didn't even want to come here for Christmas. But I insisted. The change will do us good, I said, and the fresh country air will certainly do Tom good.'

'If it doesn't give him pneumonia,' said Niall gloomily. He'd gone to the window and drawn the curtains back. 'Look at that. Pitch dark out there already, and it's still afternoon. Not a sign of life. Not a light to be seen and the only sound is that of the wind howling.'

'And a motorbike,' said Emmy defensively. She'd just heard one in the distance. 'That's a sign of life.'

Niall didn't answer, merely twitched the curtains back across the windows again.

'Thank you, Mrs Matthews. I'll give Tom a bath now, and half an hour's rest. After that we're off for supper with Niall's parents. But we'll be back quite early. I've got a girlfriend visiting me this evening. She's coming at about nine o'clock.'

'Not walking here on her own, I hope,' said Emmy thinking about the murders. Should she mention something or keep quiet? She kept quiet. No point in frightening her guests off. 'The reason I mention it,' she said hastily, 'is because there are only two lights at this end of the hard, and one of those isn't working. I have reported it to the council, twice, but they've done nothing about it.'

Christina started undressing a wriggling Tom. 'She won't be walking. She's borrowing her mother's car. Louise is a city girl. She'd be terrified of walking along a lonely lane in the middle of the country at night.'

'Very sensible,' said Emmy feeling relieved. She left them to unpack and retreated back down to the kitchen where she started to prepare supper. Mrs Smithson had gone out for a walk of all things and said she'd be back at about seven for an evening meal.

'Nothing too heavy. Something light,' she'd said. Emmy had asked if she was feeling better, and she'd said, 'Yes, perfectly well now, thank you,' in a tone of voice which did not invite further comment. She made Emmy nervous so she kept silent, and forgot to give her back the red booklet. I'll do it later, she thought, it can't be that important.

Every time she thought about the newspaper cutting in her handbag Lizzie felt a surge of excitement. She was certain that it held the answer. This was how the police must feel when they were near to solving a case. Detective work seemed much more exciting than the medical profession, and to make matters worse, evening surgery that night was very tedious. There was nothing medically wrong with any of the patients, or at least nothing wrong that she could find.

The last patient left and she looked at her watch. There was just about enough time to do some shopping and get home before Louise arrived by taxi from Picklehurst Station.

The phone rang just as she was passing the pile of patients' notes back to Sharon their new clerk. Tara answered it. 'Yes, yes, don't worry. The duty doctor will be on her way right away.'

'No she won't,' said Lizzie. 'I've done my stint for today. Stephen picks up the bleep in ten minutes. He can take it now.'

'But he's got one more patient to see,' said Tara.

'Then he'll have to be quick about it, won't he,' said Lizzie briskly and departed.

'But it's a real emergency,' shouted Tara after her. 'A woman in labour.'

Lizzie grinned over her shoulder. 'Lucky Stephen. Last time I had an emergency it was murder!'

'Oh!' Snorting with annoyance at Lizzie's lack of co-operation Tara went off to knock on the door of Stephen's consulting room. *

Problem patients forgotten, Lizzie charged around the local Waitrose with her trolley, almost coming to grief on the newly washed floors despite the sign saying WET FLOOR. She bought wine and cheese, and grabbed the last baguette from the bread basket, much to the annoyance of another woman who'd had her eye on it. 'First come first served,' said Lizzie cheerfully, before moving on to the fresh fruit and salad section where she bought some South American strawberries, a pot of clotted cream, and a bag of freshly prepared salad, then deliberated between trout or steak. Finally, settling on the trout for both of them, she felt guilty because she couldn't remember whether Louise was a vegetarian or not.

It comes to something when I don't know what my own daughter eats, she thought. How long was it since she and Louise had sat down quietly to eat together? Years. Not properly since Louise was eighteen, and had left home to go to university.

Absent-mindedly she picked up a pack of potatoes. Then realizing what she was doing put them back. There was no time to peel potatoes; she'd get some tinned ones. Making her way towards the tinned food she had second thoughts. Damn! She would do things properly for a change; she'd peel the damned things and mash them. Grim-faced with determination she put them in her trolley and marched off to the check-out, where the girl whizzed her purchases hurriedly past the electronic eye. Lizzie's fierce expression was daunting, especially to a check-out girl in her first week.

'Why, Mum, the cottage is lovely.' Louise sailed past Lizzie at the door, discarding her bag in the hall while she rushed from room to room eventually ending up in the kitchen. 'It's much bigger than I expected. I thought you said it was tiny. Compared to my flat in London it is enormous.'

It was a sharp reminder of their separate lives. 'I've never seen your flat in London.'

'I know. Not for lack of invitations on my part.'

'I know,' said Lizzie unhappily. 'I'm always so busy. I'm a rotten mother.'

Louise turned and smiled at her. 'Why the sackcloth and ashes? You've always done the best you could. It must be hell being a clever woman, having a career and a family, and always being torn between the two. And don't think that I didn't realize that you funded practically everything when I was growing up. Even now you've come out worst on the financial side of the break-up. Dad has had an easy ride. Although I think that in future he might find he's got to work a little harder now he's the only breadwinner and will soon be a father again. Amanda has given up work.'

'Do you mind?' asked Lizzie. 'The fact that you'll soon be having a stepbrother or sister?'

Louise shrugged. 'Why should I mind? I doubt that I'll see much of him or her. Anyway, there's no point in worrying about things you can't change. Worry about important things. Oh, talking about important things, my friend Alice rang me yesterday and told me not to come down here because of some murder.'

'What did she say?' Lizzie asked carefully. She took a bottle of chilled Sancerre from the fridge and poured out two glasses. 'Just one for you,' she said. 'You'll be driving later.'

'Oh, not much,' said Louise taking the wine. 'Cheers.' She raised the glass. 'We got to talking about other things. Anyway I already knew. I'd read in the weekend papers about a drug addict, Darren something, being murdered at Stibbington. It was only a small piece, but I noticed it. To listen to Alice anyone would think that there was a serial killer on the loose. I pointed out to her that in London someone is murdered every day, it's no big deal, unless one happens to be involved. And then, I imagine, it's a very big deal indeed!'

'Yes,' said Lizzie. Was finding a murder victim in your back garden being involved? She sipped her wine and smiled at Louise while her mind raced over the pros and cons. Why tell her now and spoil her first evening? She'd be safe enough in the car and she had her own mobile phone. And if her theory was right the murders had nothing to do with anyone else in Stibbington. The one person left in the equation had moved away. She knew that because Tarquin had told her. *We were inseparable until he moved away*, he'd said, and he'd been talking about Niall Walsh.

'Mother, you're not with me. What are you thinking about?' Lizzie was suddenly jolted out of her reverie. Louise was regarding her intently. 'You look as if you got the troubles of the world on your shoulders,' she said.

'My only worry is starting the supper,' said Lizzie, firmly putting Stibbington and its problems out of her mind. There was only one satisfactory way to live life and that was to concentrate on the moment. And at this particular moment supper took the priority. 'I've been rash enough to buy potatoes,' she said. 'Someone's got to peel them.'

'Me,' said Louise, with a giggle. 'I'm feeling domesticated.'

'I'm glad that someone is you, because I hate the job.' She smiled back at Louise. It was good to have her daughter in her new home, even it if was only for a few days. They must both make the most of the time. She passed the potatoes across to Louise, and started unwrapping and preparing the trout herself. 'Now, tell me,' she said. 'Who is it you're going to see this evening?'

'Christina Mallory. She's married now but I can never remember her married name. Anyway it doesn't matter; she's the one I'm going to see. She said she'd get rid of her husband. To tell you the truth I think she's got problems with him and wants to talk about it. We've been trying to fix up a meeting in London, but neither of us is ever free at the same time. Anyway, when she told me she was coming down here for Christmas, and coming early, it seemed a good idea to take time off and kill two birds with one stone.'

'I take it I'm the other bird,' said Lizzie wryly.

'Exactly,' said Louise with a grin. 'And not a bad old bird at that, for your age.' She ducked as Lizzie threw a dishcloth at her. 'Shall I put the potatoes on to boil?'

'We should do this more often,' said Lizzie. They'd finished their meal. Mozzarella, tomato, and basil salad to start with, followed by pan-fried trout in butter and almonds, mashed potatoes and mixed green salad, and for dessert the South American strawberries and clotted cream. All washed down with the rest of the Sancerre, although Lizzie was strict with Louise's ration.

'I'm glad I came,' said Louise. She reached over and took her mother's hand. 'I've been worried about you down here, all on your own.'

'I'm not on my own any more than I was in London,' Lizzie replied. It was the truth. There was nothing as lonely as an unhappy marriage, and no one knew that better than she did. 'True I've got to make new friends, but my friends in London were few and far between, and in medicine one's friends always tend to be other doctors and then they all go off and work in other places.'

'I know,' said Louise. 'Your friends used to frighten me to death. All so clever. I always felt a failure because I couldn't understand chemistry and physics.'

Lizzie felt guilty. She had, when Louise was younger, tried to steer her towards the sciences, but had eventually given up. 'You're clever too but in a different way. You're artistic. Like your father,' she added. It was only fair to give Mike some credit.

'Anyway, I'm pleased that you've settled down well here,' said Louise. 'I was a bit worried about that.'

'Whatever for?'

'Afraid of having to assume a degree of responsibility, I suppose.' Louise looked at her watch. 'Heavens, I'd better dash, otherwise Christina will think I'm not coming. Don't do the washing up. I'll help you do it when I get back. I shan't be late.'

Lizzie gave her the keys to the Alfa and her A to Z of Stibbington and district. She'd already marked the route down to the House on the Hard. 'Take care; there's no lighting in the lanes around here, and there's some lunatic who rides a motorbike without lights. I've come across him twice.'

'Don't worry. I'll find my way.' Louise hunched her shoulders into her trendy long black overcoat. Why was it the young always liked to look so funereal? Lizzie wondered.

'Got your mobile?'

'Of course,' Louise waved it. 'It's welded to my side. I'm in touch with the whole world with this thing.'

Louise had left well before Adam Maguire arrived with Tess in attendance. Lizzie was glad. She didn't want her daughter jumping to all the wrong conclusions, but all the same she felt quite pleased to see the two of them, and couldn't wait for Maguire's reaction to her news. Tess made for her spot in front of the boiler and Maguire took the Laphroaig she proffered. 'I mustn't make this a habit,' he said.

Lizzie didn't reply, but pushed the newspaper cutting across the table towards him. Maguire read it, his face impassive, and when he'd reached the end he carefully folded it up and placed it on the table before him.

'Well?' Lizzie demanded, impatient to know. 'What do you think?'

Maguire sipped his malt thoughtfully. 'I think it warrants thorough investigation,' he said slowly. 'But I'm not convinced it's the answer. It all happened such a long time ago.'

Lizzie wanted to scream with frustration. How could the damned man remain so calm? He should be rushing off to follow the clue she'd just handed him on a plate.

CHAPTER EIGHTEEN

'There's an advantage to living in one place a long time,' said Maguire.

'Pardon?' Grayson, struggling to boot up a computer, which seemed determined not to function that morning, looked up. Maguire smothered a smile. So much for IT, he thought feeling justified in his dislike of computers. It was obvious that Grayson, who loved the things, was glad of the interruption.

Without another word he spread the newspaper cutting Lizzie had given him out on the desk and indicated to Grayson that he should read it.

Grayson obediently pulled up a chair and leaned over, peering down at the faint print on paper which was yellowed with age.

20 December

JOY RIDE TO DEATH

Four teenagers from Stibbington in Hampshire, all aged sixteen, out on a drunken spree in a stolen car ended their evening by crashing into a family saloon driven by Mrs Molly Lessing. Mrs Lessing was killed outright, as were her two daughters Jackie and Chloe. The father, Giles Lessing was not with his family, but is now being treated for shock at Stibbington Infirmary. The four teenagers, Niall Walsh, who was driving his father's Rover without permission and without a driving licence or insurance, Tarquin Girling, Darren Evans, and Melinda Brockett-Smythe, all sustained injuries and were admitted to Southampton General Hospital. Police inquiries are ensuing. The chief constable of

Hampshire commented, 'This tragic accident was fuelled by alcohol. These young people had been to a party. Someone should have stopped them from driving away from it. The message is now, as at every Christmas. Don't drink and drive.'

'Bloody hell!' said Grayson inelegantly. 'Why hasn't anyone here said something? Someone in Stibbington must have put two and two together long ago.'

'You didn't,' said Maguire.

'I wasn't living here eleven years ago, I was working away. Eleven years ago,' he repeated. 'That's when this happened.' He looked at Maguire. 'And, of course, you weren't here either.'

'And I suppose most people forget,' said Maguire.

Grayson studied the cutting again, then said, 'Surely it must be more than a coincidence.'

'My sentiments entirely, Steve,' said Maguire, and immediately felt guilty that he hadn't conceded as much to Lizzie Browne. Misplaced pride, something he should have grown out of at his age. He frowned. 'Except that it suddenly seems too simple. We have to remember that two and two don't necessarily make four in this game. Sometimes they make a confusing five.' He waved the forensic report from Melinda's room, which Grayson had just handed over with many profuse apologies for its late appearance. 'And what, I wonder, has the relatively harmless occupation of smoking pot, which apparently all three indulged in, got to do with any of this?'

'You approve of pot?' Grayson sounded surprised.

'I said *relatively* harmless,' Maguire reminded him. 'I'm not recommending it.'

'I'm sorry I didn't pass it over to you yesterday.' Grayson hung his head sheepishly. 'But Ann's emergency, or what I thought was an emergency, made me forget.'

'Could have happened to anyone,' said Maguire, sounding surprisingly genial. 'What was it, by the way? Anything serious?'

'No.' Grayson looked embarrassed. 'Terrible indigestion and wind, that's all. I told her not to eat that steak and kidney pie at lunch time, but she insisted. Dr Walters was not best pleased with her.'

Maguire laughed. 'All's well that ends well,' he said. 'In more ways than one.'

'Sir?'

'You're wondering why I'm cheerful when we've got no suspects to show to the press and public and nothing but an old newspaper cutting to go on?' Grayson nodded, and Maguire rocked back in his chair, tapping a biro against his teeth. 'It's because I don't think we'll have any more murders in Stibbington. If this is the key, and I'm inclined to think it is, the killer must have moved off our patch by now. For one simple reason. There's no one left to murder.'

'There's Niall Walsh,' said Grayson, adding, 'always supposing that this theory *is* right.'

'We've got to suppose it's right. It's the only damned thing which ties these murders together. But Niall Walsh has moved away from here. So what we've got to do is find out where he went. If this is a revenge killing, then he's still in danger.'

'What about the father of the dead family, Giles Lessing? Is he still here?'

Maguire shook his head, still tapping his teeth with the biro and rocking back. 'No, I've already made inquiries on that score. According to the *Stibbington Times* he left soon after the inquest and the court case, and he's not on the electoral register here. And that's another interesting point. The court case. As the four were not yet seventeen they were not charged with manslaughter; the case came up in a magistrates' court and they got away with probation for two years. According to Danny Bayley, who remembers the case, Giles Lessing was beside himself with grief and fury. Mr Walsh, an ex-councillor and a freemason had considerable clout, and apparently used it, in conjunction with Major Brockett-Smythe, to stifle the case. Everyone knew the magistrate was in their pockets and that the case had been fixed. The four of them got off scot free.'

'If Danny Bayley remembers all that, why didn't he make the connection?' Grayson went back and pored over the torn page.

'You may well ask,' Maguire snorted. 'I've come to the conclusion that his powers of investigative journalism are nil. The only thing he's good for is writing lurid headlines.'

'What's he going to write now?' asked Grayson gloomily. 'He'll let the cat out of the bag and frighten off our suspect.'

'No he won't, at least, not yet, because the paper doesn't come out until Saturday. That's one advantage of a weekly. And he's not going to let the London press hounds have it if he can possibly help it, because he wants an exclusive so that he can sell thousands of copies. So, hopefully we've got a bit of time to track down our suspect. All I know at the moment is that Lessing sold up after the trial and moved away. I wish to hell I knew where he'd gone to. He seems to have vanished into thin air.'

Suddenly he threw the biro down on the desk and tipped his chair back into an upright position. 'But he can't have done. We've got no record of him because he hasn't committed any crime, but he must be somewhere, and someone must know of him. Start with the estate agents, Steve. Eleven years is not that long ago, and most of the firms around here have been going longer than that. They must have records of what they sold and for whom. And hopefully they'll have the forwarding addresses of their clients as well. Get on with it right away.' He pulled a notepad towards him and began writing furiously. 'I'm going to try to follow up any connecting leads with our victims. In a place like this somebody must know what they got up to before they crashed that car.

'Right, sir.' Grayson started towards the door.

'And take someone with you,' said Maguire, 'It might speed things up a bit. Take Kevin . . . what's his name?'

'Kevin Harrison, sir.' Grayson sighed.

The sigh reminded Maguire of the gossip in the station. He looked up. 'I understand that you threatened to punch him on the nose last night.' Steve nodded and looked shame-faced. 'Not a good idea. We're supposed to be upholders of the law, not unruly hooligans.' He returned to his list, adding hobbies, school friends, and youth clubs, then ran out of ideas.

'He got on my wick, sir,' said Grayson.

'A lot of people get on mine.' Maguire looked up again and gave one of his rare grins. 'But you have to put up with it, Steve. It's part of life. Or as they say in France, *c'est la vie.*'

'Yes, sir,' muttered Grayson, and went to find Constable Kevin Harrison.

During morning surgery Lizzie found it difficult to concentrate. She was annoyed. Annoyed with Adam Maguire. She thought she'd handed him the solution to the murders, on a plate so to speak, and he hadn't seemed in the least bit excited. He'd said he'd follow it up, but that was all he'd said. Of course, it was something the police ought to have discovered for themselves if they had looked in the right place, so maybe that was why he'd been so non-committal; he felt embarrassed. Meanwhile she felt impatient, even though he had phoned to tell her that Giles Lessing hadn't lived in Stibbington for years and there was no trace of him. So he *had* done something about it, but all the same Lizzie sensed he was rejecting her theory.

Her impatience showed as she sent yet another patient out without a prescription.

'A cold in the head does not warrant a course of antibiotics,' she told middle-aged Mrs Lee. There were enough articles in papers and magazines about the over-prescribing of antibiotics. Surely everyone knew a cold was a viral infection? Apparently not. The patient persisted.

'But, Doctor. I've got a sore throat and a cough as well.' Mrs Lee gave a demonstrative cough.

'Gargle three times a day with salt water, and inhale steam for your blocked nose. In three to four days' time you will be quite well,' said Lizzie briskly.

Sneaking a look at the pile of patients' notes all waiting to be seen made her feel even more gloomy. Nearly all regulars. Bad back, bad foot, piles, insomnia, plus three young mums who couldn't survive a week with their offspring without a visit to the doctors' surgery. It was only the end of her fourth week in Stibbington, and already she knew the regulars! Ah well. That was life. People thought being a doctor was glamorous. If only they knew!

Pushing the buzzer to admit the next patient, Lizzie felt impatient for lunchtime. She'd arranged to meet Louise for lunch at the Ship Inn down on the quay. The morning couldn't go quickly enough; she was enjoying her daughter's visit more than she liked to admit. Admitting it meant acknowledging that she sometimes felt lonely. A negative feeling, and one to which she could not subscribe. Life had to be full of positives.

Suddenly, Maguire's face flashed in her mind. It was a nice face, but one which held deep sadness. He had a negative view of life; perhaps that was why he hadn't jumped at the information she'd given him – he couldn't believe that it was all so simple. Ah well, that was his problem, Not hers, because that afternoon, when Louise and her friend went into

Southampton for some Christmas shopping, and she had the afternoon off, she planned to do a little detective work of her own. She'd ascertained that the library kept back copies of the *Stibbington Times*, and intended to search through them for further information concerning the joy riding incident. As well as that she was going to visit old Mrs Mills. Not something she'd mentioned to Maguire, suspecting that he would have told her to keep her nose out of police business.

The phone rang. It was Tara inquiring whether she would speak to Phineas Merryweather in between patients. Lizzie took the call.

Phineas came straight to the point. 'Dick has told me that he mentioned our little dinner party to you. If you feel up to meeting a few more Stibbington inhabitants, my wife and I would be very pleased to see you.'

'I'd love to. But, as I told Dick, I have my daughter staying with me; Thursday is our last night together. Will you forgive me if I say no this time?' Lizzie didn't particularly want to share Louise. She was already sharing her with this unknown friend, Christina.

'Of course, my dear.' Phineas sounded understanding. 'We'll make it another time. Pity, though, I was looking forward to talking about our three murder victims. You've beaten me to the scene of the crime every time.'

'Until another time then. And thank you for asking me.' Lizzie smiled wryly. Louise didn't know what a lucky escape she'd had. If there was one thing she hated it was anything of a gory nature; a cut finger was about as much as she could stomach. More by luck than good judgement, she'd managed to pass off the scene of the burnt-out greenhouse and shed as an accident which had happened before she'd bought the cottage. Louise had accepted the explanation without comment, and Lizzie had breathed a sigh of relief, reckoning that white lies never did anyone any harm.

Wednesday morning was fine, cold, and blustery. The first really fine day without black, threatening rain clouds looming overhead for more than two weeks, and the citizens of Stibbington were taking advantage of it. A steady stream of people walked along the hard, heads down against the sou'westerly blowing in from the sea, all muffled up against the cold with anoraks, hats, and headscarves.

From her guests' lounge window Emmy Matthews watched the

straggly procession: mostly pensioners, the only ones with time off at this time of the day. She was hoping that the Walshes and their baby would soon be out as well. Babies were all very well (Emmy had never had one of her own, there'd always been just her and Bert, until he passed over, and he'd been enough trouble with his muddy boots and constant pile of newspapers, which he'd insisted reading from cover to cover) but they smelled. To Emmy's sensitive nose the smell of slightly sour milk and nappies permeated the whole house. She'd already used up a whole tin of lavender spray, and was unwilling to start another one. As soon as they went out she'd open all the windows and give the place a good air. In the meantime, as there were no clouds about, she decided to wash and hang out all last week's tablecloths and sheets, which had been lingering in the laundry basket waiting for a day such as this.

It was while she was pegging out the washing at the rear of the house (never let it be said that people from the front could see her washing) that she saw Mrs Smithson lurch, yes that was the word, *lurch*, down the drive and out on to the foreshore. Hidden behind a billowing tablecloth Emmy watched through a gap in the hedge that separated the back garden from the front. The woman did not go along the hard towards the town, but turned right and followed the seaward path. Most strollers only went along as far as the end of the marina, where a stone wall had been built and half a dozen wooden seats put in place. And there they sat, taking in the view of the estuary and the saltings to the left, and the open Solent with its distant view of the Isle of Wight to the right. But Mrs Smithson didn't pause, she walked, still with an unsteady gait, past the end of the marina, past the seats with their occupants, and on towards the curve of the coastline where the coarse sea grass grew in tussocks between the salty mudflats exposed at low tide. There was just one building there – the old chandlery. Once it had been a busy place, but it was now derelict and unused. It should have been pulled down, but no one had bothered about it.

It was out of sight from the town, but in sight from Emmy's top window in the House on the Hard, where she was now (she'd rushed upstairs in order to follow Mrs Smithson's progress) with her nose pressed against the window, squinting into the brightness reflected from the sea. She saw Mrs Smithson enter the old building, and close the rickety door behind her. She thought of the leaflet down in the kitchen drawer where she'd hidden it for safety. By now she'd read it, and it had been a revelation. Previously, transvestites existed exclusively between the pages of the more lurid tabloids, and as far as she knew there were none in Stibbington. At least, none until Mrs Smithson had arrived, for Emmy was now convinced that her strange guest must be a transvestite. Why else would she have a booklet telling her in detail how to behave as a woman? It wasn't normal. But according to the booklet it was quite common, and it wasn't against the law. So what was she to do? If Mrs Smithson was a man, but wanted to pretend to be a woman, whose business was it? Emmy didn't know, but still felt it wasn't right, in spite of what the book said. Men shouldn't have those sorts of urges. Her Bert would never have dressed up like that. Well, she wouldn't have let him for one thing!

She was still standing gazing out of the window in the direction of the old chandlery when she saw a man wheeling a motorbike from behind the building along by the broken jetty. He kept to the narrow gravel path, which was always dry as the tide never reached that far, and brought the bike around to the front of the building. There he kicked it, and although she was too far away to hear, Emmy could imagine the engine roaring into life, as it must have done, for the next moment man and bike moved at a steady speed along the path and joined the tarmac road at the end of the hard. As it gathered speed, and passed the House on the Hard, Emmy suddenly remembered the sound of the motorbike at Darren Evans's bungalow, something she'd completely forgotten about until that moment. Now she did think of it she knew there was something she just had to know, and before she could change her mind, she marched down the stairs and along the corridor towards Mrs Smithson's room and opened the door. Once inside, she carefully wedged the door open, she wasn't going to be caught unawares a second time, and then began to open the drawers and cupboards, sifting through the contents swiftly and methodically.

Maguire's hopes of the media continuing to ignore events in Stibbington were dashed almost as soon as Grayson and Constable Harrison left the station. He had already fielded several calls from the national press himself that morning, refusing to give a statement. Then the superintendent stormed in and launched into a tirade.

'The press have been on to me. I sent them away, of course. But we'll have to call a press conference sooner rather than later. They're outside now, and there's a TV crew out there as well, and they're not going to go away until we tell them something. So, why the hell aren't you out there doing something? Saying something! Arresting someone! The phone hasn't stopped ringing this morning, and Headquarters have even e-mailed me.'

'Thank God I haven't got e-mail. I leave all that to Grayson.' Maguire felt that e-mails would be more than he could bear, and always let Grayson embrace all the latest technology, which he did with enthusiasm

'Find a suspect,' the super barked. 'Hold someone for questioning. Anyone,' he added.

The last remark was totally illogical, and Maguire put it down to strain. He knew, in fact everyone at the station knew, that the super had just come from yet another meeting at County Headquarters. And they all knew that he was desperately struggling to preserve the status quo. Like Maguire he had no desire to vanish into the black hole of tinted glass and concrete blocks which was County Headquarters.

'I can't hold just anyone for questioning, sir. There's got to be a reason, and I haven't got a good enough reason to hold anyone at the moment.'

'Reasons, reasons.' The superintendent paced about. 'If we don't clear this up that will be a very good reason for closing this place down and making it just another of those ghost stations, open two mornings a week for the public to come in to complain about their neighbours leaving their wheelie bins outside their front gates on the wrong day.'

'I know,' said Maguire unhappily. 'I will hold a press conference. But all I can say is that our inquiries are continuing and that there is nothing to report at the moment.'

'Do it,' said the super. 'At least that will keep them quiet for a few hours while they go away and concoct a totally ridiculous story, which we can then deny.' He strode purposefully from the room. 'I'll get DC Gordon, that new chap from the Regional Crime Squad, to set it up. He might have a few ideas of what to say. Anything to fob them off, apparently he's been trained in that sort of thing. Information psychology, it's called. A load of rubbish, but we'll do it. Be ready in fifteen minutes.'

'Yes, sir.' Maguire was not happy. He would prefer to remain silent for the time being. The press had an unhappy knack of stirring things up, a fabricated story could do damage that was hard to undo. But he had his orders to follow. He called in DC Gordon and between them they started to draft a press handout.

Half an hour later the press departed. They were not happy either. Detective Chief Inspector Maguire had not told them anything they didn't already know, but they all knew they weren't going to get anything more from him. Not today, anyway.

As soon as they'd disappeared Maguire put on his overcoat and asked DC Gordon to accompany him on the premise that two heads might be better than one. Especially as DC Gordon had never met the Brockett-Smythes. They'd go and have another word with them, and maybe Ivy James as well later on. He'd like to clear up the cannabis connection if nothing else, and there surely must be a connection, unless every other person in Stibbington was smoking pot, which was unlikely. Mrs Clackett was in cleaning the house today, so he could leave Tess for a bit longer as she'd have a run in the garden.

At midday the sheltered, cobbled yard of the Ship Inn was so sunny and warm it almost seemed like spring. One step around the corner and it was a different place – a piercingly cold wind blew a reminder that it was December – but the yard was warm and Lizzie and Louise ate their ploughmans outside.

Lizzie held up her cider watching the sunlight sparkle through the golden liquid. Her bad mood of the morning surgery evaporated like one of the golden bubbles floating free and exploding in little bursts on the surface. She took a long cool sip. 'This is what it will be like every day in summer,' she said. 'I'm glad I moved down here.'

'So am I,' said Louise, smiling. 'I'll be a regular visitor.'

They both laughed at the thought and then smiled, almost shyly, at each other. Now that she and Mike were divorced, there was no longer the need to pretend that everything was all right, and Lizzie knew they both felt more at ease. The curtain of deceit had been pulled aside, and they were seeing each other face to face. How many other families, Lizzie wondered, stumbled along in a fog of misunderstanding and fear? Fear of saying the wrong thing, always balancing carefully on the edge of the precipice before the next storm broke. She and Mike had both been responsible for that state of affairs, and they should have had the courage, both of them, to have broken free years ago. But she didn't have the courage and neither did he. It took another woman to give him the courage. But it didn't matter. She was free. They were both free.

They carried on eating. 'I'd like another half pint of cider,' said Louise. 'What about you?'

'An orange juice, please,' said Lizzie. 'I've got some driving to do this afternoon.'

Louise disappeared inside the pub and Lizzie sat alone. The dark clouds, so miraculously held at bay for the morning, began to roll in again from the west, bringing with them the threat of rain. She shivered. Thoughts of spring had been premature; this was winter, and a cold and miserable one at that. For no reason her mind slid back to the recent death of Melinda, and she shuddered. When the sun had been shining she'd been able to forget the murders for a few moments, but now the horror of all three returned in full force. The sooner the police caught this mad man the better; she was convinced in her own mind that it must be Giles Lessing. Who else would have a motive?

Large spots of rain began to splatter down, the prelude to a downpour, and Lizzie started to move towards the pub. She'd reached the door, which was on to the road leading along the foreshore, when she heard a motorbike. She felt the hairs on the back of her neck prickle in fear. Maybe it was her overwrought imagination, because it didn't seem like any old motorbike; it had a distinctive low rumble. It was the same sound she'd heard on the afternoon of Darren's murder, the night of her first visit to the Hargreaves' house, and in the lane the night Tarquin had died. For a moment she stood rooted to the spot in fear, then common sense prevailed. Motorbike engines were all the same; her imagination was just running riot. But nevertheless she stayed where she was in the shelter of the doorway and watched the black leather-clad figure ride past. The sound puttered into silence as the bike and its rider disappeared round the bend on the foreshore past the marina and was lost to view. Lizzie went into the warmth of the bar and stood as near to the open log fire as possible.

Louise came over. 'Hey, what's this?' she said. 'You look as if you've seen a ghost.'

'I'm freezing,' said Lizzie. 'It's turned bitterly cold again, and I wish I'd ordered something stronger than orange juice now.'

'You're driving, remember,' said Louise, and handed her the drink. 'You've got to keep a clear head.'

'Too true.'

Lizzie thought of her planned detective work. The answer was in that newspaper cutting, she felt certain of it. But there was more to it than that, and hopefully Mrs Mills would provide some of the answers. Finding Giles Lessing was the first priority. Lizzie wondered how easy it was for the police to find someone who had decided to disappear. It couldn't be that simple. There were cases in the papers all the time about people disappearing and never being found. What happened to them? If they were still alive how did they live? How did they get through the morass of paperwork the modern state demanded? National Insurance number, tax code, NHS number, credit card details, all these things were markers on a life. It was difficult to see how anyone could disappear unless they were dead, and she was prepared to bet a year's salary on the fact that Giles Lessing was not dead.

'Where are you?' Louise was peering into her face with a puzzled expression. 'You're looking terribly fierce again.'

'Sorry,' said Lizzie. 'I was just thinking.'

CHAPTER NINETEEN

'TELL ME, MAJOR, how do you think cannabis got into your daughter's room?'

Maguire sat opposite the major in his drawing room late on Wednesday morning. The major had offered him a low chair, which Maguire thought would have been churlish and insensitive to refuse – he was, after all, dealing with a bereaved father – so he'd sat in it. But the moment he'd sat down the major had chosen a much higher chair, and now looked down on him. Maguire wondered whether he'd done it on purpose. Did he always like to tower over his visitors? Maguire suspected so. DC Gordon had chosen to sit further away, on a spindly chair by the window. A sensible move.

'I've no idea,' came the reply. The major had a pompous voice. Something Maguire had noted before, and he found it irritating. 'And anyway what does it matter? Melinda is dead. It's neither here nor there now, is it?'

'I'll be the judge of that,' said Maguire. 'Your daughter has been murdered and I think you will agree that it would be very remiss of me not to investigate everything concerning her life and death.' As well as sounding pompous the major came across as hostile. Not in so many words, but in his manner. Maguire had the feeling that, for some reason best known to himself, the major did not want his daughter's death investigated too closely. An unnatural reaction as her end had been so violent. Most people wanted to know who had committed the crime, and what was more, most people wanted revenge on the perpetrator. The major, however, merely seemed anxious to get the formalities out of the way and give his daughter a quick funeral. And he'd given the same impression where Darren Evans was concerned. He wanted to get him buried and out of the way as soon as possible.

Maguire studied the man before him. Was he a murderer? It seemed unlikely – he was the father. Yet he was so calm in a strangely defiant way, and as Maguire knew very well, many murderers appeared calm, composed, and plausible. However, Maguire reminded himself, he was not dealing with just one murder. There were now three, and there was the link between all three victims: the accident all those years before. Although, of course, it could just be coincidence. Stranger things did happen.

The major stared back at him, and then said, 'You are thinking that I should be more upset at the death of my daughter.'

Maguire decided to be honest. 'Yes, I am,' he said, and waited.

The major continued in the same pompous tone of voice. 'Of course, I am not happy at the manner of her death, but I must be frank with you and tell you that now she *is* dead, the main feeling I have is one of relief.'

DC Gordon drew in his breath, but said nothing. There was a brief pause. The major glanced across towards him, clearly irritated by his presence.

'I see,' said Maguire, and waited again. Sometimes the less said the better. Silence had an effect on people. They often felt bound to fill it with words. And words which spilled out without any prompting were often significant.

The major leaned forward, placed one hand on each knee and said earnestly, 'You don't know what it's like to look after someone with a terminal illness. Because that was what it was. Melinda was never going to get better. No one understands how it is to watch someone deteriorate day after day.'

Don't know. Don't understand. The mere thought of Rosemary's last days and nights still brought Maguire out in a cold sweat. Watching her fade away, hour by hour, losing control, losing her dignity, until eventually she became a faint shadow of the person she had once been. 'I understand better than you may think,' he said quietly. 'My wife died of cancer.'

That took the wind out of his sails. The major sat back, suddenly deflated, no longer quite so defiantly superior. There was a long silence, then he said, 'I'm sorry.'

'Let's get back to the point,' said Maguire. 'How did your daughter get the cannabis? Don't deny it. The forensic evidence is there. She was ill and didn't go out, so therefore someone in this house must have procured it for her. What I want to know is who got it, from where, and why?'

'Very simple, really,' said the major, the pomposity suddenly evaporating, as an air of resignation crept into his voice. 'Darren recommended that we try it. Did you know that cannabis has been used as a medical remedy in some countries for years?' Maguire shook his head; he didn't know that. 'And yet here,' the major continued, 'it is not even legal for a doctor to supply it.'

'Why did Melinda need it?' DC Gordon asked.

'To control her moods. I've already told the chief inspector that as the years went by she got more violent. She was strong and aggressive. I must admit that often I was afraid of her, and my wife certainly was. Melinda seemed to hate her, my wife, I mean. She was her stepmother; my first wife died when Melinda was quite small.'

'You got the cannabis for Melinda from Darren Evans,' said Maguire, trying to keep the major on track. 'I assume he kept in touch, then, after the accident?'

The major sighed. 'I wondered when someone would put two and two together. It was all such a long time ago, but then when these murders started it brought it all back. Yes, he kept in touch.' He paused, then said, 'As best he could. But he dropped out of life after that accident, took to drink and drugs, although he still had some feelings for Melinda. He was her boyfriend once, you know. Before the accident. Then after she became ill he helped us. We couldn't have managed without Darren.'

'And after Darren's death Tarquin Girling offered to keep on supplying cannabis to you?'

The major's head jerked up. 'How did you know?'

'Simple, really,' said Maguire echoing the major's words. 'We saw him leaving here the day he was murdered, and there were burned cannabis plants around his remains.' The major was silent.

DC Gordon moved his chair a little and the legs scraped on the polished wood of the floor. 'How well did you know Tarquin Girling?'

'Not well at all.' The major leaned back and put his hands together to form a steeple. Maguire could see he was gradually relaxing. 'Of course, Melinda knew Tarquin when they were all young, but we didn't. He was a friend of Niall Walsh, and spent most of his time at the Walshes' house. Never came here. In fact, had never been here before the day you saw him, the day he was killed. I didn't recognize him, but when he offered me the cannabis I said yes. We were desperate for another supplier.'

'Desperate, you say. So when Tarquin was murdered you had a real problem. There was no other supplier.'

Maguire watched the man before him carefully but was disappointed. Years in the army had taught the major to give little away, and he gave nothing away now, merely said, 'I would have found another supplier. These things can be done, you know.'

'Unfortunately I do,' said Maguire. He looked out of the window. It was raining again. Hard, slashing rain. He picked up his raincoat, which was lying beside him, stood up, and nodded to Gordon to do the same. He knew now about the cannabis, but the knowledge was useless as far as the murders were concerned. Except. Except. It didn't quite fit. He looked at the major, who had also risen, and was standing in front of the fire, his hand on the greyhound's head. The man had desperately needed another supplier, he had admitted as much. What if it proved more difficult than he'd thought? Maguire had a deep-seated feeling about Melinda's murder. Not only was it different in method, it could well be that the motive was different. But if he followed that line, it threw the revenge theory for the other two out of kilter.

'Are you going to arrest me for buying cannabis?' asked the major.

Maguire shrugged his shoulders into the heavy raincoat. 'Not at the moment,' he said. 'But I would like to talk to your wife.' He looked at his watch. There were one or two things he wanted to talk to Phineas about and as it was just after lunchtime he'd be taking his postprandial nap and should be free. 'I've got some appointments now,' he said, 'so I'll talk to her later at the station if that's convenient. Let's say at about four o'clock this afternoon.'

'But she's told you all she knows.' The major's bland tone dropped. He was on the defensive again.

'It never hurts to go over things several times,' said Maguire quietly. 'And I've not formally interviewed her and recorded it. This afternoon would be a good time.'

'I shall come with her.'

'Come with her if you wish, but I shall talk to her alone,' said

Maguire. He intended to follow a hunch, a luxury he seldom indulged in because they rarely paid off. At least not for him. But this time the feeling was so strong he couldn't ignore it.

Once outside DC Gordon quizzed him. 'Why do you want see his wife? She seemed a scared little rabbit of a thing to me when I met her.'

'Ridiculous as it may seem,' said Maguire, 'I'm sure that Mrs Brockett-Smythe knows far more about her stepdaughter's death than she is saying.'

Back at the station he phoned Phineas Merryweather. 'Good God, man,' said Phineas, sounding slightly sleepy. 'Don't you ever rest? After a good lunch one should always have forty winks.'

'I haven't had any lunch,' said Maguire, 'never mind about a good one, and forty winks in the middle of the day is a luxury I'm saving until my retirement.'

'At the rate you're going you'll drop dead long before you get there,' said Phineas grumpily. 'Now, tell me what you want.'

Lizzie was greeted with a rapturous smile by Mrs Mills. 'Why, my dear,' she said, balancing on her Zimmer frame, 'how nice of you to come and see me when I'm not ill. I made a cinnamon cake this morning and was wondering how I was going to eat it all by myself. But now you're here, we can have a piece each.'

Lizzie followed her down the narrow hall feeling guilty. It wasn't an altruistic visit on her part, but one for her own inquisitive purpose. In the living room a blazing log fire was crackling in the hearth, and the elderly cairn was fast asleep in front of it, pink underbelly exposed to the warmth. He didn't stir when they entered. 'Not a very good guard dog, is he,' she said.

'No, dear. No good at all. Deaf as a post, he is. But I wouldn't be without him. He's the last little bit of my Harry I've got left. I don't know what I shall do when he turns up his little toes and departs this world.' She swivelled the Zimmer in the direction of the kitchen. 'Now, you sit there and I'll just go and put the kettle on.'

'I'll help.'

But Mrs Mills was firm and wouldn't allow it, so Lizzie sat beside the sleeping dog and hoped he wouldn't turn up his toes, as Mrs Mills had said, for a very long time. There was something sad about old people and old animals. Either one would be devastated when left alone. I wonder if I'll be like this one day, she thought; an old woman, alone, longing for someone, anyone, to knock on the door so that I can talk to them. The thought was disturbing because the uncomfortable truth was that it was all too possible. For anyone, not just herself. Children grew up, and went away, and when they got married or took up with stable partners then they usually went even further away. It was natural. Their lives would be full of their own doings. The world was full of lonely people. Suddenly she thought of Maguire. He was lonely, with only an old dog for company, although, like her, he did have his work, but that wouldn't last forever. Then she thought of the man whose wife and children had been killed by the youthful joy riders. Giles Lessing. Was he still alone? Was he alone and bitter? Bitter enough to go on a vengeful killing spree?

'My goodness, you look serious.' Mrs Mills re-entered, this time with the wooden trolley, set out as before with a tea tray and cups and saucers. On the bottom shelf sat a cake, with a crunchy brown sugar topping. Lizzie could smell the cinnamon as soon as she entered the room. The tea was poured out, and two pieces of cake cut, before Mrs Mills lowered herself carefully down into a chair. She leaned forward, took another log from the brass log box beside her, and threw it onto the fire. A shower of sparks flew up the chimney, catching on the soot at the back of the fireplace and lingering for a few seconds. A tiny red firework show. 'People going to church,' said Mrs Mills. 'That's what my mother always used to say.' Then she smiled at Lizzie a smile of infinite sweetness and wisdom. 'Now, tell me,' she said quietly, 'what have you come to see me about?'

Lizzie found Mrs Mills a mine of information. She learned about the four when they'd been at primary school, how they'd formed an unlikely friendship together, which lasted even when they split up and went to different secondary schools; Niall and Tarquin to the private grammar school, Darren and Melinda to the local mixed comprehensive. In those days, Mrs Mills had been an active member of Stibbington's Church and Women's Institute. She'd followed the lives of her ex-pupils with interest and with an insight which made her notice more than most.

'Darren Evans and Melinda Brockett-Smythe,' mused Lizzie. 'I find it difficult to believe that Melinda's father approved of Darren.'

'Oh, Darren was different in those days. His mother was alive, and she came from good county stock. Her family were well known commoners. Everyone in the New Forest knew them. They had a small-holding and let their cattle loose in the forest. She had no money, of course, as she'd married beneath her, but her family were good enough for the major. And he had just married again and was taken up with his new wife.'

'What about the others, Tarquin and Niall?' asked Lizzie.

'They say Tarquin won a scholarship to the grammar school, but I never believed it. He was bright, but not that bright. Niall was the clever one. No, I think Mr Walsh fixed it and paid for him to go there.'

'He did,' said Lizzie. 'Tarquin told me that. He said that he was company for Niall.'

'Company,' said Mrs Mills, and smiled. 'Yes, I suppose you could call it that. They were like brothers, and there were always rumours. They were so close.'

'Did you think they were brothers?'

Mrs Mills didn't answer immediately. Instead she looked thoughtful as she struggled to her feet and poured two more cups of tea.

'I'm not sure about that,' she said slowly. She paused and looked quizzically at Lizzie. 'But why do you want to know all these things? Three of them are dead, and the other one moved away years ago. What has it got to do with you?'

'Nothing,' Lizzie was forced to admit. 'Except that I have a theory that these murders are revenge killings, and that the only person likely to want revenge is Giles Lessing.'

'The police should be asking me all these things.' Mrs Mills began to sound slightly disapproving.

'I know they should,' said Lizzie quickly. 'And I've told them what I think, even given them the evidence in the form of an old newspaper cutting. But Detective Chief Inspector Maguire doesn't believe me. He thinks I'm just a meddling female.'

'And are you?'

Crunching on her last piece of cinnamon cake Lizzie swallowed, considered, and then said, 'Yes, in a way I suppose I am. But I can't help it. It's the way I am. I want to know why these murders have been committed, and who the perpetrator is.'

Mrs Mills looked serious. 'You've already made up your mind on that score, haven't you? You think it is Giles Lessing.'

'Yes,' said Lizzie. 'I do, so what can you tell me about him?'

Mrs Mills deliberated for a moment, and then said with a sigh, 'Very little. He went to pieces after the death of his wife and daughters. Well, who could blame him, poor man. His whole family taken from him in one moment of madness. Your predecessor, Dr Burton, spent hours and hours with him. Counselling they call it nowadays, but then it was plain old-fashioned compassion. He was a kind man, Dr Burton, I mean, and he advised Giles Lessing to try to start a new life somewhere else. There was nothing to keep him in Stibbington, and money wasn't a problem; he'd always had a private income and sold antique books as a sideline. He left here not long afterwards, and as far as I know, no one has ever seen him since. At least, no one from Stibbington.'

It was a disappointed Lizzie who eventually took her leave of Mrs Mills, no nearer to finding Giles Lessing. 'You've been very helpful,' she said. 'Thank you for answering all my questions.'

'Hmn!' said Mrs Mills. 'I'm not sure that I've done the right thing. Maybe I should have kept quiet, because if you've got any sense, young woman, you'll leave well alone. Murderers are for the police to catch, not lady doctors.'

Lizzie smiled. 'It's years since I've been called a young woman.'

'When you get to my age everyone is young,' said Mrs Mills wryly. 'Would you mind fetching my Zimmer frame from the kitchen for me, dear? I'll come with you then as far as the front door.' Lizzie duly obliged, helping to hoist the old lady onto the frame before they set off together towards the hall. 'I do remember something else about Giles Lessing,' said Mrs Mills, 'although I doubt it's important. He was mad on motorbikes. Old ones. He used to ride them around the lanes at night without lights. Everyone said it was a wonder he wasn't the one who was killed. But there you are. He survived, although his family didn't. No justice in this world, is there?'

'None,' said Lizzie, speaking with difficulty. A cold, hard ball of fear had lodged in her throat. Giles Lessing *was* in Stibbington. He was the man on the motorbike she'd seen driving away from Darren Evans's cottage, and now she realized it must have been his motorbike she'd heard on the night of Tarquin's murder. He must have stayed around long enough to make certain his victim was dead. But she'd forgotten to mention the motorbike to the police, something she ought to rectify now. Remembering Steve Grayson had given her his mobile phone number when they'd first met, she sat in the car with the interior light on and fished in her handbag for her phone.

Finding the number she called it, but a disembodied voice informed her that the phone was switched off and she should try again later. Lizzie sat for a moment and considered. The fact that Giles Lessing rode a motorbike was not going to tell the police where he was, and anyway, he was he was hardly likely to be advertising his presence. Dr Burton had been his doctor and confidante; maybe he'd kept notes, so perhaps she'd find a clue to Lessing's whereabouts in amongst them. If anyone had told Lizzie she was venturing further and further into police investigative territory she wouldn't have listened. The adrenalin was pumping, she was on the trail, and she was going to follow it until she got to the end. Turning the key in the ignition she started down the forest track, turned left at the main road and headed towards the Honeywell Health Centre.

All the old records were amazingly easy to find. When Lizzie asked Tara if they still existed she merely took her to a room at the end of the corridor, opened the door, pointed towards stacks of boxes on the shelves and said, 'There you are. No booting up to do, no disks to search, just take out the boxes and look through the old Lloyd George Cards. I've always preferred them to the computer. There's something satisfying about a bundle of brown cards.'

Lizzie laughed. 'Tara, you're too young to be so nostalgic,' she said.

Tara shrugged. 'We're not all geeks,' she said as she closed the door leaving Lizzie inside.

Praise be to God, thought Lizzie, for people who don't believe in the paperless society. The Lloyd George Cards, the old-fashioned brown medical cards, were all there. Everything had been noted. Patients who had died thirty years before still featured large amongst the piles of notes, and it was not difficult to find Giles Lessing's records. In the days when patients' records were for a doctor's eyes only, it was possible for private anecdotes to be written secure in the knowledge that no one else would ever see them, and Dr Burton had liberally sprinkled his patients' notes with information of a non-medical nature. Lizzie learned that Giles Lessing's private income came from properties he owned in the London area and let out by the room, and that when he left Stibbington he had moved back to a flat he owned near Regents Park canal. The address was in the notes. He'd also owned and let out, according to the notes, various farm properties, and boathouses, in and around Stibbington, although there were no specific addresses.

'Pity,' said Maguire rifling through the notes Lizzie had handed over to him. 'Pity,' he repeated, 'that we don't know where the Stibbington properties were. Because if he's here that's maybe where he is.'

'But you have his London address in there,' said Lizzie. She was feeling guilty about handing over the records.

'No wonder none of the estate agents here knew where he'd gone to,' said Grayson. 'We found the one who sold his house,' he told Lizzie, 'but we couldn't trace a forwarding address'. He picked up a page of medical notes and began to read. Lizzie snatched it back. 'You do realize that patients' notes are confidential, even though the man's a murderer.'

'He's a suspect that's all, nothing more at this stage,' said Maguire dourly as Lizzie gave a derisive snort. 'And you shouldn't break the rules, either, if you're worried about it, and neither should you jump to conclusions.' Lizzie opened her mouth to protest, but Maguire silenced her with a sharp bark of, 'Steve!'

'Yes, sir?' Grayson who'd been leaning against a filing cabinet, jumped to attention.

'Take this,' he handed him the paper with Lessing's last known address on it, 'and find out if he still lives there and if he does where he is at the moment.'

'He's here. In Stibbington,' said Lizzie. 'I know it. He's been riding his motorbike around. I've seen him. And what's more I saw a motor-cyclist riding away from Darren Evans's bungalow the day we found his body; I suppose he'd gone back to check that he really was dead. And I heard a motorbike when I got back to Silver Cottage and found Tarquin's body. Plus I've seen it going along the shore road near the House on the Hard.'

Maguire pushed the bundle of notes across the table. 'Take these and put them back where they belong. I'm not interested in his medical conditions, past or present; I've got the information that's useful. And as far as the motorcyclist is concerned, what you've seen is a man on a bike, and that doesn't prove it is Giles Lessing. And, you should have told me earlier about seeing it at the Evans bungalow.'

'I know,' said Lizzie. 'Sorry.'

Maguire picked up the notes and held them out. 'Take them,' he said.

'Aren't you going to say thank you? You've got an address, which you wouldn't have got without me.'

'Thank you,' said Maguire. He looked at Lizzie sternly. 'Now go back to your doctoring, and leave the police work to me and my colleagues. Murder is a dangerous business. Leave it alone. Don't get mixed up in it.'

'But I *am* mixed up in it,' said Lizzie, resenting his tone of voice.

'Leave it alone,' Maguire repeated, losing his temper. Leaning forward he banged the palm of one hand flat on the desk. 'For God's sake, woman,' he shouted, 'this isn't a cosy TV series where a clever amateur uncovers the murder under the nose of some dumb policeman. We're probably dealing with someone who is seriously deranged here. Don't get involved, or your own life might be in danger. Leave the police work to the experts.'

Lizzie glared at him. She didn't like being shouted at by men. It reminded her too much of Mike.

She stood up, picked up the notes, and made, what she hoped, was a dignified exit. But she couldn't resist having the last word.

Pausing at the door of his office she said in dulcet tones, 'I was only assisting the police, something I believe every citizen is encouraged to do.'

Maguire didn't answer. He didn't need to. He slumped back down in his chair, his ferocious glare saying it all. Even Grayson looked worried.

CHAPTER TWENTY

'WELL, TESS,' SAID Maguire to the dog, who was sitting on her special mat beside him. He'd gone home to take her for a walk and then bring her back to the office as it looked like being another late night. 'I've well and truly put an end to any invitations for us to have supper at Silver Cottage again. Dr Browne did not like being told what to do!'

Tess looked back at him, her brown eyes full of undemanding affection. Undemanding and non-judgemental, that is the good thing about dogs, thought Maguire. If only more people could be like that. Rosemary had been, but she'd been exceptional, and indeed there were times during their marriage, if he were honest, that Maguire had felt irritated by her lack of what he termed 'spirit'. But all those feelings had been swept away by her illness. Then, her courageous acceptance of her fate seemed almost saint-like. Now, Maguire didn't allow himself to think of her as anything other than perfect. Lizzie Browne certainly wasn't in the same mould, he mused bad-temperedly. She was a clever, interfering, infuriating woman who couldn't have been easy to live with. No wonder she was divorced.

'Not that I had anything other than the occasional pasta supper in mind. Divorced and acerbic Dr Browne might be, but she is also a damned good cook.'

'Sir?' Steve Grayson popped his head around the door. 'Oh, you are alone. I thought you had someone with you.'

'Just talking to the dog,' said Maguire, guessing, rightly, that Grayson was thinking, poor old sod, reduced to talking to the dog because there's no one else.

'Major and Mrs Brockett-Smythe are here, sir.'

'Good. Escort her down to the interview room; I'll be down in a moment.'

Grayson's eyebrows shot sky high. 'Interview room? Do you suspect her?'

'Let's say that I suspect she is not telling me the truth, the whole truth, and nothing but the truth, and that if she did it would help us enormously in our inquiries, Steve.'

Grayson grinned. 'Amen to that.'

A few moments later, after he had deposited Tess with WPC Jones, who loved dogs, Maguire sat down in the interview room by the side of Grayson and opposite a clearly very nervous, Mrs Brockett-Smythe.

'I'm sorry to have to drag you in here,' said Maguire, switching on the recorder. He had no desire to terrorize the poor woman, but he had to get at the truth. 'Have you any objection to this conversation being recorded?'

'No, I suppose not. But you've already spoken to me once, and I can't tell you any more.' Her voice was high-pitched, and trembling.

'I know.' Maguire was soothing. 'But at the time you were, understandably, very upset, and we didn't record the interview. There are certain rules and regulations which we, as policemen, have to abide by otherwise we should all lose our jobs.'

'I understand you went shopping yesterday morning,' said Grayson consulting his notes. 'It wasn't your usual day, was it?'

Mrs Brockett-Smythe nodded. 'No, Ivy usually comes on Wednesdays and Saturdays.'

'So why did you change it to Tuesday?' Maguire spoke very quietly, in a matter-of-fact kind of voice, as if it didn't really matter. He smiled at the nervous woman opposite. 'We have to put everything down, no matter how small and trivial it may seem.'

'I'd run out of toilet rolls. I know I could have phoned Ivy and asked her to bring some up. She would have done, she's always so helpful, but I wanted to get away, get out.' The words came out in a rush and when she'd finished speaking Mrs Brockett-Smythe leaned back in her chair as if exhausted.

'It must have been a terrible strain for you, looking after Melinda,' said Maguire. 'I can understand you wanting to get out.'

'Yes.' The woman opposite relaxed a visible slackening of facial muscles and body position. 'She wasn't my daughter, you know, and she wasn't ill when I married the major.'

'Would you have still married him if she had been ill?' asked Grayson.

Maguire shot him an irritated look. That, he thought, was putting it too bluntly; it was the kind of thing they could find out by other means. But too late now, Grayson had blurted it out.

However Mrs Brockett-Smythe didn't appear to take offence, rather the opposite. She became almost confidential. 'The answer to that is almost certainly no,' she said. 'I would not have married him. But by the time Melinda became ill it was too late.'

'You could have left him,' said Maguire.

A pair of pale blue eyes stared back at him in surprise. 'But I'd married him, and I loved him. I still do love him. I'd made my promises so I couldn't go back on them, although sometimes I must admit I have prayed that she would die soon.'

'And now she has,' said Grayson.

'Yes, but I didn't want it like that.' The reply came swiftly. Mrs Brockett-Smythe shuddered. 'No one could want it to end like that. It was horrible.' She shuddered again.

'I understand your husband was at the back of the house repairing a fence when you left to go shopping,' said Maguire.

She nodded. 'Yes. The fence had been blown down in the gales of the previous week. It's a long way from the house, behind the hazel copse at the far end of our land, so I didn't bother to tell him I was going. Ivy James arrived, and I left her making herself a cup of tea in the kitchen.'

'Were the outside doors locked?'

'Oh no. We never bother, not when we're there. There's no need. There's not much crime around here.' The understatement of the year, thought Maguire in view of recent happenings, but he remained silent and let her continue. 'Melinda's room was locked, of course,' she said. 'From the outside. But you already know that.'

'So anyone could have got into the house,' said Maguire.

'Oh yes,' she said quickly. 'Well, they must have done, mustn't they? How else could Melinda have been murdered?'

'How else indeed,' said Maguire and, leaning slightly forward just to emphasize his words, said, 'interview with Mrs Brockett-Smythe ended at 5.35p.m.'

Mrs Brockett-Smythe almost fell out of her chair. 'Is that all?'

Maguire smiled. 'Yes, you may go now, and I would advise you and your husband to go to the Royal Oak and have a meal. You deserve a little relaxation this evening after all you've been through.'

She stood up. Maguire noticed she was still trembling. 'Yes, perhaps we will,' she said. 'Yes, that's a good idea.'

'Tell me,' said Maguire, just as she reached the door. 'How did you acquire that nasty bruise just under your hairline on the right side of your forehead?'

A hand instinctively flew up to it, and tugged a piece of hair down. 'Melinda hit me,' she said. 'Yesterday morning, before she was killed.'

'Sounds like she was telling the truth,' said Grayson after she'd gone. 'Perhaps Lessing did get at Melinda and do it.'

'Yes.' Maguire ran the tape back to the beginning. 'But if Lessing killed Melinda why the hell didn't he shoot her? Why slit her throat?'

'Quieter,' said Grayson. 'Ivy James was downstairs, and the major was somewhere in the garden. A shot would have been heard by both of them.'

'I know that's the logical reason, but somehow it doesn't feel right.'

'Sir?' Grayson was clearly puzzled.

Maguire left the interview room to collect Tess. 'Don't worry, Steve, I was in danger for a moment or two of letting a gut feeling get in the way of plain common sense. Come on, we've got to track down Lessing. Much as I hate to admit it, I think Dr Browne is right and that he is still here in Stibbington. Although God knows why; the Walshes left years ago.'

'The parents have moved back,' said Grayson. 'Ann told me. They've bought one of those luxury flats down by the quay.'

Maguire stared angrily at his younger colleague. 'Why the hell didn't you tell me that before?'

'I only found out myself today. When I went home for a sandwich at lunchtime Ann and I talked about the murders and then she told me. And we've been busy ever since. Besides, I didn't think *they* were in danger. After all, it was their son who was involved in the crash not them, and he's not here.'

'God knows how you ever got to be made a detective.' Maguire stomped angrily from the room, followed by the now very anxious Grayson. He collected Tess and went back to his office. 'Forget about going home for supper,' he told Grayson. 'I want to know the whereabouts of Giles Lessing, pronto. Get those two they've sent down from Winchester on to it, and just make sure the three of you come up with a result.'

'Where are you going, sir? The super might ask.'

'Out,' said Maguire, 'and pass me that damned phone. I suppose I'd better take it with me. Call me as soon as you find out anything. And I do mean *anything*.'

'He's bound to find out sooner or later.' Joan Walsh stood at the large bay window of their apartment and looked out across the darkening windswept harbour. The serried masts of the yachts in the marina lurched about haphazardly in the wind. Even the water in the inner harbour was choppy, white horses curling and spitting on every scrap of open water where the wind caught and snatched it up. Normally a peaceful scene, it looked out of control. Dark and menacing, exactly the way Joan was feeling , as though her life was beginning to spiral out of control. But of course Geoffrey would never think that. 'We can't keep three murders from him,' she said. 'He's bound to find out.'

Geoffrey suddenly surprised her. 'Perhaps it might be safer if he went back to London,' he conceded. Joan nearly wept with relief. To get Niall away from Stibbington was her one aim now. Back to London and to safety. Her husband joined her at the window. 'But you'll have to think up some excuse,' he said. 'Say you're feeling ill, can't cope with the family, and it would be better if they went back and had Christmas on their own. Say Tom is getting on your nerves. Niall knows you've always suffered with your nerves.'

And whose fault is that? Anyone married to you and treated the way I've been would have nerves! But of course the words were silent, just a noise in her own head. Geoffrey never heard them, wouldn't even have heard them if she'd screamed them at him. 'But I like Tom,' she said, disagreeing with him once again, and noting with a degree of satisfaction that she seemed to be better at it since they'd returned to Stibbington. Geoffrey glanced at her, and she could see he was annoyed. 'And I want to spend Christmas with them,' she continued defiantly. 'We can go to London as well. Stay at their house in Primrose Hill.'

But Christina wouldn't even consider going back. 'You'll pick up in a couple of days, Mother,' she said blithely. 'It's just a little bug and Tom has got to be exposed to those. Besides, it's so lovely here beside the sea.'

Joan hugged Tom, who'd been deposited on her lap.

'Tell you what,' Christina continued, 'you give me a list tomorrow, and I'll do all the shopping for Christmas, and then we'll only have to get odd things in on Christmas Eve. And if you're still feeling under the weather, which I'm sure you won't be, I'll help with the cooking. Niall agrees with me, don't you Niall? We ought to stay here.'

Yes,' said Niall, without looking up from the book he was reading. He seemed to do nothing but read these days, Joan had noticed, his conversation merely consisting of monosyllabic grunts.

She longed to shout, *But three of your friends have been murdered! You are in danger!* but as usual, kept silent. The habit of years was impossible to break.

'And another thing,' Christina rattled on, seemingly oblivious to her husband's lack of interest in things. 'We are going out tonight to a barn dance at Steepletoe Village Hall. We've been counting on you to have Tom to sleep over; I don't want to leave him with that Mrs Matthews at The House on the Hard, or that rather creepy Mrs Smithson. My friend Louise is coming as well, and between the two of us we've managed to persuade Niall to come. Haven't we, Niall?'

'Yes,' said Niall again.

Smiling, Christina came over and tickled Tom under the chin. You are the only one in this room who is happy thought Joan, and didn't know whether to be envious or angry.

'The band is Peter Pod and the Peas,' said Christina. 'It should be a real hoot.'

It was settled. Baby Tom would stay overnight, and Niall would drive the three of them to Steepletoe, which was about eight miles away through the forest further along the coast. Joan tried to comfort herself with the thought that Niall would be safe because he would never be alone. The apartment was safe with all of them there, and he had Christina and her friend Louise with him this evening. The other murders had all been committed when the victims had been alone. It couldn't happen to Niall. She cuddled Tom close to her, resting her head on his silky golden hair, and tried not to worry.

Three hours later Niall still sat in the lounge overlooking the quay, eyes glued to a book he was not reading, and wondered why neither of his parents had even mentioned the deaths of Darren or Tarquin. Did they know about them but were afraid to mention them because of the possible connection with himself? Or did they know and not care? Or had they blotted out the past so firmly from their minds that they hadn't even made the connection? Niall didn't know. His father had always been something of a stranger to him, impossible to get close to. But now even his mother seemed to be holding back.

'Hold him for me while I start getting dinner.' His mother dumped Tom on to Niall's lap. 'If the three of you are going to this barn dance, and Louise is going to eat with us, we'll need to eat a little earlier. I'd better get started whilst Christina is picking up Louise from Silver Cottage. And I must say, dear, I do think you were a little awkward refusing to go and fetch her with Christina. You know the way much better than she does.'

'Louise is her friend, not mine.'

Silver Cottage, Deer Leap Lane. If only his mother knew how difficult it had been restraining himself from driving out to his old home. But it was someone else's home now, and would be different, and besides, he didn't think he could bear to see the place where Tarquin had died. Burned. The newspaper had said he had been shot dead before the fire, and he'd said a silent prayer hoping that it had been so. Shooting was quick, no time to think; being burned alive was too horrible to even contemplate. He shut it from his mind, and like his mother took comfort from burying his head in Tom's soft golden hair. He smelled sweet and clean, was a warm, round wriggling bundle. Suddenly he felt near to tears. What lay in store for this small human being now held safely in his arms?

Christina and Louise erupted into the apartment. 'Oh, heavens,' said Louise. 'I forgot to tell my mother I was going out.'

'Phone her.'

'No point. She's won't be in yet, and she never leaves the answerphone on, and she switches her mobile off when she's off duty.'

'Talk about incommunicado,' said Christina. 'How very inconvenient.'

Louise agreed but added, 'It's a habit she started as a GP in London. It doesn't do to let people get you on the answerphone or mobile, not the sort of people my mother dealt with, anyway – most of them were weird. I'll phone from Steepletoe – she'll be in then – and tell her what we're doing. She won't mind.'

Christina took Tom from Niall. 'I'll feed him and put him down for the night. He's sleeping in the carry cot in your parents' bedroom, that way we won't have to worry about him while we're enjoying ourselves.'

While *you* are enjoying yourselves, thought Niall resentfully, watching the two girls. It was all a great big laugh for them, a village barn dance, full of country yokels, or so they thought. Once village affairs had been the highlight of his week and no doubt if he'd stayed they still would be. The people of Stibbington and Steepletoe were not yokels, as Christina had called them; they were different to the people of Primrose Hill, less sophisticated, but somehow, Niall felt, more real. He'd been different when he'd lived in Stibbington. In fact, if he were honest, he grieved for the person he'd left behind in Stibbington all those years ago.

When Lizzie stalked out of Maguire's office she resolved to do nothing more with the knowledge she had acquired concerning Giles Lessing. Maguire had been right. This wasn't a cosy TV series, and she wasn't a clever amateur. She was a doctor and should leave well alone. She would leave it to the police now that she'd told them all she knew.

That resolve lasted until she got back to the Health Centre. The centre was still busy; a glowing island of light in a darkened street, car park full, three surgeries running, and Maddy for once running a clinic instead of attending some high-powered meeting. Tara, alone at the reception desk, was struggling to deal with patients' telephone calls as well as making appointments on the new computer system, which, she complained, made the work much slower. So Lizzie didn't ask Tara to put the notes away as she'd intended, instead she let herself into the cupboard at the end of the corridor to do it herself. Standing on the stool to reach the highest shelf where the Lessing notes belonged, she lost her balance and dropped the bundle of notes. The elastic band holding them together broke, and notes, letters, old hospital report cards, all spilled out across the floor. Cursing, she got down on her hands and knees to gather them together. It was then that her resolve not to get further involved evaporated. She should have gone home as she was off duty, but she didn't.

Kneeling down on the cold lino tiles amidst old paper clips and balls of fluff, her excitement grew as she sifted through the paper detritus of Giles Lessing's life. She found the address of the doctor in London to whom he'd been transferred, and she also found a hospital haematology report, which showed that Giles Lessing had developed leukaemia before he had left Stibbington. Dr Burton had written a personal letter to the GP he was transferring to, a Clifford Beeston, and kept a copy in the file. Sitting back on her heels Lizzie gathered the notes together and started thinking. It wasn't the most aggressive form of leukaemia, but he'd had it now for almost ten years. Giles Lessing would either be in remission or he'd be dead. She had to find out which.

A surge of adrenalin tingled. It was significant. She was sure. Never mind what Adam Maguire said about gut feelings, she had one and was going to follow it. Deciding her wits needed refuelling, she grabbed a cup of Tara's ghastly coffee from the communal rest room, then took the notes and the coffee and slipped into her consulting room, where she switched on and booted up the computer.

Surely the London practice would have a website. She tapped in the address, Regent Canal Corner Health Centre, waited, and then almost clapped her hands with glee. Not only was the practice there, but Clifford Beeston had his own website and e-mail address. She sent an exploratory e-mail informing him of who she was, what she wanted to know, very vaguely referring to the possibility that it might be connected to a homicide case. She had to think about that: what were the rules of libel or was it slander when it came to e-mail? But she took a chance and was rewarded with a phone call.

'Your e-mail intrigued me,' said Clifford Beeston. 'I'm off duty and as it happened was playing around with my computer. Taking into account that you are not in the deepest depths of Arizona I thought I'd phone you back.'

Giles Lessing, so Dr Beeston informed Lizzie, had been in and out of remission for years, and his life had been saved several times by using his own plasma, which had been taken and stored while he was in remission. However, lately things had not been so good and he knew his days were numbered.

'What kind of man is he?' asked Lizzie.

There was a long silence, then Clifford Beeston said, 'He has never confided in me, not about his life before he came to this part of London, nor about how he feels about his illness. All I know is what Dr Burton told me in that initial letter. I was prepared to help him, to counsel him, but he has always kept me at arm's length. At first I thought he was deeply unhappy, after all he has good reason to be, but now I don't think he is. He's beyond that. It's almost as if he's devoid of feeling, cleaned out of emotion for himself or anyone else. He knows he's going to die soon, and he doesn't care.'

A shiver crept slowly along Lizzie's spine. *Devoid of feeling, cleaned out of emotion for himself or anyone else.* But perhaps not devoid of hatred. A hatred so deep, so intense that it blotted out all other feelings. She thought of herself; how would she feel if Louise was killed and her killer got away with it? Distraught, vengeful, that's how she would feel. But life would have to go on; she'd have to come to terms with it. But what if life was not going to go on? Terminal illness altered one's state of mind. Life itself would become pointless. With nothing to lose, perhaps the termination of another life could seem logical.

'Strange thing is,' Clifford Beeston's voice made her jump, she'd forgotten she was still sitting there holding the phone in her hand, 'in spite of the fact that his blood count is far from good, he's gone away. He told me he was taking a holiday for a couple of weeks. The oncologist at the local hospital asked me to try to persuade him to stick around here, near to the hospital, but he wouldn't.'

'Do you know where he went?' She asked the question but was already sure of the answer: he'd come to Stibbington.

'No, but I think it must be in Hampshire. I do know that he had some of his own plasma transferred to a private hospital near Southampton. For insurance purposes, he said. I suppose he's hoping that if he suddenly starts to come out of remission the plasma will help him.'

'You've been very helpful,' said Lizzie. 'I'll be in touch later.' She put the phone down and thought hard. She ought to ring Maguire and give him the information. It confirmed, as far as was possible, that Lessing was in the area. But he'd told her to keep out of it, and anyway that was the job of the police, to find out things. No, she decided, she'd leave it for the time being. The damage was done; three people had been murdered but at least the fourth was safely tucked away in London somewhere. There was no urgency. Then conscience got the better of her and she rang Maguire.

'It's Lizzie Browne here,' she said, 'and I've got some more information for you that indicates that Lessing is, or certainly was, in this area recently.'

'And I've got news for you,' said Maguire. 'Mrs Brockett-Smythe has come back to the station and confessed to the murder of her stepdaughter.'

'Confessed?' Lizzie found it difficult to believe. 'I can't believe it. You must have frightened her into saying it.'

Maguire snapped. 'Frightened her?' He thundered down the phone so loudly that Lizzie held the phone away from her ear, 'Those are not my tactics. Believe me she was not intimidated. She wasn't even here, had gone back home, in fact. Then she just arrived back at the station out of the blue, on her own, and confessed. We've had to arrest her, of course.'

'Well, of course, I suppose you had to.' Lizzie thought Maguire was beginning to sound despondent. His next words confirmed it.

'I was just beginning to think you were right with the Lessing theory,' he said, 'and now we've had a hole blown right through it.'

CHAPTER TWENTY-ONE

'D O YOU WANT me to take her statement, sir? And shall I phone and tell Major Brockett-Smythe now?' Grayson waited in Maguire's office. 'Bit of a sod, this,' he said, pacing about anxiously. 'Just when the pieces of the puzzle were beginning to slot together and make some sense, she comes along and messes everything up.' He was obviously fed up with the turn of events, and Maguire knew he was itching to get home to Ann and a cosy supper. But it was not to be; they were both likely to go hungry tonight, a quick snatched take-away if they were lucky. He wondered if Grayson ever regretted coming into the CID. A desk job or the Traffic Division had more predictable hours. Grayson was evidently thinking along the same lines. 'There they go,' he said, nodding towards the window as a police car drew out of the car park, 'off to put up the flood warning signs, then they'll be going home.'

'On call, though,' said Maguire. 'Give them some credit for working. We may not have motorway pile-ups around Stibbington, but we do have floods.'

'Yes, but they're on call at the end of a telephone,' said Grayson gloomily.

'Pretty boring job, though.' Maguire looked at the notes on the desk before him. Mrs Brockett-Smythe had certainly thrown one enormous spanner into his theory.

Grayson suddenly grinned. 'Too right. Their job is boring, and this is getting more exciting by the moment.'

'Unpredictable is a more apt word, I'd say,' said Maguire.

Grayson started towards the door. 'I'd better ring Ann and tell her to expect me when she sees me.' He paused, nodded in the direction of the interview rooms and said, 'Do you honestly think she did it?'

Maguire thought for a moment. Did he? He had suspected that she was holding something back, but somehow had doubted that it was murder. He couldn't bring himself to believe that she was the murdering kind, but on the other hand there was plenty of evidence littered through the annals of criminal history to show that fact was very often stranger than fiction. It was never possible to be sure of anything unless the evidence proved it beyond any shadow of doubt.

'It's possible,' he said, 'although at the moment there's no forensic evidence to support it. We'll have to go over that room and the house and garden again with a fine-tooth comb. And she'll have to be examined by forensics as well.' He thought about the woman now sitting quietly in the interview room. She looked so frail. Would she have had the strength to have slashed the throat of a crazed girl, who, according to her father, was strong and aggressive? 'Yes, and you'd better tell the major and get him up here, and get a WPC to stay with her and make arrangements for forensics and a doctor to examine her thoroughly. But keep the major in another room; don't let him talk to her until we've got everything we want.'

Outside there was a flash of lightning followed by an enormous clap of thunder. 'Storms in December,' said Grayson. 'It's not natural.'

'There's a lot in this world that's not natural,' said Maguire. He was thinking of the three murders. Were they linked or was it just coincidence? The link was a more comfortable theory as it meant they knew who they were looking for; it meant that the killer was not killing at random. But if the deaths were not linked then it was altogether a more chilling prospect. Psychopaths were notoriously difficult to catch; they always led, on the surface at least, such normal lives that no one ever suspected them. So far there hadn't been a vociferous public demand for the police to *do* something, because they'd managed to keep the lid, more or less, on the press. The deaths of two dropouts and a mentally ill girl hadn't excited Fleet Street. If it had been the deaths or abduction of children, then, Maguire knew, that would have been an entirely different matter. Half the TV crews and press reporters in the United Kingdom would have been camped out in Stibbington. And as for the population of Stibbington itself, it was a small community, and everything had happened so quickly, that people had hardly been given the chance to take it all in. But that wouldn't last. Maguire guessed that by the following day, if not sooner, the press would be howling at their door, demanding to know what was being done. 'Her confession has pushed us back to square one. Back into unknown territory,' he said. 'It's a bloody nuisance.'

'I know.' Grayson was sombre. 'Are you going to tell the super and give a press statement now that she's confessed?'

Maguire walked outside to the corridor, where a coffee machine resided with a permanent pot of coffee stewing on a hotplate. Usually, he didn't bother to drink it, as it tasted foul, but today thought it better than nothing, and he needed something to stimulate his brain. He poured himself a cup and contemplated the situation as he walked back into the office. The super should be told – he'd asked to be kept informed on any progress, and this was progress, although not in the direction Maguire had envisaged. If anything he'd put the major in line as a suspect, not his downtrodden little wife. He took a sip of coffee; it was bitter on his tongue, but hot and reviving.

'No,' he said. 'We'll not tell anyone until tomorrow morning. We haven't got her official confession yet. We'll let the doctor and forensics get their work done, then we'll wait a bit; let her stew for a while. Sometimes that can have a miraculous effect.'

'What sort of miracle are you expecting, sir?'

Maguire gave a half smile. 'None, to tell you the truth. But it will give us a little more time to sort things out.'

'Yes, sir.' He sounded doubtful.

Grayson departed, leaving Maguire in no doubt that he didn't think they would make any progress as far as sorting things was concerned. Maguire felt the same. Where the hell did they go from here?

Lizzie left the surgery and went back to Silver Cottage. The storm was in full swing by the time she arrived. A brilliant display of nature's pyrotechnics might be awe inspiring, but it was rather nerve wracking when one happened to be in the middle of it. A tree was struck before her very eyes; forked lightning spreading its fiery fingers down the trunk and along the branches. Had it been summer the tree would have probably exploded into flames, but now in winter and in the pouring rain nothing so dramatic happened. All the same Lizzie was glad to arrive in one piece and shut the cottage door gratefully behind her.

'Louise?' she called out expecting an answer. She was also expecting the cottage to be warm and welcoming. But it was cold; the stormy winds had blown the pilot light out on the gas boiler and the central heating was off. Neither was Louise there. The house was empty, and Lizzie was worried.

Lying flat on her stomach, the only way to get the pilot light ignited, Lizzie squinted at the instructions printed on a small metal plate on the bottom of the boiler. She followed them religiously, down to the last comma. Turning the gas off, turning the gas back on, pushing the button, holding it in then slowly releasing it. The flame died every time. Outside, the storm built in intensity and inside, Lizzie's frustration increased as it became clear that she was not going to get the boiler going. And where was Louise? Why hadn't she rung her to say where she was?

She scrambled to her feet and went to look at the answerphone, but the light wasn't blinking. No messages. But of course there wouldn't be. Out of habit she hadn't switched the damn thing on. Then, she remembered, neither had she switched on her mobile. Another habit: off duty, out of range had always been her motto. Now she wished it were different.

The phone rang and Lizzie snatched it up thinking it must be Louise but it wasn't, it was Emmy Matthews.

'Dr Browne,' she said, 'can you come and see me?'

'I'm off duty,' said Lizzie angrily. 'You know very well you should ring the Health Centre and you'll be put through to the duty doctor.'

'It's not about me. It's about . . . well,' she hesitated, and Lizzie could tell she was nervous. 'I rang you because your daughter is friendly with them.'

'Friendly with whom?' Lizzie felt her stomach muscles tighten, an involuntary spasm of apprehension. Why was Emmy Matthews ringing about something to do with Louise? What on earth could be the connection?

'With Niall and Christina Walsh.'

The words shot through Lizzie like an electric shock, jerking her body straight. She found she was holding the phone so tightly that she could see her knuckles shining white beneath the skin. Niall Walsh! Christina! That must be his wife, Louise's friend. Why had she never mentioned the surname? The answer was simple of course: there'd been no reason why she should, and now she remembered Louise saying that she always forgot it.

Niall Walsh was the only one left of the four occupants of the car involved in the accident. He was the next to be murdered, and Louise was involved with his wife. Lizzie's thoughts galloped ahead. To say she was on the point of panic was putting it mildly. All her maternal instincts throbbed with terror. Louise could be in danger as well, because, now Lizzie was absolutely certain Giles Lessing was in Stibbington. It stood to reason. He hadn't finished his task. The one person he needed to complete the quartet, Niall Walsh, was here in Stibbington, too.

'What is it you want to tell me? Is it something to do with Giles Lessing?'

She heard Emmy's sharp intake of breath and knew it was. She could almost feel Emmy's fear slithering down the phone line. 'It's difficult to explain over the phone,' said Emmy, sounding breathless. 'I've got some things to show you. I think I know where he is.'

'You must tell the police. Now!'

'No.' Emmy sounded stubborn. 'I can't do that. Not before I get some advice. I need advice; it's about Giles Lessing, and you're a doctor. You can help.'

'But you must—'

'No, don't ask me to ring the police. I'll talk to you or nobody. I *must* talk to you.'

It was obvious that the woman was not going to impart any more information over the phone, and Lizzie didn't stop to think. 'I'm on my way,' she said.

Before she left the cottage she carefully switched on the answerphone and left a message for Louise on the kitchen table in case she came in. Thinking carefully, or as carefully as her racing brain allowed, Lizzie tried to word the note casually so as not to alarm Louise when she read it: *Where the hell have you been? Luv Mum.* Adding as a postscript, *Boiler pilot light gone out. If you can light it you're a better man than I am, Gunga Din! PS I have switched my mobile ON. Ring me.* Then she switched on her phone, put it in an accessible place in her handbag, reluctantly shrugged herself back into her wet raincoat, and scuttled across to the Alfa.

Driving conditions were a nightmare, compounded by the fact that the dampness from her raincoat steamed up the inside of the car. Even with the heater on full blast, and the fan going so violently that she could hardly hear herself think, the windscreen stubbornly refused to clear.

The shore road leading to Emmy Matthews' house was flooded. It was high tide, and the force of the wind combined with the tide sent an ugly grey sea surging across the road, bringing with it great swathes of seaweed torn from its roots way out in the estuary. Lizzie kept the Alfa going as fast as she dared while at the same time trying to avoid letting water surge up and into the engine. The lights of The House on the Hard were blazing in the downstairs rooms, and the end window was wide open again, the curtains being sucked out by the wind, flapping frantically as if trying to escape.

Lizzie parked the car and ran to the front door. There was no need to ring the bell, the door was open. Not wide open, but ominously ajar, which made her nervous. 'Mrs Matthews?' As she called out she was suddenly aware of the harsh sound of rapid breathing, and then realized it was herself. Stopping for a second she willed herself to take long slow breaths. Keep calm. Keep calm. 'Mrs Matthews, it's me, Dr Browne.' She called once more. The only reply was the wind soughing through the skeletal branches of the trees at the back of the house, and somewhere a door banged. Bang, bang, banging in the cold darkness of the night.

Lizzie stepped into the brightly lit hall. From where she stood she could see into the kitchen, the door of which was also open. Crossing the hall quietly she pushed the door open wide and called out again. Still no reply. Slowly edging around the kitchen table Lizzie found that she was clasping her black doctor's bag tightly against her chest in a defensive position. Stop being so ridiculous, she told herself, and lowered it into a more normal position, not that it helped to stop the beads of sweat she could feel slowly trickling down between her breasts. She knew something was wrong, and found out the moment she edged around the other side of the table.

Emmy Matthews lay in a half-sitting position, wedged between the fridge and a cupboard. Her arms were behind her and her eyes were wide open, as was her mouth, which was a blueish hue. Her tongue lolled against the side of her mouth and was the same colour as her lips.

Slowly, Lizzie sank to her knees. There didn't seem to be any point in hurrying; Emmy was clearly dead, but formality dictated that she feel for a pulse. There was none. The body was still warm. She checked her watch. The time was 7.35p.m. She must have knocked the body slightly, because it toppled sideways revealing that Emmy had been clasping something behind her back. It was still in her hand. It was a small maroon-coloured booklet. From the position she was in it looked to Lizzie as if Emmy had been hiding the book from whoever had attacked her. For a moment she hesitated then, remembering that somehow Louise was involved and also in potential danger, she broke all the rules and took the book from Emmy's lifeless hands. Maguire and the police force could do what they liked; the safety of her daughter came first and this might be a clue.

To her astonishment she found she was looking at a SHAFT publication. Although she'd never personally worked with such patients she had seen and read the publication before. It was the handbook for male to female transsexuals, and those concerned with their care and treatment. But why had Emmy got it, and why was she hiding it? Emmy had called her because she said she had something to tell her about Giles Lessing. Slowly, the unpalatable truth began to filter through into Lizzie's mind. Was Maguire looking in the wrong place and for the wrong man? Should he have been looking for a woman? She turned the book over and over in her hands. Was this the answer? Was Giles Lessing posing as a woman? For a moment she felt numb.

The door still banging at the far end of the corridor jolted her back to the present. Wasn't that the room that Emmy had told her on a previous visit Mrs Smithson occupied, the room with the window open tonight and the night of her earlier visit? Perhaps Mrs Smithson was Giles Lessing. It would certainly account for the fact that nobody had seen a strange man about, only a strange woman. Lizzie knew she ought to ring the police. *Now. This instant.* The sensible part of her brain insisted. But she didn't. Instead she walked purposefully towards the room with the banging door. The priority right now, as far as she was concerned, was to find out where Giles Lessing was. Instinctively, she felt that the room might provide an answer.

The first thing she saw was evidence of someone leaving in a hurry. Drawers were open, the wardrobe door swinging, underclothes scattered about on the bed, and on the floor was a pair of shoes. Lizzie recognized them immediately: they were the shoes the woman on the train had worn, the woman who she'd trodden on. This was Mrs Smithson's room, but that didn't prove she was a transsexual, and certainly didn't prove that she was, in fact, Giles Lessing. She turned to leave the room, but something dark at the back of the wardrobe caught her eye. Pulling it out she looked more closely, realizing with a raw horror that it was a black leather motorcycle outfit, and that on the floor of the wardrobe was a wig; a woman's wig. The evidence clinched it. Motorbike leathers: Giles Lessing was known to have been a fanatic for such vehicles, and a woman's wig. Now she was certain. Mrs Smithson was Giles Lessing. The knot of fear in her chest tightened but Lizzie forced herself to breathe slowly. Had he killed Emmy Matthews this evening and now gone out to kill again? She didn't know, but whatever happened she had to keep her head.

At that very moment her mobile rang from the depths of her handbag, which she'd left on the kitchen table. Racing back along the corridor she tore at the handbag to open it and retrieved the phone.

'Yes?'

It was Louise. It was difficult to hear her against the noise of chatter and music in the background. 'Mum? Hi. You sound as if you've been running.'

'Where are you?' Lizzie tried hard to keep the fear from her voice and sound normal, but obviously didn't succeed.

'What on earth is the matter, Mum?'

'Where *are* you?'

'Well if you must know I'm at Steepletoe, and don't get all irate. I did try and phone you earlier but as usual you didn't have either your mobile or the answerphone on. Christina and I, and Niall, that's her husband, have come out here to a village barn dance. I'm using her mobile. So don't worry about me. I'll be home late. Niall will drop me off.'

'Louise, listen to me. Niall is in danger. You are all in danger. Leave there and come home to Silver Cottage now. You'll be safer there.'

The connection cut out, then picked up a faint signal again. 'I can't hear you, Mum.' Louise's voice was broken up and faint. 'It's a terrible signal. Must be the storm. See you later.'

The phone went dead. Lizzie shook it in exasperation. Then pressed the recall button. But the number didn't show. Dammit, must be barred. No chance now of getting back to Louise as she didn't know the number. There was nothing else to do. She had to go to Steepletoe herself, wherever that was. She thanked God she still had the borrowed sat nav in the car, but to be sure she looked at the map in her handbag and searched for the village. Trying to ignore Emmy's intent sightless stare she found Steepletoe on the map. It was not far from the water-splash on the other side of Stibbington.

Maguire. Maguire. The name flashed through her brain. Of course, she must tell Maguire what had happened here at the House on the Hard and also about Niall Walsh being at Steepletoe and that Giles Lessing was posing as Mrs Smithson. She dialled Stibbington police station only to find that the automatic answerphone was on. A mono-tone voice gave her options of pushing various buttons depending on her need. In a panic, Lizzie scrolled through the numbers and found the one for the Blackberry Grayson usually carried. She called it, and waited impatiently, praying that it wasn't switched off.

'Maguire.'

Maguire had answered. Lizzie almost wept with relief. 'Lizzie Browne here.' The words tumbled out in a rush. 'Emmy Matthews has been murdered; her body is in the kitchen at The House on the Hard. Strangled, I think.'

'Stay there. We'll be there in five minutes.' If Maguire was surprised he didn't sound it. The words came rapping out, staccato, businesslike.

'No.' Lizzie could hear her voice trembling, she was losing control. 'I can't stay. I'm going to Steepletoe. To the village hall. Niall Walsh is there with my daughter, and Giles Lessing alias Mrs Smithson is going there. Don't ask me how I know, I just do. There's evidence here to prove it, but I can't waste time telling you now. I've got to go.'

'Look, wait. Don't go there. It could be dangerous.'

'Which is exactly why I *must* go. My daughter is there.'

Without waiting for his reply, Lizzie rang off, picked up her bag, and ran out of the house.

Outside, the storm had increased in ferocity but Lizzie hardly noticed. She drove hunched over the steering wheel, peering through the darkness and lashing rain. She could hear the gravel from the hard, driven there by the force of the wind and waves, slashing like so many nails against the side of the car, and breathed a small sigh of relief when she reached the tarmac surface of the quay road. The quickest way to Steepletoe was through the water-splash if it wasn't too flooded. She decided to risk it.

Once out of Stibbington, and in the total blackness of the country lanes, driving became even more hazardous. Lizzie concentrated hard and then noticed when she was on a relatively straight stretch of road that there was a motorcyclist ahead of her. A motorcyclist without lights. Her heart started thumping erratically: ectopics, she thought (part of her doctor's mind was still on duty), too much adrenalin. She lost concentration for a second and the wheels of the car very nearly lost their purchase with the road's wet surface, but she recovered it and the Alfa raced on following the motorcyclist into the darkness. They passed a junction; the white-painted wooden signposts showed up in her head-lights: one pointed to Warnford Down and the other to Steepletoe. The motorcyclist took the Steepletoe road. Lizzie followed.

The flood warning notice was in the road before the water-splash but the motorcyclist went on, and so did Lizzie. There was no turning back now, and in her feverish state of mind she was thinking that if only she could catch him maybe she could actually knock him off the bike. A mad thought but one worth trying. Anything to stop him.

The water-splash came into view. Surely the water was too deep for a motorbike? Lizzie hesitated, and slowed down. What to do? She'd get out of the car and tackle him. That's what she'd do, and pray that she was fit enough to floor him. And pray, too, that he didn't have his gun handy. She didn't allow herself to think about that. Gun or no gun, she had to stop him. That was the only important thing. The Alfa rolled to a halt and Lizzie had the door half open when she saw that he wasn't stopping. He was crossing the water-splash; not on the road through the flood, but by riding across the narrow wooden foot bridge at the side. She heard the machine revving up, and then he was over the bridge and away into the night.

Nothing for it now but to try to cross the stream herself. Without hesitation Lizzie drove at speed into the water-splash, which by now was a small turbulent river. Halfway across the Alfa stalled, which was not surprising as the car was half full of water. I'm going to drown. The thought hammered through her head as she struggled to undo her seat belt and open the door. But luckily the force of the flood water was flowing into the passenger side and as she managed to open the driver's door the force of the water took it and pushed it open wider. The current was strong, pulling her into the icy water. Submerged for a moment, she swallowed great mouthfuls of muddy river water, and then managed to get her head up and gulp in a breath of air. More by luck than judgement Lizzie found herself swept down just below the pedestrian bridge and hurled against the branch of a tree, which had fallen into the water. Clinging hold of it, she pulled herself hand over hand, eventually managing to make her way to the relative safety of the bank. Once there, she scrambled up its muddy sides, and from there she got on to the road.

Exhausted, but knowing she had to go on, she began to run. Running, stumbling, gasping from the pain of stitch in her side, Lizzie staggered on towards Steepletoe's village hall. She could see the lights, hear the music, but it all seemed so far away. In another world. A world separated from her. A dream world and she was in a nightmare.

CHAPTER TWENTY-TWO

MAGUIRE SLAMMED THE phone down. Damned stupid woman. Who was she to take the law and possibly her life into her own hands? But he knew the reason why; he'd tried to persuade her to go against maternal instincts and failed. Her daughter was in danger, which was all she could think about. He knew he'd have probably been the same if he'd had a daughter, but now Lizzie Browne had put both of them in danger.

'Steve!' he roared, at the same time dialling Phineas's number.

'Sir?' Steve Grayson came running. It wasn't often Maguire shouted. 'The major's making a fuss, sir. He says we've got to take a statement from his wife so that he can take her home, he says—'

'Damn the major. Tell him we can hold her for tonight, and will do so, and get WPC Jones on to it. Make sure the woman is comfortable. In the meantime we've got another murder on our hands. Emmy Matthews down at The House on the Hard.'

'Bloody hell,' said Grayson.

'What's that? Emmy Matthews murdered?' Phineas had picked up the phone and heard Maguire's last remark.

'Yes, another murder, Phineas. This place is going mad. Grayson is going down there with another officer.' He nodded at Grayson, 'Take DC Gordon.'

'He doesn't know much about the case,' objected Grayson. 'And we've never worked together.'

'We don't have a case, as you call it. All we have is a series of murders which seem to be spreading like a bloody epidemic. Don't just stand there; find him and get going. I'll organize Phineas Merryweather and forensics. Go!'

The last shouted word galvanized Grayson into action. 'Yes, sir.'

'And where are you going?' asked Phineas still listening in on the phone. 'What is more important than the scene of a murder?'

'The scene of a potential murder,' said Maguire. 'I'm taking young Kevin Harrison and two squad cars and going to Steepletoe village hall. And if I don't get there quickly there could well be a disaster.'

'Are you sure? Disaster's putting it a bit strongly, isn't it?'

'Of course I'm not bloody sure,' shouted Maguire. 'I'm not sure of anything, and am getting less sure by the bloody minute, but I can't risk not going.'

'Hold on, my dear chap, I—'

'Goodbye.' He cut Phineas off in mid-sentence. There wasn't time for a discussion. Phineas didn't know what he knew. A few swift phone calls, and within ten minutes – much too long for Maguire's liking – three police cars were on their way to Steepletoe. Once he had the facts the super hadn't quibbled, just given orders, and four officers had drawn weapons. Maguire hated using guns, and, like Grayson, hated working with men he didn't know well, but with the possibility that Lessing was carrying a weapon they couldn't take chances. No sirens were blaring, Maguire had ordered silence, but the flashing blue lights were on illuminating the tangle of branches and piles of debris caused by the storm as they sped along. They went the long way round. Everyone knew that by now the water-splash would be completely impassable.

Maguire sat in the passenger seat and thought. Lizzie had said Giles Lessing alias Mrs Smithson. If the man was in drag no wonder no one had seen him. But no one had seen a woman near any of the murder scenes either. But a man on a motorbike was another matter. Why the hell hadn't anyone mentioned it before? Of course, Lizzie had eventually, but he'd dismissed it. Surely Emmy Matthews must have seen the bike as well. Too damned late to ask her now; if she had mentioned it maybe she'd still be alive. Maguire was certain in his own mind that Giles Lessing must have murdered Emmy Matthews. Obviously, she'd found out too much. But proving it – that would be a different matter altogether. Strangled, Lizzie Browne had said. Why hadn't the man kept to his preferred method of murder? Shooting! Strangulation was another complication to an already complicated case.

He wondered what Lizzie Browne was doing. He found himself thinking of her as Lizzie, a distraught mother, not a scientist, or a cool, calculating doctor. But he prayed that her normal presence of mind would prevent her from doing anything silly, such as putting her own and other people's lives in danger. A man and a gun was a dangerous combination.

It took nearly fifteen minutes before the lights on the outskirts of Steepletoe came into sight, and then a few seconds later the brightly lit village hall itself. The cars skidded to a halt.

'The music's still playing,' Maguire said to the assembled officers, 'that's a good sign. Nothing can have happened.'

They spread out to a pre-arranged plan; the armed officers had their orders and knew what to do. Maguire strode towards the main door of the hall.

Lizzie stood in the doorway of the ladies' lavatory out of sight of everyone in the hall, which was just as well as she was dripping all over the floor, and her breath was coming in shallow, ragged gasps.

'Can I help you?' An elderly woman wearing an apron and carrying a tray of teacups stopped by Lizzie's side. 'You look a little wet, dear.'

'No, you can't help me,' hissed Lizzie in between gulps of air. 'Go away.'

The woman went off in the direction of the kitchen, teacups rattling. 'Well, I was only trying to help,' she said huffily.

Afterwards Lizzie couldn't remember how long she'd stayed there out of sight, trying to get her breath back, and trying to concentrate. There was a lull in the music, and the room was full of people milling about, talking, and laughing. She couldn't see Louise. It was difficult to pick anyone out, there were so many young people all dressed in jeans and T-shirts, and the lighting was dim. Then she tried to find Mrs Smithson – or Giles Lessing. Suddenly, panic struck, making her shiver. She'd be able to recognize him if he was dressed as a woman but had no idea of what he looked like as a man. Giles Lessing could be anyone in the room. Anyone at all. Oh, please God let him be dressed as a woman, she found herself praying.

The band, consisting of three elderly men playing an accordion and two guitars, started up again, and the caller grabbed the microphone, clapping and shouting in time to the music. The noise was ear-splitting, and Lizzie felt her strength draining from her. How would she ever find Louise here? The noise was stopping her from thinking straight.

Whooping and laughing, the entire room began circling right and then left. It was then that she saw Louise. She was laughing with her partner, a tall, blond young man with glasses. There was something familiar about him, but Lizzie couldn't pinpoint what it was. Not a first. But it only took a few seconds for her to realize what the familiarity was. The hair was not as golden, or as long, but the sensitive face was the same. Except for the glasses he looked like Tarquin. But how could he? They were not related, although Mrs Mills had hinted there was gossip. But none of that mattered now. Lizzie felt as if her mind were wrapped in cotton wool. Thinking was so difficult. Concentrating was so difficult. She felt exhausted. But hammering through her head was the certain knowledge that Louise's partner was Niall Walsh, and that somehow she had to get her away from him, get them both away from danger. But her first concern was for the safety of Louise.

She hung back. Hesitant. What to do for the best? She couldn't rush out across the dance floor in the state she was in. It might precipitate Giles Lessing into doing something drastic. Oh, where was he? Was he in the hall or lurking outside somewhere waiting to come in? Clinging on to the door jamb of the lavatory Lizzie tried to think clearly. It was more and more difficult. She felt so tired; her limbs were leaden from her struggle through the flood, and the music seemed to get louder and louder. It echoed round and round in her head, threatening to submerge her in noise.

'Dozey to the right, basket to the left,' the caller shouted in a broad Hampshire accent. 'Take your partners and around you go.'

The dancers swirled around the room in a big circle as the music rose to a crescendo. Lizzie thought her head would split. She couldn't bear it. Exhausted, she closed her eyes for a moment, still hanging for strength to the doorway. Then she opened them and looked straight across the room at Giles Lessing. He was standing against the far wall in a woman's brown tweed suit, clasping a large leather handbag. It seemed to Lizzie that everything was happening in slow motion. His hand moved into the handbag slowly, oh so slowly, and then Lizzie saw the glint of metal as he took his hand out of the bag. Feeling as if she were standing outside of herself, witnessing the scene from afar, Lizzie opened her mouth to call out. She could almost feel the separate muscles of her face move as she mustered up the effort to shout. From somewhere, she never knew where, Lizzie dredged up the strength to scream at the top of her voice, over the top of the music, over the top of the caller 'Louise, Niall, he . . . she's got a gun. Get down!'

Then she snapped back into action. This time fast forward. The assembled company turned as one and looked at her as she ran, screaming at the top of her voice, across the floor to where Louise and Niall were standing.

She saw the gun come up. Why weren't they lying down? At the back of her mind old TV films wound in silent slow motion. That's what one had to do when guns were going off. They had to lie down. 'Lie down,' she screamed. 'Everyone lie down!'

A bright light exploded in her head. Somewhere there was screaming. Lizzie felt a gush of warm liquid down her face. I've been shot, she thought. Then there was darkness.

Maguire saw Lizzie stagger across the floor towards her daughter. He also saw the woman opposite take the gun from her handbag. Powerless to do anything about it himself, other than run after Lizzie and try to restrain her, he prayed that his men were on the ball, and had seen everything, and could prevent the gun being fired. They had. Almost before the gun was raised an officer was there, his hand on the woman's arm jerking the gun upwards. But it was not quite soon enough. The gun was fired and Lizzie collapsed on the floor in a pool of blood.

'Mum, Mum!' Far away Lizzie could hear Louise calling her name. There was the sound of weeping. She wanted to say don't worry, but couldn't because she was trapped in darkness just the other side of consciousness. She tried to hang on, claw her way towards the voice, but couldn't and wearily let go.

'Come round, you stupid woman. Didn't I tell you to mind your own business, and that murder was dangerous?'

It was the *stupid woman* that did it. How dare he! Indignant, Lizzie ferociously clambered back into consciousness. She opened her eyes to find Maguire kneeling over her, his hand on the side of her neck. He was checking for vital signs. 'I'm not dead,' she said crossly, spitting the blood out from the corner of her mouth.

'You damned well deserve to be,' he said.

'You needn't have shouted at me,' said Lizzie.

'Well, we couldn't leave you lying asleep on the dance floor for ever. Lie down.' He pushed Lizzie, who was struggling to sit up, back down, before he was elbowed out of the way by Louise and a paramedic.

'Mum,' she cried. 'Oh, Mum.'

'Out the way, miss,' the paramedic said. 'Your mum is off to the infirmary. You can talk to her later.'

An oxygen mask was clamped over her face and Lizzie drifted back into semi-consciousness again, dimly aware of a mass of people around her. Maguire was in the background and Louise was holding her hand. Above her the roof beams moved past in regular procession, and then it was dark. It had stopped raining, and she could see the stars. But only for a moment. Then she slept.

CHAPTER TWENTY-THREE

GILES LESSING CONFESSED to all three of the murders, which caused a bit of confusion as Maguire now had two confessions to Melinda's murder. When he'd questioned Mrs Brockett-Smythe again she'd just collapsed into an incoherent quivering heap, and eventually a frustrated Maguire reluctantly gave up trying to find out what had really happened and took Giles Lessing's word for it. But not before he had confessed his doubts to the superintendent, who told him to be thankful for small mercies and close the case.

'Keep your doubts to yourself,' said the super. 'This is between the two of us'. So he did, although it all seemed a little too neat to him and Grayson.

'But I suppose orders are orders,' Grayson observed as they watched the major escort his wife home. Later that day, Giles Lessing was charged with all three murders.

The funerals of Darren, Tarquin, and Melinda were held together, one week later, just four days before Christmas. The major arranged and paid for all three, and had even bought three plots so that they could lie side by side in the new grassy cemetery, which had been built beside the coast road to Keyhaven.

Maguire attended with a reluctant Grayson. For once in his life he was glad that the major had been able, through his various business and freemasonry contacts, to bring pressure to bear on the authorities. Major Brockett-Smythe had wanted all the necessary business over and done with as quickly as possible and it had been. The post-mortems, the inquests, the paperwork, everything had been done in record time. 'Just shows,' he said to Grayson, 'that these things can be hurried if people put their minds to it.'

'An indecent haste, if you ask me,' muttered Grayson. He did not approve of anyone being able to exert any pressure on anyone else, and certainly not ex-magistrates and freemasons, who he regarded with equal suspicion.

'Nothing of the kind,' said Maguire. 'Tell me, what good does it do in hanging around, prolonging the families' agonies? Prolonging *our* agony. You know a case is never shut until the last T is crossed and I dotted.'

'That's true.' Grayson looked more cheerful. 'At least now it's done we can have a decent Christmas.'

Maguire looked over to where Lizzie was standing. He had not expected to see her there. But there she was, looking pale with a large dressing plastered to the side of her head. Louise was standing close to her, fussing a little, holding on to her arm. Almost losing her mother to a gunman's bullet had evidently given their relationship a new dimension, reflected Maguire wryly. For the moment Louise was the carer; she was in charge, and was scuttling around Lizzie as if she were a very precious object indeed.

Maguire and Grayson stood a little apart from everyone else. Not that there were many people there, just the major and his wife, Mrs Girling, Niall Walsh, themselves, and Lizzie and Louise Browne. The press had stayed away, which didn't surprise him. No story in funerals. And anyway the national journalists had moved on to other, more exciting, events; a Minister of State had been caught hiring high-class prostitutes in one of the classiest hotels in London. The tabloids were having a field day. Even Danny Bayley of the *Stibbington Times* hadn't bothered to turn up, although he did send a photographer, and no doubt, thought Maguire, he'd fabricate a nicely touching little piece for the weekend's bumper Christmas edition.

The small party followed the hearse from the tiny stone chapel situated within the cemetery to the graveside. The weather had changed completely. It seemed that the heavens had emptied themselves of rain, for now it was brilliantly sunny, dry and frosty. Standing on the short-cropped turf, his breath steaming in the bitter cold, Maguire looked out across the sea, thinking that the view was almost too beautiful to be real. The smooth surface of the Solent gleamed like glass beneath the morning sunlight; now and then the smoothness melted into treacherous swirls where the current was fast and deep. Beyond was the Isle of Wight with the great jagged rocks of The Needles and the red and white striped tower of the lighthouse, marking where rocks lay beneath the water. The scene stood out clear and sharp in the frosty air. It was when he looked at such a view, and breathed in the fresh sea air, that Maguire knew he could never go back to a city job. Promotion palled into insignificance. He would stay put, here in Hampshire, no matter what happened.

'You know, there's something I've been puzzling about,' said Grayson in a low voice. They were standing far enough back for no one to hear them. 'And that is Melinda's murder. Tell me what you think. Honestly. Do you think Mrs Brockett-Smythe killed her stepdaughter or was it really Lessing? I know he's confessed, but somehow I couldn't help thinking that he just said it because he didn't care what happened once we'd caught him.'

'Very astute of you, Grayson.' Maguire watched the Brockett-Smythes. They both looked ghastly. She was pale, with dark circles under her eyes, as if she hadn't slept at all since the murder, and he looked sick with worry. He felt an immense sorrow for them both. They'd lived with the demon of Melinda's illness for years, and now, suddenly, that had gone. But, he wondered, how long would it be before they'd realized that all they'd done was to exchange one demon for another? How long? Minutes, days, a week? A demon that they had created themselves, and one from which there would be no escape. Maguire knew only too well that it was possible to batten down the mind for so long, but every now and then, the thing you'd battened down, whatever it was – pain, loss, guilt – would escape, rear up, and confront you. In their case it was guilt. A peaceful old age was not to be their lot in life. Dark secrets were not conducive to tranquillity.

Yes,' he said eventually. 'I do believe she killed her. But I don't think it was murder. I believe it was a ghastly accident, and she wasn't really certain whether she was dead or not, and then she panicked and left Melinda on the floor, where she bled to death. It was just as she told us when she first confessed. But then her confession was annulled by Lessing's. And you're right about him. I don't think he *did* care. Why should he? He's at death's door anyway and he'd admitted to two murders, so what is one more? And there's no doubt in my mind that he did intend to kill Melinda, and unwittingly he did. But now he's so ill, it's unlikely that we'll be able to question him enough to ever find out the truth.'

Grayson was puzzled. 'How do you work that out? That he unwittingly killed her?'

'When Lessing killed Darren, and then Tarquin, he cut off the supply of cannabis the Brockett-Smythes bought for Melinda. It was this fact that triggered her violence. The violence that caused her to attack her stepmother with a knife. There was a struggle, and it ended up with Melinda herself being killed.'

'If Mrs Brockett-Smythe had told us that straight away it could have been proved it was self-defence. No jury would have convicted her of murder on that. It would have been manslaughter,' Grayson mused out loud. 'But,' he continued, 'the fact that there's no forensic evidence, no knife, no bloodstained clothes must mean that the major was involved as well.' Grayson turned to Maguire. 'Surely you don't think she could have covered up everything by herself?'

The priest was saying the final words at the graveside and the three coffins were being lowered simultaneously by the pall-bearers into the waiting graves. Maguire and Grayson stopped talking and waited in silence. The major stepped forward and dropped a sod of earth into the graves of Melinda and Darren, and Mrs Girling did the same for Tarquin. A few more words from the priest and the short service was over. The small company turned and walked back to the waiting cars, leaving the cemetery to the two grave diggers, who'd been leaning on their shovels at the far end of the sea wall having a quiet cigarette.

'Yes, the major must have been involved as well,' said Maguire, picking up the conversation where they had left off. 'Not in the killing, but he must have come back and tidied things up before coming back yet again, when he was told his daughter had been murdered, and feigned convincing shock horror. But that was the problem. It wasn't quite convincing enough for me. There was no doubt that he was horrified. But that sharp, initial burst of grief and shock I was expecting wasn't there. And it wasn't there because he was prepared. He already knew what had happened to Melinda. As for the clean-up, there are plenty of places to hide things in that rambling garden of his. For instance there's a deep well that hasn't been used for years. He probably threw the knife down there; we'd no doubt find it if we cared to look, but there's no point now. And then there's that bonfire he had; I assume any bloodstained clothing went on that.'

'Forensics wouldn't have any difficulty in proving clothing had been burned. We ought to do something about it. Find the knife and the clothing. They ought to be punished.' Maguire thought Grayson sounded a little pompous and smug. It irritated him, but then he told himself Grayson was young, and the young were inclined to see things in black and white instead of shades of grey, which was the way life really was.

'They are being punished,' he said quietly. 'They'll have it on their consciences for the rest of their lives. And you're right. Forensics would have proved it if we'd had more time. But events overtook us, and now we've got a confession from a confirmed murderer. Do you think the super or the CPS are going to be very happy if we start throwing alternative scenarios down in front of them? It's difficult enough to get them to proceed with a prosecution of any kind, and now we've presented them with an open and shut case they will want it left that way. And as the murderer in question is at death's door himself, there will be no expensive trial. Everything is cut and dried, and most importantly in these days of tight budgetary control, it will be cheap.'

'But surely, if Lessing lives long enough, he'll be brought to trial.'

'Yes,' said Maguire. 'He will, *if* he lives long enough. But that, according to the medics, is very unlikely. So the powers that be will want us to leave it for a while, then when he dies, the case will be quietly closed. The files put away and forgotten. A case solved. The accountants and the statisticians will be pleased.'

They started to walk down the incline towards the police car standing by the gate which led into the cemetery, their footsteps crunching on the grass still brittle with the hoar frost. 'I suppose you're right,' said Grayson. Then he suddenly changed tack. 'Well, as I said before, thank heavens we've got it all out of the way before the holidays. At least now we can relax and have a good Christmas, always supposing everything goes back to normal and stays quiet. Ann is pleased. She was beginning to think I'd be staying down at the station all over the festive period.'

Maguire smiled. 'And this conversation will remain strictly private, I hope,' he said. 'Just between the two of us. It doesn't do for policemen to have views that don't follow the official line.'

'Strictly private,' said Grayson, still looking a little doubtful. Then he relaxed and grinned. 'I'm looking forward to a bit of a rest. Let's hope the citizens of Stibbington behave themselves for a few weeks. By the way, Ann said if you'd like to join us for Christmas Day you're very welcome. It will be just us, and her mum and dad.'

'Thanks, Steve, but I've already accepted another invitation,' lied Maguire. He didn't relish a family Christmas with Steve's mum and dad. 'It's very kind of Ann, thank her for me.'

'Will do.' Grayson made no further inquiries. 'Shall I get Tess from the car for you? Looks like Dr Browne and her daughter are waiting for us.' Maguire fished the car keys from his pocket and handed them over.

'Let's wait for them. I want to know what's going to happen to Giles Lessing.' Louise tugged at her mother's arm. They stood and watched the major and his wife climb into their Land Rover and Niall slide into his BMW. He turned back, looked at them for a moment, then gave a faint wave before driving off. Maguire and Steve Grayson caught up with them.

'How are you?' asked Maguire. 'I came to see you in hospital with the mandatory bunch of grapes and a bouquet of flowers, but you'd ske-daddled and gone back home.'

Lizzie smiled at Maguire, and felt absurdly pleased that he had been to the hospital. 'I suppose you've eaten the grapes,' she said.

'Of course. Couldn't let them go to waste.'

'I wanted her to stay in longer,' said Louise.

'There was no need,' said Lizzie firmly. 'Hospitals are dangerous places; one can pick up all sorts of nasty things there. I should know, I'm a doctor. Besides, the bullet only grazed my head. I collapsed with concussion, nothing more dramatic than that, plus a little blood loss, of course.'

'As far as I could see there was an awful lot of blood,' said Maguire. 'Maybe you ought to do as you're told for a few days.'

'Nonsense,' snapped Lizzie. 'I'm quite capable of doctoring myself.' Then realizing that sounded a little ungracious she added in a more mellow tone of voice, 'I'm glad we met you today, because I haven't had a chance to thank you.'

'What for?'

'For saving my life. If you and your men hadn't got there when you did, God knows what might have happened.'

'Never mind about God knowing. *I know*,' said Louise. 'You would have been shot dead, and probably Niall as well. Not to mention a dozen or so other people.' She threw her arms up in a melodramatic gesture.

'Only another five,' said Grayson. 'There are only six bullets in a barrel.'

'Are you always this pedantic?' said Louise, cross that her moment of drama had been squashed. Maguire and Lizzie laughed and Steve looked grumpy.

'I don't even know what pedantic means,' he said huffily.

Lizzie took pity on him. 'Don't take any notice of Louise being difficult,' she said. 'She's glad you were there too.'

'But I wasn't there,' said Steve gloomily. 'I missed all the excitement because I was sent down to The House on the Hard to a murder that turned out to be natural causes. I didn't get to be involved in any of the excitement.' He started off towards Maguire's car. 'I'll collect Tess.'

Lizzie turned and looked at Maguire. 'What did he mean? I saw the murdered woman with my own eyes. What do you mean natural causes?'

'It's true. I thought you knew. The post-mortem revealed that she had died of a heart attack. Or a coronary occlusion, to use Phineas's words. Apparently, she had a congenital abnormality of the heart. The stress of everything just proved too much for her. So to all intents and purposes Lessing did murder her.'

'Oh my God. Poor woman!' Lizzie felt a stab of guilt; she and all the other partners at Honeywell Practice had regarded Emmy as a nuisance with her imagined illnesses. Now she wished she'd given her more of her time, and she wished she'd hurried more that night Emmy had called. 'If I'd got to her sooner,' she said slowly, 'Maybe I could have prevented her death.'

'Perhaps,' Maguire said. 'But it's all history now, and we can't change it.'

Lizzie didn't feel convinced. 'It's illogical, I know, but somehow I feel responsible for Emmy's death.' She was sure there'd been no mention of heart disease in her notes, she would have remembered it. The answer was that they had all missed something because the woman was a nuisance. She always turned up with such trivial complaints that the main concern of everyone in the surgery was to get rid of her as soon as possible. 'I've got to go to her funeral tomorrow,' she said miserably. 'Not that it will do Emmy much good.'

'Stop thinking about it,' Maguire said again. 'Phineas said she could have dropped dead at any time, and it's a wonder she hadn't done so before.'

Lizzie felt perilously close to tears. Must be the reaction to that damned blow to the head, she told herself crossly.

'So stop thinking about it. And that's an order,' Maguire added.

'My mother is not very good at following orders, only at giving them,' said Louise.

'I had noticed.' Maguire gave a wry grimace.

'But she's going to do as she's told this Christmas, because I'm staying to look after her,' Louise said firmly.

Lizzie turned and saw Grayson leading Tess towards them. She was pulling on her lead, and bobbed down to pee on a grave. She laughed. It lightened the moment. 'That dog hasn't got any churchyard manners.'

'True,' agreed Maguire. 'But I don't think the occupants of this place will object too much.' He took Tess's lead from Grayson. 'Take care. And let that daughter of yours look after you for a few days.' He raised his hand in a gesture of farewell before he and Grayson made their way back to the car the long way round so that Tess could have a bit of a walk.

The day after the funeral Louise and Lizzie went shopping in a hired Ford. The sporty Alfa, Lizzie's pride and joy, had been towed from the water-splash and according to Stan at Forest Garage (Repairs, MOTs, General Maintenance, nothing too small or too large) was a complete write-off. So a hired Ford it was for the time being.

'Much more sensible,' Louise had said. 'Although, what you really need for around here is a four-wheel drive vehicle with a cattle bar on the front.'

They met Niall and Christina and baby Tom in the supermarket. They both looked more relaxed and Christina was holding Niall's hand.

'It's funny,' said Louise later when they were out of earshot, 'how no one guessed that Tarquin was Niall's half-brother, and Niall got himself into such a state worrying that his mother would find out about his father's infidelity. And now it *is* out in the open, it's brought Niall and Christina closer, and even Niall's mother doesn't seem to mind.'

'She doesn't mind because she's always known, and kept quiet for

Niall's sake. Dick Jamieson told me about it. Niall's father bullied both Mrs Girling and his wife into silence, and since he found out Niall has never forgiven him. Then to make matters worse he quarrelled violently with Tarquin because it was Tarquin who'd been driving the night of the accident. They never spoke again once the court case was closed.'

'So that's why Niall never wanted to come back to Stibbington.'

Lizzie nodded. 'Guilt and fear, I think.'

'And now there are three more people dead,' said Louise sombrely. 'But that's the end of it. No more murders.'

Arriving back at Silver Cottage they unloaded the Christmas shopping. 'Well, that's that,' said Louise. 'We'll be on our own for Christmas Day, although we could ask Maguire to lunch. He'll probably be on his own. What do you think?'

Lizzie smiled. Did Louise think she couldn't read her mind? The girl was so transparent. She was trying to pair her off with the local widower, and she had no intention of being paired with anyone. But it was true, Maguire probably would be on his own with only Tess for company, and Christmas was not a good time to be alone.

She compromised. 'You can invite Tess,' she said. 'I daresay she'll bring her master along.'